HOT-BLOODED FIGHTING MEN AND TEMPESTU... ...EN CARVING OUT A FUTURE F... ...ND

RENNO—Born... ...eneca, his fighting spi... ...in the fires of the Am... ...looded desire for a dusk... ...nerable to treachery . . . and a betrayal that would force him to choose vengeance as his destiny.

DALNIA—A woman so sensuous, so desirious that no man could resist her. Honey sweet lips, dark alluring eyes, a ripe, voluptuous body masked the ruthless ambitions that made ruin, dishonor, or death the price of her love.

RATTLESNAKE—Choctaw name of the half-breed **DAVID SIMPSON**, son of a notorious British spy slain by Renno. To avenge his father, Rattlesnake would strike at the Senecan, not in open combat . . . but with a venomous perfidy that made passion the poison that killed.

EMILY JOHNSON—Golden-haired, high-spirited daughter of brave frontier Colonel Roy Johnson, she could lose her heart to a courageous Indian warrior, but her pride and her heritage could forbid her to chose the way of the Senecas as her fate.

CAPTAIN BEN WHIPPLE—A skilled soldier driven by twin emotions of jealousy and hate, he wanted to possess the beautiful Emily at any cost, and his vicious cowardice would tragically change the life of Renno and the Indian nation forever.

AH-WEN-GA—Proud grandmother of Renno and widow of the Great Sachem, Ja-gonh. The Manitous have granted her wisdom critical to the Bear Clan's survival . . . and have sent in the winter of her life an unexpected love.

The White Indian Series
Ask your bookseller for the books you have missed

The White Indian Series
Book XI

CHOCTAW

Donald Clayton Porter

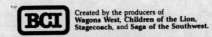

Created by the producers of
Wagons West, Children of the Lion,
Stagecoach, and **Saga of the Southwest.**

Chairman of the Board: Lyle Kenyon Engel

BANTAM BOOKS
TORONTO • NEW YORK • LONDON • SYDNEY • AUCKLAND

CHOCTAW

A Bantam Book / published by arrangement with
Book Creations, Inc.

Bantam edition / July 1985

Produced by Book Creations, Inc.
Chairman of the Board: Lyle Kenyon Engel

ISBN 0-553-24950-9

Published simultaneously in the United States and Canada

PRINTED IN THE UNITED STATES OF AMERICA

O   0 9 8 7 6 5 4 3 2 1

For the American people, whose debt to their forebears since Colonial times is immeasurable.

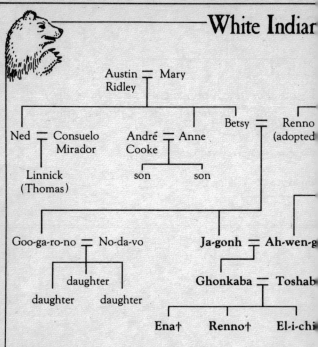

White Indian

Austin — Mary
Ridley

Ned — Consuelo   André — Anne   Betsy — Renno
Mirador   Cooke   (adopted

Linnick   son   son
(Thomas)

Goo-ga-ro-no — No-da-vo   **Ja-gonh** — **Ah-wen-g**

daughter   **Ghonkaba** — **Toshab**

daughter   daughter   **Ena†**   **Renno†**   **El-i-chi**

* The parents of Renno, the original white Indian, were Jed and Minnie Har
they were killed by the Seneca when Renno was an infant.

† Named for an ancestor.

© 1984 BOOK CREATIONS INC.

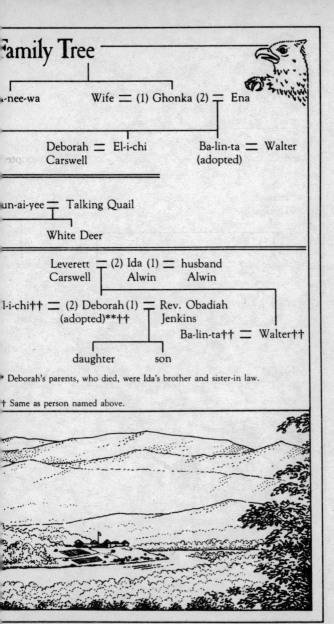

Family Tree

-nee-wa   Wife = (1) Ghonka (2) = Ena

Deborah = El-i-chi   Ba-lin-ta = Walter
Carswell   (adopted)

-un-ai-yee = Talking Quail

White Deer

Leverett = (2) Ida (1) = husband
Carswell   Alwin   Alwin

l-i-chi†† = (2) Deborah (1) = Rev. Obadiah
         (adopted)**††   Jenkins

                      Ba-lin-ta†† = Walter††

daughter   son

* Deborah's parents, who died, were Ida's brother and sister-in law.

† Same as person named above.

RON TOELKE '84

CHOCTAW

Chapter I

The wilderness in the land of the Cherokee—which some American settlers were beginning to call Tennessee—was quiet, serenely peaceful. Living among the Cherokee were several hundred Seneca from upper New York State, most of them members of the Bear Clan. The two tribes, fighting as brothers, had recently won a great victory over the nearest

1

neighbors of the Cherokee—the Creek and the southern branch of the Tuscarora. An abiding peace had been established here and almost everywhere throughout the new United States.

With the defeat of the British at Yorktown in Virginia in October 1781, the active phase of America's war of independence had ended; now only the peace treaty remained to be negotiated and signed. A commission of prominent Americans had landed in France and already was engaged in serious negotiations with representatives of Great Britain, the former mother country. It appeared likely that the American Revolution finally would end in this new year, 1783.

But thoughts of war, the fear that a new conflict was imminent, were foremost in many minds. None was more concerned with this issue than Loramas, the white-haired Grand Sachem of the Cherokee. On a late-winter day, he sat cross-legged on the skin-covered floor of his dwelling, his chiseled features solemn. He studied the equally sober demeanor of his son, Wegowa, the competent military leader of his nation, and then turned to Ghonkaba, the leader of the Seneca contingent who, in effect, acted as its sachem. Seated nearby was Ghonkaba's trusted friend and counselor, Casno.

"Some of our hunters who have strayed into the land of the Choctaw report that they suspect the Choctaw are preparing to launch a fresh war. Since we are the only nation that stands between them and domination of the entire region, it seems safe to assume they are planning to attack us. Do you have any information to share?"

"I sent three scouts there," Wegowa replied. "Two have returned. Both say the same thing as our hunters."

"My son Renno," said Ghonkaba, "went into their territory on my orders. He approached so close to one of their towns that he was directly outside its palisade. Warriors of the Choctaw go in large numbers into the wilderness each day to practice with the tomahawk, bow and arrow, and less often, with the muskets they received from the British. He was convinced this activity means they are planning a hostile move. I share his judgment."

"What do you propose then?" Wegowa asked.

"Prepare as best we are able for what we believe is going to burst upon us," Ghonkaba said. "If the American settlers are available to join us, we will stand united once again against a common foe. But, in my opinion, we are mistaken to try to fight a battle before we ever go into the field. A reasonable step, it seems to me, would be to seek the advice of General George Washington, who has commanded the Continental Army through so many difficult situations."

"He actually will advise us?" Wegowa asked.

"He will do at least that much," Ghonkaba promised. "He is well aware of the worth of these lands across the mountains from the coastal states. I feel sure he wants to take no chances that the frontier will fall into the hands of the British."

At this point, Casno spoke up for the first time. He was participating in this council as war chief, though he frequently set aside his military function to perform ceremonially as medicine man, a role that was increasingly close to his heart.

"I agree that such a mission is indeed advisable," he said forcefully.

"And," he added, turning to Ghonkaba, "though you yourself would be hesitant to say so, I take the liberty of proposing that it be Renno who will be sent to explain our situation and ask for the general's counsel. He will know how we can best prepare for whatever test awaits us."

Renno, son of Ghonkaba and great-grandson of the famous white Indian whose name he bore, was rousing from a sound sleep on a bed of pine boughs within a forest glade. His conscience bothered him, and he had been sleeping fitfully. The darkness was encompassing, and he knew from the position of a sliver of moon through the trees that the hour was not long past midnight.

Lying next to him, with her head resting on his shoulder and her body pressing close to his, was Dalnia, the beautiful Seneca to whom he was betrothed.

He was restless, and he realized that Dalnia was at the root of his problem. Her physical appeal was so overwhelming that he found difficulty in resisting her frequent, ardent advances. On the other hand, he was uncertain whether he really loved her. He often had the unpleasant feeling that she was still maneuvering him, hurrying him further into a relationship for which he doubted that he was really prepared. He realized that she was aware of her hold over him and used it to get what she wanted. Their deep involvement was premature, he thought, but he saw nothing that he could do to forestall their headlong plunge toward marriage.

Instead of living in her parents' house or in the longhouse with other unmarried women of the Bear Clan, Dalnia had contrived to establish her own home. She had argued successfully that inasmuch as she expected to be married soon, she should prepare a house for that time. Even so, on several evenings such as this, she and Renno had elected to go off together after dark. Leaving the town behind, they sought an undisturbed night in the peaceful forest.

As Renno stirred, Dalnia slowly came awake. She smiled lazily and pressed still closer to him. The intimacy of their contact eliminated everything else from his consciousness. Within moments, they were making love. Then, as their ardor cooled, a state of drowsiness crept over them, and both slept again.

Only when the first light of dawn appeared, awakening Renno for the day, did he fully realize what had occurred during the night. Their lovemaking was a fitting farewell before he left on a mission of high importance.

Running to a nearby lake, he went for a refreshing swim and then applied yellow and green war paint, his proud signs of his identification as a Seneca. After shaving his head on both sides of his scalp lock, he inserted into it three hawk feathers, symbols of his rank of war chief. He had received that coveted rank after killing Anthony Simpson, the most dangerous of British agents, in personal combat during a battle with the Choctaw. He was the youngest Seneca to receive this high rank since his great-grandfather.

When Renno returned, he was surprised to find that Dalnia, who was not ordinarily an early riser, had prepared a meal of broiled fish and corn bread.

"You are going to travel a great distance across the mountains, far from your new home," she said with a smile. "It would be less than fitting if I allowed you to leave without the benefit of good food that will stay by you on the trail."

For a time, she watched in silence as he ate. "Will you go to one of the cities of America to see General Washington?" she asked at last.

Renno shook his head. "The general," he said, "has been in winter quarters on the Hudson River, and I assume he is still there. So it is in the colony of New York that I shall seek him at his encampment."

"Do you intend to race the wind in order to reach his side quickly?"

"My mission is not that urgent," Renno told her. "Besides, I am to be accompanied by several Cherokee warriors, who will be assigned to learn from observing our unique wilderness travel. They will be taught by the Seneca warriors who will comprise my escort. We will therefore require more time for travel than we would otherwise need."

He failed to note the relief that crossed her face fleetingly. Even if he had seen it he would not have understood its meaning. The fact was that Dalnia had made up her mind to follow him secretly. Ever since she heard that Renno was to be sent on a special mission, she had seen it as a means to promote her selfish ends.

She realized that she was regarded as a pariah by the Seneca women, largely because of her behavior with Renno. Rather than suffer their snubs and insults during Renno's absence, she had decided to start alone on the long journey.

She found it reassuring that Renno was not intending to travel so rapidly that she would be unable to maintain the pace.

Only when he and his warriors had progressed too far to turn back would she reveal herself; then Renno would have little choice but to allow her to accompany them. She regarded it as possible that, once they reached their destination and he had conferred with General Washington, he would be ready to marry her then and there. Especially after he saw the admiration with which she was received at Washington's camp, she assumed he would be far more inclined toward marrying her immediately.

When Renno finished eating, he picked up his weapons, and with them, a bag of parched corn and another of jerked venison. These emergency rations would accompany him on the journey, in keeping with the practice of warriors of the Seneca on their forays into the wilderness. He was ready to join his companions and depart after a fitting farewell to his family.

His older sister, Ena, was clearly envious of his opportunity to make the long and important journey, but she overcame these unworthy feelings and presented him with one of her own treasures, a steel

knife that she had carried on her numerous successful scouting expeditions.

El-i-chi, two years younger than Renno, was
likewise full of admiration; his envy was lessened
only by the knowledge that his time as a war chief
would come. Occasionally, he had difficulty in curbing his impatience, and at such times his behavior
bordered on the undisciplined conduct of youths of
lesser stature. His attitude toward his parents, too,
sometimes was churlish, causing them despair as
well as irritation, and bringing upon himself well-
deserved rebukes and warnings. But this morning he
was in one of his sunnier moods, and he could not do
enough to make certain that Renno's preparations
were adequate. He, too, had a small remembrance
that he proudly offered. From a willow limb, he had
carved a whistle that his brother might be able to use
as a signal.

Toshabe, disappointed that Renno would not be
able to more than taste the elaborate breakfast she
had prepared, was content to stand in the background,
smilingly observing the departure scene. With her
was the family's shepherd dog, Lyktaw, who also was
disappointed. He wanted to be part of this journey.

Renno turned to his father, who touched his
own forehead as an intimate gesture of recognition,
and then they silently clasped one another's wrists.

"My son," Ghonkaba said, "I dispatch you on
this mission with confidence in your stamina and
valor. I know that you will succeed at least as well as
we are hoping. My one further observation is that in
addition to feats of bravery and physical ability, of

which we have no doubt, these qualities sometimes need to be leavened with discretion and self-knowledge by the true Seneca hero."

"I hear you, my father," Renno responded with equal gravity, accepting the gentle admonition with proper respect for his elder and superior. "I assure you I shall keep in mind the advice that you present me. I am grateful for the opportunity to serve you and our Seneca, and also the people of the Cherokee, in this manner."

It was customary for Seneca women to refrain from showing emotion at the times that their men marched off, and they avoided physical contact with the braves on these occasions.

But Dalnia daringly set out to defy tradition. Her slender arms slid around Renno's neck, and her lips parted to receive his kiss. She snuggled up to him, her breasts separated from his naked chest only by the thin fabric of her shirt. One leg lifted enough to press into his groin.

When he reacted, she instantly became demure. "May the manitous watch over you and protect you from all harm," she murmured.

Shaken by the intimacy of their embrace, Renno thanked her for her good wishes and bade her farewell.

"We will meet again when I return," he said coolly, seeking to hide the embarrassment he felt at his evident lack of self-control.

Turning away quickly, he walked to the town gate, where he would meet the other warriors.

Dalnia gave the expedition a start of nearly an

hour, then followed at a distance, making sure she remained far enough behind so as not to be discovered. Walking silently, she remembered to obey all the many rules of the wilderness she had learned as a child. She, too, was a Seneca. And she saw her future as more promising than that of any warrior.

Sir Nigel Durward, holding the dubious title of His Britannic Majesty's high commissioner for the lands west of the Appalachian Mountains, sat in his tent and shivered slightly. Even in the Kentucky wilderness, where Sir Nigel had come with a strong escort of Ottawa braves, he felt a recurrence of the chill he had experienced all winter in Quebec. The atrocious herb brew that his Ottawa cook constantly prepared had failed to warm his blood.

Huddled in his greatcoat, he kept a long woollen muffler wrapped around his neck and a thick wig firmly on his head.

As for his nearly naked visitor, Sir Nigel's flesh crawled at the mere sight of him. The man's skin was almost as pale as his own. He was, in fact, half white. Known as Rattlesnake to the Choctaw, he was the son of Anthony Simpson, the British agent, and a squaw of the Choctaw nation. Young David Simpson, who had inherited his father's ferretlike face and unpleasant disposition, chose to live as an Indian and, consequently, wore no clothing above his waist. It was beyond the Englishman's comprehension that he could be comfortable.

The visitor spoke earnestly. "Is what I have been hearing true?" he asked. "Is it a fact that Britain will sign a peace treaty this year with the revolutionaries who have delighted in bringing her to her knees?"

"I am not privy to the current status of the negotiations," the high commissioner replied, "but I daresay your information is reasonably accurate. The terms, to be satisfactory to both sides, are being hammered out, and I think it likely that a treaty concluding hostilities will be signed before long."

"That leaves your country with a simple choice, as my father sagely observed," Simpson said dryly. "You can give up a rich chunk of your empire for all time. Or you can seek to return it to the fold."

Sir Nigel made a wry face as he drank the dregs of his herb tea. "The choice you suggest is far more easily said than made," he interjected with a touch of asperity. "We beat the Americans many times in battle, but they simply refused to admit defeat. No matter how hard we stomped on them, they seemed to bounce back all the harder. We just grew tired of the mounting casualty lists and the terrible expense of the war. His Majesty's government is determined to end the hostilities. I hope I make myself clear, Mr. Simpson?"

"No, sir, you do not," was the prompt, intense reply. "And by the way, you must know that I prefer not to be known as David Simpson. At least until I have found satisfactory revenge for the fate of my father, I shall be called by my Choctaw name—Rattlesnake."

Sir Nigel peered hard at this forceful young

man. "Perhaps you have a suggestion for ending the dilemma?" he suggested sardonically.

"Indeed I do," the half-breed replied. "As I read in a book that has become my favorite, 'Unlike an individual, a state is not bound by limitations of conscience—it acts only in its own best interest.' "

He seemed humorlessly unaware of the incongruity of a half-naked brave in the wilderness quoting maxims of abstract political philosophy.

Sir Nigel smiled grimly.

"To me, that means your nation," Rattlesnake continued, "would be wise to accept the terms of peace—but only on the surface. Your commissioners should swear that Britain will uphold the terms of the treaty. But in actuality you must strive to disrupt the treaty and to work for the overthrow of the new American government and the return to the British Empire of the land she claims. That should be Great Britain's unalterable rule, no matter what misleading stories you tell that will deceive the world."

The high commissioner felt a reluctant admiration. "How is this goal to be accomplished?" he inquired.

"As my father repeatedly made clear in everything he stood for," Rattlesnake said, "the key to America's future lies here in the West. Whether the United States succeeds or fails will depend on whether she has the strength to seize and hold the unoccupied lands on her western frontier. If she can take them and bend them to her purposes, she faces potential greatness. But if these territories fall into the hands of Great Britain or any European power, America is doomed and will surely die."

"You are proposing," Sir Nigel summed up, "that Great Britain take possession of these western territories, prevent the Americans from occupying them?"

"Exactly!" Rattlesnake nodded emphatically. "And, by rolling back their waves of expansion, regain possession of the colonies that you have lost."

"I approve of your thinking," the high commissioner said, "just as I admire the strategy developed by your father. But you failed to take into consideration one important element. That is the dilemma in which we long have found ourselves. We are unable to fight a war thousands of miles from home, especially when the colonies are united against us."

"Great Britain is lax in her use of natural allies," Rattlesnake persisted. "The Indian nations resent encroachment by the colonists on their hunting grounds and other lands. In the big region to the south of you, no nation is the equal of the mighty Choctaw. Strong tribes like the Creek and the Tuscarora freely admit our superiority, and obey us. Only the Cherokee remain opposed to us. When the weather grows warmer and the trees are once again in full leaf, we will destroy the Cherokee. We could accomplish this more speedily with the aid of the British, if you decide to help us. Then, after the entire region is ours, we shall drive out the colonists who have dared to settle here. We will admit no foreign troops to the area—except those of Britain, of course. And those who were colonists will be excluded for all time."

Sir Nigel was silent. "What help do you want from Britain?" he asked at last.

Rattlesnake's reply was prompt and vehement.

"Give us arms! All right—if you wish, give us blankets, pans and kettles and pots, and mirrors, as you always have in dealing with Indians. But what will really matter are modern weapons, so we can wage war as you British wage it!"

Sir Nigel's mind worked rapidly. The cost of accepting the scheme outlined by the half-breed would be relatively small. In return, Great Britain might have a chance to regain the colonies. Suddenly, the chance seemed well worth taking.

"It is agreed," he said after only momentary reflection. "From our own stores right here, we will provide you with the arms you seek. As your end of the bargain, your Choctaw friends will drive the Cherokee from the region. And after they are gone you will expel the Americans. Can I count on that?"

Hints of an early spring were in the air, game began to reappear in the forest, and the braves in Renno's Seneca and Cherokee escort were young. In no great rush to reach their destination, they took their time on the trail. They brought down small animals in the forest and ducks that appeared overhead on the flight north. In lakes and streams they passed, fish were plentiful.

Their relatively slow pace made it easy for Dalnia to keep up, and she remained no more than two miles behind them. Reluctant to light a fire, she had to refrain from shooting game or catching fish that would have to be cooked. To augment her emergency rations, she looked repeatedly for roots and early spring fruit to be found in the wilderness. She could survive on such basic fare, but daily existence was none too pleasant. She looked forward eagerly to the day when she would be able to reveal her presence. As the distance traveled grew steadily greater, she reasoned that she would need to wait, at the most, only a few days longer before she caught up with the party.

They were now too far from home for Renno to take her back without losing too much travel time.

Meanwhile, she made her way with nimble ease, pleased that her childhood training was making it possible for her to carry out the journey without undue difficulty. Most Seneca children were required to undergo rigorous exercises in the forest; in recent years girls as well as boys had been included, and Dalnia had been among them. For the first time in her life, these lessons, which Dalnia had resented and resisted, were serving her well.

She did not realize that Renno's party had passed out of the hunting grounds of the Cherokee into a wilderness corridor generally conceded to be within the Choctaw realm. She knew only they were moving far more rapidly and apparently were taking greater care to make no sound. Her own task unexpectedly became difficult, and she was forced to devote her full attention merely to keeping up.

Her surprise was complete when three Choctaw, wearing the black and white war paint of their nation, suddenly ambushed her as she passed through a small ravine. One dropped a rawhide lariat over her head and pulled it tight, while two others seized her arms and legs.

Dalnia fought valiantly, using her fingernails as claws, and biting and kicking viciously. She instinctively struggled with all her might, giving no quarter as she strove to free herself.

"Bind only her hands!" a deep voice behind her commanded. "Do not tie her ankles. She is to walk under her own power. We will not carry her. And control her with a noose around her neck. If she fails to respond to an order, draw it taut, and as she begins to choke, she will decide to do whatever you wish."

As the warriors immediately obeyed, Dalnia turned to see a tall young man in the war paint of a Choctaw. Significantly, his feathered bonnet showed that he was no ordinary warrior. His rank undoubtedly was higher than that of a war chief. Noting this, she instantly stopped resisting capture. This was a man on whom she could hope to use her wiles successfully.

The Choctaw smiled cynically. "You show great good sense for a woman—and for a Seneca."

She was amazed that he knew her origins, but he gave her no opportunity to speak.

"We will begin our march now," he said. "If you make any sound, my men will not hesitate to silence you with a knife blade in your heart."

Speaking to his companions, he continued, "Keep in mind how badly we are outnumbered by the two times ten Seneca and Cherokee who went this way a short time ago."

The Choctaw promptly began their march. Dalnia was half led and half dragged with the leather thong around her neck and her hands bound tightly behind her back. She did her best to maintain the pace set, but she struggled in vain. Occasionally she stumbled and fell; twice she tripped on a tree root and plunged headlong on her face. No one helped her arise, however, and she climbed wearily to her feet and resumed the rapid march. She had no idea where her captors were taking her, but because of the position of the sun she realized they were going toward the southwest, exactly opposite to the direction Renno was taking.

At last, late in the afternoon, the group halted. One of the braves went off to hunt game for supper, and his two companions walked to the bank of a nearby pond to swim. The leader, apparently feeling assured of his safety, slashed the bonds at her wrists and removed the lariat from her neck.

"I am Solomba, the sachem of the Choctaw," he announced. "In our tongue, my name means Bird-Who-Eats-Flesh."

Dalnia considered it useless to try to flee—and, besides, Solomba's high rank fascinated her. She set about a subtle flirtation with him as she gently, almost meaningfully massaged her aching feet.

"I am called Dalnia," she replied in a soft voice, "and I am betrothed to Renno, the Seneca war chief who leads the party you saw today."

Solomba's expression remained unchanged, but a hint of awe entered his voice. "Renno of the Seneca—the one descended from the white Indian of that name?"

Smiling ingratiatingly, Dalnia nodded affirmation.

"Then he is the man who killed Anthony Simpson!"

"That is he," she agreed proudly.

Solomba chuckled quietly. "It would be interesting," he said, "to observe Rattlesnake when he sees you and learns that you are betrothed to the very man who is responsible for his father's death. In fact, perhaps you will find it preferable not to mention this to him."

Suddenly his attitude became stern. "You were following him through the wilderness. Why?"

"If you must know," she said haughtily, "life among the Cherokee is so dull that I was following Renno in the expectation that when I caught up with him he would take me on a journey he is making to a leader of the Americans."

Solomba began to fit together the pieces of the intricate puzzle he saw before him. As he did so, he reached the conclusion that the various parts could be employed to his advantage and that of the Choctaw. This woman was far more important than he had imagined.

The two warriors who had gone swimming donned their breechclouts and made a small fire, where they sat down to complete drying off.

Dalnia leaned toward Solomba, her lips parted suggestively. "Are you intending to swim?" she asked demurely.

"Now that you mention it," he said, "I think I should consider doing just that. Perhaps you would accompany me to the pond?" The last was added in a hopeful voice.

"May I go into the water, too, then?" she asked, smiling in a helpless fashion. "You need not think for one moment that I would try to escape by jumping from the water and running away."

Solomba gave the matter no more than a moment's hesitancy. His captive's charms had swayed his judgment and normal reserve completely. As he rose to his feet, Dalnia got up and began disrobing. Side by side, they walked to the water's edge, where Solomba removed his garments. They plunged into the pond at what appeared to be its deepest point. Dalnia was a natural swimmer, completely at home in the water. Solomba followed her free-spirited example, and soon both were laughing and shrieking as they swam on the water's surface, then below it, and back up again several times. For the next half hour, they played enthusiastically in the water, climaxing it with a game of tag.

Only the approach of the two Choctaw warriors called a final, reluctant halt. When they appeared with fishing lines made of vines and hooks fashioned from thorns, Dalnia and Solomba climbed from the water. He gave her a blanket to wrap herself in as they dried at the fire. Encouraged by her questions, and what he construed as her sincere interest, he began to speak about his experiences as a man of war.

Dalnia deliberately appeared fascinated by his recital. As he told her about his exploits, the blanket slipped from her bare shoulders. She seemed to be so interested that she neglected to pull it higher. She sat near to him, their knees and legs occasionally touching. Her full, ripe lips were parted as she listened to his tales of bravery and bravado.

Neither that night nor any other on their journey farther into the land of the Choctaw did Solomba consider it necessary to bind Dalnia's hands behind her back or to drop a rawhide lariat around her neck. She assumed she was on her way to becoming without question a favored member among Solomba's entire complement of family as well as warriors and counselors, and she showed great alacrity in living up to the role that she regarded as rightly hers.

Renno's party had one major stroke of good fortune on its mission to confer with the commanding general of all American ground forces—an encounter that saved days of travel.

They had traveled across the Appalachian range, choosing this time to follow the river that flowed westward through great gaps. They marched across the hazy ridges that descended in gradual craggy slopes to the Piedmont region of what had become known as the Old North State.

From Carolina, they moved with increasing tempo, turning northward into the tidewater region of Virginia, where some of Renno's white ancestors had been important planters, traders, officers, and statesmen. He wondered whether Renno, his great-grandfather, had walked these same paths, whether his great-grandmother, member of a leading Virginia family, had known the same sights he was viewing. Though the Seneca branch of the extended family had fallen out of touch with the Virginians, Renno was generally aware of the relationships, and he briefly speculated that perhaps one or another of the riders they occasionally saw in distant fields was a cousin. He was too preoccupied with the purpose of his mission to give the entire matter much thought, though he did think that one day he would return and inquire, in the hope of tracking down members of the Virginia family.

They had crossed the James and other rivers of the fertile lowland when they halted to bivouac late one day near the Rappahannock.

Shortly after sunset, a small knot of mounted militiamen rode up, changing their course somewhat after spotting the unusual-looking encampment a couple of hundred yards off their intended trail.

As they approached the Seneca and Cherokee camp, small and hurriedly but efficiently put together in anticipation of a short stay and early departure, Renno stood up from his crouch near a fire and prepared to confront the newcomers.

Their leader, a sharp-eyed, bearded man who had to lift his head in order to see Renno clearly from under the brim of his slouch hat, waved a friendly salute. He awkwardly stumbled into an effort to mimic what he thought was a greeting suitable for an Indian's ears.

Renno smiled broadly. "Good evening," he said, emphasizing each word with particular clarity to add to what he knew would be the other's discomfiture. "It was good of you to detour so that we savages might have an opportunity to make your acquaintance. With that in mind, permit me to introduce myself.

My name is Renno, and I am a war chief of the Seneca nation. Accompanying me are warriors of the Seneca and also of the Cherokee. They are acting as my escort by designation of my father, who is descended from the Great Sachems of the Iroquois League."

Taken aback, his surprise evident, the militiaman removed his hat and dismounted. For a moment, it seemed that his amazement would be enough to render him speechless.

Finally, he managed to stammer out a response. "I beg your pardon," he said with an attempt at a smile that would match Renno's. "I'm afraid that I did improperly presume what I had no business in presuming. You may be sure that I will be more scrupulous in the future in remembering that appearances are not always what they seem. . . . Now, may I have the honor of introducing myself."

He snapped his heels together and saluted once more, this time formally and with military precision.

"At your service, sir, Cap'n Jack Collins, and six of the finest riders of what we proudly call the Virginia Irregulars."

At once, the entire gathering, Indians and Virginians alike, were at ease, and the slight tensions that had accompanied the coming together of strangers disappeared altogether. Renno and Captain Collins then completed the lengthy ritual of making known the identity of each member of the two companies. With that done, the two leaders began to exchange information as to the respective reasons for their presence.

When Renno explained that he and his escort were en route to an anticipated audience with General Washington at his encampment on the Hudson River, Collins's eyes widened, but he said nothing until Renno had finished. He then held out a cautionary hand, placing it on Renno's arm as though to restrict his movements. His words made quickly evident what he had in mind.

"I gather that you did not know," he said in a voice that conveyed quiet amusement and pleasure at his being able to bring news to the Seneca, "that General Washington no longer is in Newburgh.

"In fact," he continued, "we left him within the past three hours, having served as part of his escort from New York down here to Virginia."

As Renno's face expressed amazement, the captain explained. "He had been experiencing some of the aches and pains that go with the cold weather of that region. Finally, he was persuaded that—the troops being in satisfactory condition and the outlook probable for continued quiet on all fronts—he should for once take care of himself and retire for a period of two or three weeks to a more favorable climate. Right now, he is undoubtedly enjoying himself mightily over at Mount Vernon—his home, you know. A visit there is a luxury that he has had very little of for the past eight years. It was a great pleasure, I assure you, to see how his whole appearance began to improve as soon as he got within sight of that plantation."

Renno's plans had begun to change drastically even as Captain Collins was speaking, and by the time the Virginia horsemen departed with renewed expressions of good wishes on all sides, he was prepared to change the direction of the march appropriately. He was pleased that many days' travel to the north would be avoided, with as much additional time saved on their return. He would be able to complete his business with General Washington more speedily than he had planned, and to report to his father earlier than either of them had hoped. Wrapped up completely in thoughts of the errand to which he had been entrusted, and concentrating on fulfilling it satisfactorily, he never had time to think of his betrothed and how she might be faring.

Mount Vernon was the most extensive private estate that Renno could imagine. Set on a bluff overlooking the rolling hill country of northeastern Virginia, it included numerous buildings and extensive lawns, as well as large, well-tended fields. Ample room was available in the mansion to house not only General and Mrs. Washington, but also various relatives and a steady stream of guests from all thirteen of the new states who constantly sought the counsel of the commander. Behind the dining room stood a large, handsomely equipped kitchen in a separate building. It was widely reported that the Washington cooks could provide a meal for fifty guests on short notice. Behind the mansion were servants' quarters, the stables, the carpentry shop, and a score of other outbuildings. Mount Vernon was virtually self-sufficient, and in order to survive and thrive, its occupants needed nothing that could not be made on the property.

Renno's escort of Seneca and Cherokee was quartered, as they requested, in a patch of nearby woods. The braves prepared their meals in the open with food provided from the Mount Vernon larder.

Renno was housed in a pleasant chamber in a guest wing of the residence and took all his meals in the dining room, as was expected. In deference to his host, he underwent the sharp change in appearance that so startled anyone unfamiliar with his family. Instead of appearing in war paint and scalp lock, he wore a powdered wig. Rather than buckskins, he put on a suit of satin, complete with breeches, waistcoat, and swallowtailed coat, white stockings, and buckled shoes. At his side, he carried a short sword. He had learned to use such weapons of civilization as a small boy, at the insistence of Ja-gonh, his grandfather.

Renno had to await his turn to see Washington and seek his advice. Having arrived at Mount Vernon early one afternoon, he was unable to make the desired appointment until late the following morning, when one of the general's aides informed him that he was scheduled to eat and confer alone with Washington at the noontime meal.

They sat down to a table laden with mounds of fried oysters, which were among Washington's most favored foods.

Renno, unfamiliar with the delicacy, nonetheless found it appetizing.

As they ate, washing the delectable fare down with schooners of light ale, Renno began to describe the situation that existed in the mountain areas of

Tennessee. He was hardly surprised to find that the general already was familiar with the problem.

"I hear regularly from Jack Sevier," Washington said. "He receives weekly reports, I gather, from his Tennessee militia commanders. He tells me just what you are saying. The territory, as you undoubtedly know, has been quiet since Sevier's regiment combined with the Cherokee and your Seneca to defeat the Creek and Tuscarora so decisively, and then took on the Choctaw, too, in that battle."

"We see it as a deceptive quiet, General," Renno put in. "My father instructed me to state that in his opinion the quiet is only on the surface. He and Wegowa of the Cherokee have gathered a great deal of evidence that suggests the Choctaw are planning to launch a major campaign. In fact, I witnessed some of it myself, and reported as much. We assume the attack would be aimed first against the Cherokee and the Seneca, then, after our defeat, would be turned against the white settlers."

"I'm sure that Colonel Sevier must be well aware of that, and so would be his battalion commanders, like Lieutenant Colonel Johnson, one of the best, I understand. You realize, I assume, that Sevier's militia is severely handicapped?"

"Perhaps you should explain what you mean, General," Renno replied tentatively.

"After our men have spent so many years fighting the redcoats, they've grown weary of war making. They're ready for the peace treaty. And they're reluctant to take up arms again. Whether we like it or not—and frankly, I don't care for it in the least—

each state is going to be responsible for its own safety. It would be able to call on other states for help only in a supreme crisis. By the time a situation in your area could be recognized as an emergency, it might be too late."

Renno made a gesture to show he appreciated the general's candor.

"Therefore," Washington went on, "John Sevier's frontier regiment must stand on its own feet and look after its own interests. The same is true of the fighting men of the Seneca and of the Cherokee nation. I will gladly do everything I can to encourage the settlers and the friendly Indians to work together and to fight together. But I can offer little in the way of material help. The Treasury is empty after all these years of war, and we need a period of peace in order to replenish it."

"If America loses the West to the Choctaw, who are allies of Great Britain," Renno said, "the victory that we won in the war will be hollow. The states will be helpless to protect themselves. Before they even realize what is happening, they could become British colonies again."

"You have touched on a point I want to make," Washington agreed. "The best I can offer to anyone, be it our own settlers or an Indian nation with whom we are friendly, is intangible. It's liberty—personal liberty, freedom of conscience. Opportunity, may I say, to live in what I think of as the American way. That way, incidentally, owes much to the Indians who were here long before we came from Europe and settled in the New World. I encourage Sevier's regiment, the Cherokee, and the Seneca to lock arms and form a common front against their common foe. They will not need to stand alone indefinitely. When the rest of the United States become aware of the gravity of the danger, they will join in expelling from our soil all who would deny us our freedom. And as I said, however, I can only trust that such help would not be too late in arriving."

Detecting an inquisitive look on Renno's face, Washington stopped, and said in a kindly way, "I see that I have not provided a satisfactory response to some matter that is on your mind. It would be well for you to speak up candidly."

Renno felt chagrined that his thoughts had been so plainly evident on his face that he had inadvertently caused the general to become perplexed.

"Sir, I meant no disrespect," he said ruefully, and was relieved to see Washington's hands move as if to brush away any thought of apology.

"I guess that what is on my mind, sir," he began again, "is the hope that you will offer some counsel bearing directly on our military situation. I believe that my father and his Cherokee colleagues are hoping that I will return with some advice from you relating to the proper strategy for our limited forces. Your suggestions would bear heavily on our behavior in the immediate future—and beyond."

The commanding general straightened his posture in his armchair until he was almost leaning toward Renno. With his hands, he gave expressive emphasis to his words.

"Though, as I have said, it will be necessary for

you to carry through on your own, without material help from outside, I believe that you can improve your prospects by one very effective and time-honored device. That is the element of surprise and initiative. If I have one piece of advice for your father at this great distance, it is this: promptly seize the opportunity and strike! Do not hesitate, and above all, do not wait for your enemies to move first. You will have by far the greater advantage in picking the time, the place, the circumstances, and the deployment of your available men. Throw in the additional element of taking the Choctaw by surprise at a time when they are unprepared, and you can readily see the tactical benefits."

Washington paused and gave a small smile, as though reflecting on some inner, unspoken thought. After a moment, he resumed, still gazing reflectively about the room as he spoke.

"I should add, I suppose, that I speak not on the basis of textbook theory, but rather through experience—hard-won experience, at that."

Noting Renno's questioning look, he explained.

"In the light of all the campaigns during this long struggle from which, I suggest thankfully, we now appear to be emerging, I can see with the benefit of hindsight where my own errors occurred. They were hand-in-hand with hesitation and procrastination. Sometimes I was saved because an opposing general staff delayed even more than I did. Unfortunately, such was not always the case. On the other hand, when I had the good sense to analyze the situation decisively and to act with dispatch, the results were good. Or, at least, they were happier than otherwise might have been the case."

Renno was listening attentively, his imagination captured by the contrast the general was painting so vividly. He understood fully the significance of the advice and resolved on the spot to do his best to see that such sound counsel was followed by his superiors in the leadership of the Seneca and Cherokee.

"And so," Washington was saying as he stood, signaling that the audience had come to an end, "I say, strike! Strike hard! Strike with determination! Strike with all you have! And, above all, strike first!

"As to what else you might say to my friend Ghonkaba—tell him from me to persevere in what he is doing. I shall lend such assistance as I can, but until it is forthcoming, tell him that, like Jack Sevier and a handful of others who guard the West for America, he must stand as a sentinel for our liberties!"

In spite of her failure to arrange a permanent liaison with Solomba, Dalnia had good reason to believe she stood high in the favor of the Choctaw. She soon discovered the reason for his sudden loss of evident interest in her as their party approached its destination. Then he began to turn a deaf ear to Dalnia's further blandishments. When he arrived home,, his behavior suggested that he hardly knew her.

Despite her disappointment and irritation, she could not blame him. His wife, a mildly attractive woman, reputedly had a sharp temper. It was easy enough to imagine her raising a storm of protest if he

was known to have strayed and become untrue to his
marital obligations. Dalnia thereupon accepted without a murmur his change of attitude and behavior.

As she realized, she was fortunate indeed. Most
female captives of the Choctaw would have become
prostitutes who were forced to service fighting
warriors. Or, at best, they would have become servants for a high-ranking family. As a household slave,
she would have been compelled to obey the orders
of a demanding mistress and her children, all of
whom might beat her if she failed to please, no
matter how hard she worked from daylight until
sunset, every day of the week.

Instead, to her surprise, she occupied a small
house of her own, set apart from other dwellings.
Daily, a silent, middle-aged brave brought her fresh
meat, vegetables from the communal gardens, and
fruit and roots from the forest. She was given as
many pails of water as she wished, and apparently no
reasonable request would be denied. Her nearest
neighbors ignored her presence, but she noticed that
a number of men eyed her surreptitiously; the desire
for her that appeared in their eyes could not be
concealed.

She continued to keep up her meticulous appearance, using berry juice to stain her lips and
cheeks red, and using charred sticks to enhance her
eye makeup. When she walked, her hips swayed in a
manner that was hardly the manner of a captive.

Dalnia was reminded of her strange status princi-
pally on the occasions when she tried to go outside
the town palisade. Then the sentries halted her and

reminded her that she was confined to the community and was not permitted to go beyond it. She wanted to protest to Solomba, but her attempts to see him were politely rebuffed. She had to content herself with the idea that her treatment was indeed special, and that perhaps she was being saved for some obscure purpose that had not yet been revealed.

One afternoon, after her midday meal, Dalnia sat alone in her small clay house, brooding on the events that had led to her present predicament. If she had stayed at home, she would have been safe and protected. When Renno returned from his trip she would have become, without question, the wife of the heir to leadership of the expatriate Seneca. Surely that was preferable to sitting on the dusty ground as a prisoner of the Choctaw!

Suddenly the animal skins that covered the entrance to the house were pushed aside. A man called out, in the language of the Seneca, "I wish to enter."

"You're already in," Dalnia replied, making no move.

She looked up and saw a young man who, at first glance, reminded her somewhat of Renno. He, too, was part Indian and part white. His Indian side predominated, however. His pale brown hair was cut in a scalp lock and his eyes looked out from behind beetling light brown eyebrows. His torso, bare to the waist, was smeared with the paint of the Choctaw, but his webbed, brass-buckled belt and tailored breeches were those of the British army. Instead of moccasins, he wore the low, hand-sewn boots of a British traveler in the New World. His polite bow, too, resembled that of an Englishman.

"I am Rattlesnake," he announced. When he saw no reaction in her face, he asked, "Do you know of me?"

Dalnia thought he was too haughty for his own good and immediately decided to take him down a peg. "No, should I?" she inquired negligently.

"My father," he said proudly, "was the renowned Anthony Simpson, the principal liaison officer of Great Britain with the Indian nations in these lands claimed by the United States. After he was killed—through trickery—by Renno of the Seneca, I was appointed by Great Britain to succeed him. Today I am responsible for the procurement of arms, munitions, and other supplies by nations that ally themselves with Great Britain."

Dalnia looked at him with increased interest, her manner thawing.

Again he bowed. "May I sit?"

She waved him to a place on the floor.

Dalnia seated herself opposite him, ineffectually tugging down the abbreviated skirt of her doeskin dress.

"It was your misfortune," Rattlesnake said, "to be made captive by none other than the leader of the Choctaw. But you actually are far luckier than you know. Your gods are watching over you. Instead of being placed in miserable slavery, you are in an enviable position. You bewitched Solomba sufficiently to have assured yourself that no harm will come to you. As you may have gathered, he insists that you be treated with every due consideration."

This reassurance was welcome to Dalnia, and she treated Rattlesnake to her most dazzling smile. Even the wily half-breed could not totally escape its impact.

"I have had some rather daring, complex plans for quite some time," he said, "but a lack of the right people has prevented me from putting them into operation. It may be that you are just the individual I am seeking."

She folded her hands in her lap and looked at him demurely.

"By any chance," Rattlesnake asked, "are you acquainted with this Renno?"

Having no intention of revealing that they were betrothed, she replied equally casually. "I have been acquainted with him ever since childhood." She thought it strange that Solomba apparently had not revealed to Rattlesnake what she had told him of their true relationship and wondered about the seeming omission—what might it mean.

"What do you think of him?"

She was silent for a moment and then said what she thought he wanted to hear. "Renno is naive, gullible, and easily led."

He smiled, pleased by her answer.

"Why do you ask?" she went on.

"Suppose you were to return to the land of the Cherokee and take up residence again with your fellow Seneca," Rattlesnake suggested. "Do you consider it possible that you could use your talents in such a way that Renno would become interested in you, as a woman?"

Dalnia had to exert considerable willpower to prevent herself from laughing aloud triumphantly. She realized that she had been correct in not telling him that Renno was madly in love with her. Instead, she would go along, step by step, with this self-satisfied half-breed.

"Renno has long been a close friend of my family," she said, "and I am sure very little effort would be needed on my part for us to become intimate, if I cared to. Would it be worth my while?"

Rattlesnake looked hard at her and hesitated for a time before he said, "I hope your optimism is justified. I can foresee how your close relationship with him could bring great benefits to all concerned."

"I am quite certain my optimism is fully justified," she replied with great self-assurance. "I have good reason to believe I can obtain information from him, if that is what you mean."

"Well," he said. "I can see you number a beautiful face among your assets when you speak of influencing a man's actions. Are there other assets?"

She was annoyed but answered readily, "Indeed there are," and wriggled out of her single garment. To give him the full effect of her figure in the nude, she stood in the bright sunlight cast through the hole in the roof that provided an outlet for smoke.

Amazed by her boldness, Rattlesnake did his best to respond to it suitably. "I see what you mean," he murmured, "and—and you are quite right."

Disregarding her nudity, she seated herself close to him.

Her lack of clothing was a powerful aphrodisiac, and he found difficulty in concentrating on the business he had in mind.

"Have you ever wished for more in life," he asked unsteadily, "than the simple pleasures that await a woman who lives out her days in a village such as the ones you know?"

"I'm not sure I know what you mean."

Rattlesnake smiled.

"Quebec in Canada is an interesting city," he told her. "It has many attractions, including a great many dressmakers, who fashion clothes to order. They undoubtedly could make some spectacular gowns for a figure like yours. New York, too, is an interesting town, but it will undoubtedly revert to the United States when the peace treaty is signed, and my allies the British will evacuate it. Then there is London, the greatest of all cities. I am certain that I shall be welcome there, as my father was before me, whenever I choose to sail across the Atlantic. And a warm greeting will be extended to anyone I bring with me."

"I see," Dalnia murmured, and let a forearm drop until it draped across his thigh.

Rattlesnake pretended to be unaware of the physical contact. "It is possible," he said, "for one who is farsighted and ambitious to earn many benefits that are not available to the ordinary brave or squaw."

Her fingers crept along his leg; he found it

impossible to continue their conversation and promptly began making love to her.

Presumably, Dalnia had temporarily won their undeclared contest, distracting his attention from what he had intended to say and relying on her sex appeal to make him malleable. All the same, Rattlesnake considered himself the real victor, and he rejoiced, even as he began to relish the intimacy. His plan for betraying and conquering Renno and the Seneca, delicately conceived and tentatively broached, was going to bear rich fruit.

Chapter II

In the land of the Seneca in the Finger Lakes region of New York, elders sent children and their dogs beyond the community's palisade to play in the open fields and the forest that stretched in every direction. Every Seneca was intent on maintaining a suitable decorum, their mood serious and hearts heavy. Conversation was held to a minimum, and those who found it necessary to communicate spoke in muted voices.

Ja-gonh, Great Sachem of the Iroquois League, son of the renowned Renno, heir of the famous Ghonka, was dying. He faced the end of his days on earth with the equanimity of one who had devoted his entire life to his family, his clan, and his nation.

"My time is at hand," he said calmly to Ah-wen-ga, his wife of a half century. "I am being called to the land of our ancestors, and there I will await you."

Ah-wen-ga prepared for the sad event with little show of emotion. First she summoned the chief medicine men of the nation. While they came to Ja-gonh's side and began to chant and dance solemn rituals, she called for the relatives who were still living in the land of the Seneca.

Prompt to appear at the house were Ja-gonh's sister, Goo-ga-ro-no, and her husband, No-da-vo, the sachem of the Seneca. For nearly sixty years of both war and peace, he had been Ja-gonh's constant companion and aide. They gave a touching farewell to their great leader, who consoled them in keeping with his stoic courage. Their three daughters tried to virtually surround them as a way of insulating them from the great sorrow that lay ahead. Also on hand were the principal elders and the war chiefs of the nation. Gathering in a chamber adjacent to Ja-gonh's, they joined in the chants of the medicine men.

Other than the medicine men, only Ah-wen-ga remained in the room where Ja-gonh lay with his hands folded on his chest. It was her right, her duty, to stay at his side. She lowered herself to the floor beside his pallet and fixed her gaze on him.

Ja-gonh suffered no pain and was in no distress. His travails behind him, he maintained a serenity that was monumental. His eyes were open, fixed on a distant place that only he could see. Though his lips moved, and Ah-wen-ga could hear his voice faintly, she could hardly make out his words.

She listened closely for a time, then rose swiftly and walked to the doorway. Those in the adjoining chamber chanted more softly.

"The end is near," she said quietly, her poise remarkable. "Already he is endeavoring to speak with those who await him in the land of our ancestors. . . ."

Ja-gonh stood on the near shore of a broad, swiftly flowing river, its presence concealed in a thick fog. As he waited, the mist began to lift, and he recognized great trees of elm, oak, cedar, maple, and pine. This wilderness was completely unfamiliar, yet it held no terrors for him. He was convinced that he knew this forest, even though he had never set foot in it.

A blackness enveloped the land. For that instant, Ja-gonh felt that he was suspended in space, that he was teetering on a high precipice, and then that a sudden gust of wind was blowing him off the edge.

But he did not fall. Neither did he float or fly like a bird.

Light appeared again and ultimately the sun was visible. Its rays were so dazzling that Ja-gonh's eyeballs ached and he blinked his lids rapidly.

Somehow, in a manner that he could not understand, he had been transported across the Great River. He stood now on what he had regarded previously as the far bank. The fog had been dispelled; every leaf, each blade of grass, was clear and bright.

The shiny leaves of a large bush parted and a shaggy brown bear came into the clearing.

Directly facing him, it reared and stood on its hind legs, at least a head and a half taller than the brave. Its weight was several times that of Ja-gonh. A single swipe of an oversized paw could incapacitate an opponent.

But Ja-gonh felt no fear. He knew, with absolute certainty, that this gigantic creature was his father's close boyhood friend, also called Ja-gonh. He himself had been named for it. How this animal happened to be present was beyond Ja-gonh's ability to determine, but no menace or threat appeared to be involved. The animal's presence seemed so natural he accepted it without question.

The bear beckoned, moving its head back slightly before plunging into the bushes.

Ja-gonh followed without hesitation or fear, stepping into the underbrush.

They made their way through the forest, the bear walking swiftly, the man using the Seneca trot, a rapid jogging pace, in order to keep up.

At last they came to an area where the trees had been cut down, the soil broken for agriculture. Many cultivated plants were growing. As nearly as Ja-gonh could judge, these fields were vast, larger by far than the farming grounds of the Seneca. He assumed the population was several times the size of the community that he knew.

The trail passed close to the shore of a large lake. Its waters seemed so cool and inviting that Ja-gonh involuntarily glanced down at his reflection in the water. What he saw caused him to stop and peer harder in openmouthed wonder.

No longer was he white-haired, infirm, and thickened through the middle. Indeed, the image that stared back at him was that of a man at least forty years younger. It occurred to Ja-gonh that this was probably how he had looked at about the time when Ghonkaba, his son, had been born.

A palisade came into view beyond the green fields. The great bear vanished from sight as two couples moved out of the gate and started toward him.

In the lead came a young couple of about the same age he himself appeared to be in the lake's waters.

Ja-gonh first noticed the woman. She was blond, fair-skinned, and indescribably beautiful. She looked just as he recalled Betsy, his mother, from the dimmest recesses of his memory.

At her shoulder came a warrior with a yellow scalp lock, his skin deeply tanned, his eyes a pale shade of blue. Ja-gonh needed a moment to realize that he was actually seeing his father, the great Renno, the white Indian about whom songs and fables were still being written.

Throwing her arms about him, Betsy hugged and kissed him. In spite of Ja-gonh's lifelong training to hide his deepest emotions, he was severely shaken and was on the verge of weeping. Through the years, he had not allowed himself to realize how much he had missed his mother. "We have long waited for your coming, my son," Betsy said softly.

His father awaited him. They clasped forearms in the formal Indian fashion, and then Renno enveloped him in a bear hug. Ja-gonh was so overcome that he was incapable of speech.

"We have watched your development and your progress in the land of the living, and we are proud of you," Renno told him. "You have added to the glory of our heritage."

Ja-gonh now turned his attention to the couple standing behind Renno and Betsy. For a moment he did not recognize them, though they, too, were vaguely familiar, despite being much darker than his parents or himself. The woman was supremely self-contained, although a suspicious hint of moisture was visible in her eyes. The burly, square-shouldered warrior beside her was the most powerfully built man Ja-gonh had ever seen; he conveyed an air of great strength and purpose.

With a shock, Ja-gonh realized they were Renno's foster parents, Ghonka and Ena, looking as they would have before he had been born. He went to them and kissed Ena with great reverence.

"Welcome, my grandson," she said. "We will have much to discuss with you about affairs in the land of the living."

Ghonka reached out and grasped Ja-gonh's wrist

in a grip so firm and tight that the younger man's whole arm ached.

Even now, Ghonka was a man of few words. "Welcome!" was all he said, though his voice was full of meaning.

"We thought it only fitting," Renno said, "that he for whom you were named should lead you to us."

"I look forward to becoming acquainted with him, after all these years," Ja-gonh replied.

Renno laughed. "All in good time. Nothing is hidden from him who is patient."

Even Ghonka smiled slightly.

Betsy and Ena linked their arms through Ja-gonh's and started to walk with him toward the town. "Come," his mother said, "we will go now to eat the feast that we prepared to welcome you."

Ja-gonh hesitated before he asked, "Will Ah-wen-ga come to join us in eating the feast?"

Betsy shook her head. "Her time has not yet come."

"They still have a need for her wisdom," Ena added, "in the land that lies across the Great River."

"You will be enabled to observe what she does and occasionally even to enter into her thoughts," Betsy told him. "You must be content with that until her time comes."

"Exercise the patience, my son, for which you were renowned in the land of the living," Renno urged. "You and Ah-wen-ga will be together here for all eternity. Do not begrudge her the few years that she must spend with those who need and want her across the Great River."

"I am content to wait," Ja-gonh said quietly. . . .

The Seneca gathered silently in the large clearing set aside for the purpose of bidding farewell to those who had preceded them into the land of the ancestors on the far bank of the Great River. Seasoned wood had been stacked on the ground, and dried corncobs had also been brought forward to be added as fuel to the funeral pyre.

The elders of the Seneca were the first in the nation's ranks, leading the procession into the clearing. After them came the medicine men, wearing the Great Faces, hideous representations fashioned of wood and leather that only faintly resembled the faces of human beings. Having been taken from the building in which they were permanently housed, these were worn for the funeral of the league's leader.

The active warriors were next. After them came the squaws. Bringing up the rear were children, solemn and unusually quiet. On such an occasion, no one needed to monitor them.

Representatives of the Mohawk, Oneida, Onondaga, Tuscarora, and Cayuga, the other nations of the Iroquois League, were on hand to join in bidding farewell to their Great Sachem.

At the rear of the long line marched Ja-gonh's relatives, led by No-da-vo. Bringing up the rear, walking alone, was Ah-wen-ga, who needed no help as she trudged silently, her step heavy. The mourners took their places in a circle around the hut in the

center of the clearing. Ah-wen-ga walked to it to look
inside an opening and to gaze at Ja-gonh for the last
time. She stood motionless, her face devoid of
expression. No one dared guess her private thoughts.
As she stepped back, drums began to throb, softly at
first, but gradually their insistent beat became louder
until it seemed to enter the bodies of everyone
present.

The medicine men now were dancing, the masks
of the Great Faces making them look grotesque as
they gyrated and cavorted. They carried urns of sacred ashes collected from the funeral pyres of Renno
and of Ghonka. They sprinkled these on the body of
Ja-gonh.

The principal medicine man kindled a fire with
the aid of the rays of the noonday sun. From this fire
he lighted a torch. When its flame was crackling,
growing higher and higher, he thrust the torch into
the hands of Ah-wen-ga, who stood alone at the foot
of the pyre. Without hesitation, she thrust the torch
among its logs. They caught instantly, and as the
flames began to mount, the entire assemblage started
to chant.

Ah-wen-ga, however, made no sound. She would
have been permitted, on this occasion, to join in the
chanting. Instead, she believed she was bidding only
a temporary farewell to her husband, and therefore
behaved in the ordinary Seneca manner—silently
and with great dignity.

In just a few minutes, the pyre was completely
ablaze. As its flames mingled with the smoke, the
body of Ja-gonh was consumed.

Peering into the fire, Ah-wen-ga was not surprised to see a vision of her husband. She often had heard it said that those who had departed from the land of the living sometimes favored those whom they had left behind with such a final appearance. It was then that she heard his voice addressing her alone. No one else was aware that he was speaking, any more than they realized that he was visible to her.

He spoke succinctly, as he had in life; every word was clear. As he had done for so many years, his thoughts were not on himself, but centered on the welfare of others.

"Send word to Ghonkaba in the land of the Cherokee," he told her, "and let him dispatch an escort to take you to him and to Toshabe. You have no useful function now in the land of the Seneca. But you are needed there. Our grandchildren require your presence and your guidance."

As the pyre continued to burn, the flames gradually subsiding, the vision of Ja-gonh faded slowly from Ah-wen-ga's view. The steady throbbing of drums seemed to match her own heartbeats.

Roy Johnson hardly looked or acted like a man of fifty years, much less a man entrusted with dealing out justice in the mountainous area where colonists were establishing a foothold adjacent to the land occupied by the Cherokee. Clad in buckskins, he led an infantry patrol through the wilderness. Carrying his frontier rifle as though it were a part of him, he made no sound as he swiftly made his way, following

the faint trail left by a party of Indians. Every now
and again he halted and pointed downward at a
flower or a blade of grass bent by a human foot or a
broken twig.

One by one, the nine members of the patrol
examined the sign that Lieutenant Colonel Johnson
was pointing out. The march resumed only after each
of them had seen it and affirmed that he understood.

As one of the more renowned officers in the
regiment led by Colonel John Sevier, Colonel Johnson had his own method of teaching his scouts. It
was his boast that when a member of his command
completed a course of scouting instruction, he should
be the equal of Daniel Boone of Kentucky.

Believing it the duty of every frontier dweller to
take an active part in the defense of his home and
country, he set the example for his neighbors. This
quiet man, who dispensed justice with an even hand
in the frontier version of a court, became quite another person when he led his men into the field.

The young men of his patrol, most of them no
more than half his age, did not dare to voice their
feelings about his treatment of them. Working on the
theory that soldiers were always complaining of being
either tired, cold, or hungry, he was notoriously
short-tempered with any member who dared to hint
at being required to labor beyond his capacity or
endurance.

In addition, the scouts were not forgetting that
the colonel was the father of the most popular belle
in that part of the country. The competition for the
right to walk Emily Johnson home from church on

Sundays was so intense that the scouts assumed that it could do them no harm to win favor in her father's eyes. Accordingly, they put up with "Indian fare," parched corn and jerked venison. They endured marches so long their legs almost gave way and did not complain audibly about receiving so little rest that sleep became a luxury. Each man saw it as reasonable to hope that any soldier for whom the colonel developed a liking and respect would gain a great advantage over his many rivals for Emily's hand.

The scouts worked day and night, therefore, extending themselves to the utmost, and never uttering an objection. Colonel Johnson finally was beginning to feel satisfied that he had brought together a superior group of scouts.

By the fourth day in the field, the patrol's members were tired and privately looking forward to the return to their fort on the following evening. The thought of a full, hot meal and sleep in a real bed appealed to them enormously. Unfortunately for those dreams, that happened to be the morning the colonel picked up the trail of a party of Choctaw braves.

"We're obliged to see this through to the finish," he told the men. "Not only is it going to be excellent training for you, but we cannot afford to let any unfriendly tribe of Indians come closer to our fort. We are in a no-man's-land between territory we've clearly marked as our own and the hunting grounds of the Choctaw. I don't mind, naturally, if they stay in their own territory, but once they begin to nibble away at the ground near our fort, it could become tempting to launch an all-out attack on one of the outlying frontier settlements. To hold such incidents to a minimum, I believe in launching an attack on any party that might dare to cross into territory that we regard as our own. We must find this band of warriors, lads, and teach them a lesson."

By noon, it became evident that they had come across no ordinary Choctaw hunting party. As Colonel Johnson pointed out, a number of what resembled the prints of horses' hooves could be seen on the trail, as well as those of human feet. The animal prints seemed smaller than those ordinarily left by horses. This led the colonel to conclude that they might be mule prints.

"It's very possible," he said, "that we have stumbled onto a pack train, one carrying supplies to the Choctaw nation."

"I doubt they carry on an extensive trade with any other Indians," a young sergeant dared to object. "Besides, what Indian nation has mules to use as pack animals? It doesn't seem to make sense."

"The picture holds together," he was told, "and makes sense only if the present trading partners of the Choctaw turn out to be the British. We will find out after we learn what goods are being transported."

The Choctaw, laden as they were, seemed unable to move rapidly. By midafternoon the scouts had gained on them so much that the supply column came within sight. Gathering his men together for final instructions, Johnson ordered them to spread out on both sides of the trail. "Do not fire too quickly," he instructed. "I don't want the pack mules to be hit. Once they grow panicky and begin to scatter, the cargo they're carrying can be lost in the forest. We will open fire as our final tactic. And when we do, confine your shots to Choctaw, not the pack animals."

Using the methods most generally employed by the Indians themselves, the party of settlers silently advanced on a broad front, each ready for action but—following the colonel's orders—not initiating a fight.

Johnson, occupying a position in the center of the line, caught a glimpse of two pack mules at the rear end of the Indian column. Both were heavily burdened, and behind them marched two braves wearing Choctaw war paint. Determining what arms they carried was difficult because, at that moment, an arrow sang through the air close to Colonel Johnson and was buried in the trunk of an oak. Immediately making use of the tree as a cover, he stepped behind it, and from there could see the guard for the pack train who had fired the arrow. Now the guard was searching for another glimpse of him. The oak would provide only temporary cover.

Johnson had learned through long experience in forest warfare the defensive value of a strong offense. He raised his long frontier rifle, took quick but exacting aim, and fired.

The Choctaw died silently, making no sound as he slid to the ground.

But the sound of rifle fire alerted his companions, a number of whom dropped back to ward off whatever assault was being made. Though the Choctaw were armed with muskets as well as their traditional bows, they proved clumsy and inept in handling the weapons. Their shots went wild, landing nowhere near their targets.

The semicircle of the militia patrol closed in more tightly and cut off the enemy's ability to maneuver. Without exception, they were expert marksmen.

A second brave died, and then a third. The rest of the Choctaw rear guard fled, none taking the time to rally their comrades to make a determined last stand.

Johnson did not need to give any orders. His men's seasoning soon proved itself in their effective efforts. They maintained a maximum pressure, moving up in unison from tree to tree so rapidly that their foes had no opportunity to reorganize.

Caught off guard and unable to employ the Choctaw's own favorite tactic of seizing the initiative, the pack-train company fell back in a flight that soon became a stampede. Losing all sense of discipline, they hurried away.

The mule train continued to plod ahead on its own, but the lead mules, finding themselves abandoned, became confused. Soon, some fifteen of them were milling around and starting to move off in all directions.

Seeing the foe vanishing in disarray, Colonel Johnson called off all attempts to follow and annihilate the Choctaw. It was better, he reasoned, to let the remaining enemy escape and, rather, to concentrate on salvaging anything possible from the supply train.

As it happened, fortune smiled on his militia.

Virtually the entire train could be saved. The mules could not move rapidly in the forest, so the soldiers found it a relatively simple matter to catch up, surround, and halt them. Their packs contained large quantities of British muskets, ammunition, and various household goods.

"This is one load of British merchandise," Colonel Johnson said grimly, "that will never reach its destination. We will distribute the weapons and goods to anyone back at the fort who can make good use of them."

The colonel decided to march all night, if necessary, in order to reach the log palisade safely, before the much larger company of Choctaw could reorganize and counterattack.

He theorized, correctly, that the weapons and supplies must have originated at a point farther to the north, where a British outpost continued to function, maintaining contact with the main force in Canada even though it was almost surrounded by hostile Americans. The mules could not have traveled much farther than that distance, and it was reasonable to assume that the arms had been stored there, awaiting just such a troublemaking disposition as the mule train had been intended to initiate. Colonel Johnson had never met Sir Nigel Durward, but his intuition probably would have enabled him to envision that Englishman. As to who might have arranged for the transfer from British hands to the Choctaw, the colonel could only hazard a guess.

Like the Indians who were their enemy, the frontier settlers recognized no limits in their war to

the finish. Colonel Johnson made a point of looking
the other way when three of his soldiers claimed the
scalps of Choctaw braves who had fallen.

Renno and his escort did not tarry on their way
back to the land of the Cherokee after they left
Mount Vernon. He knew that his father and Loramas
would be eager to learn the contents of General
Washington's message. When they crossed the mountains and headed west, they were within a two-day
march of the fort where Colonel Johnson's troops had
originated. The fort was located at the junction of
two rivers that united to form one much larger in the
western foothills of the Great Smokies range.

One of his Seneca scouts came to him and pointed
out something strange in the forest: five pairs of
footprints leading toward the southwest. Four were
obviously the prints of male Indians wearing moccasins, and the fifth was a recurring set of small
footprints of a female or child. Renno was sufficiently
intrigued to order a brief delay in their journey, and
he gave the command to follow in the same direction
as the footprints.

The braves immediately increased their pace
and made such good progress that by late afternoon
they approached the party. Renno ordered his men
to surround it and to refrain from firing unless first
attacked.

His escort promptly changed directions and traveled in a wide circle. Within a short time, the hooting
of an owl in the forest told Renno that the maneuver
had been carried out and that the party was sur-

rounded. He increased his own pace in order to close the circle.

He was not overly surprised, a short time later, when he saw four braves wearing Choctaw war paint. With them was a captive, a young white woman with wheat-colored blond hair streaming down her back. Her face was forlornly unhappy, and her hands were securely bound behind her back with a rawhide thong. Occasionally, one of her captors prodded her in an attempt to force her to walk faster.

One Choctaw became aware of the Seneca and gave the signal to his companions by drawing his tomahawk and hurling it with all his might. The weapon came perilously close to Renno, glancing off a tree between him and the closest companion to his left. The Choctaw had struck the first blow.

Renno drew an arrow from its quiver, fitted it into his bow, and let fly. His aim was true, and his arrow lodged in the chest of the Choctaw, killing the brave instantly.

Two other members of the escort fired at a second Choctaw, who also went down, fatally wounded. The surviving pair promptly took to their heels, managing to break out of the circle forming around them. Showing far more speed than grace, they raced off through the forest, making no attempt at concealment.

By this time, Renno had reached the side of the captive. After drawing his knife from his belt, he slashed her bonds and freed her hands.

Rubbing her chafed wrists, she looked at Renno angrily, her pose defiant. "If you are expecting me to thank you," she said, "you have another thing coming. I refuse to be grateful for being hauled from one tribe to captivity in another!"

Renno looked at her gravely, curbing a desire to laugh. He startled her by bowing from the waist. "I am Renno of the Seneca," he told her, "and I do not make war on women, not even those whose tongues are sharp."

She stared at him in openmouthed astonishment. His English was as faultless as her own.

"Perhaps," he continued, "you will be good enough to let me know the location of your home, so my companions and I can return you there. We have a mission of considerable importance to complete, and thus we have no time to waste." He glared at her expectantly.

"I live some distance away, at a fort on the bank of the Tennessee River—perhaps you know of it," she said, her attitude adamant. "But please do not put yourselves out for my sake. I am perfectly capable of returning home."

"I am sorry to disagree with you," he said, shaking his head, "but you have already demonstrated your inability to take care of yourself in these woods. You need protection, which my men and I will gladly give to you."

She knew he was right but was willing to admit it only grudgingly. "Thank you," she conceded ungraciously. Apparently realizing how impolite she had been, she allowed her anger to dissipate somewhat. "You are very far from home," she observed, "if, as you say, you are of the Seneca."

Renno saw no need to discuss his circumstances with her. "Whom do I have the honor of addressing?" he asked formally.

His good manners stunned her. "I am Emily Johnson," she said.

"I don't suppose," he asked, "you are from the family of Lieutenant Colonel Johnson, commander of a battalion of militia?"

Emily Johnson's wonder grew. "Yes," she said faintly, "he is my father."

"I know him by reputation," Renno said. "I have heard much about him from men who fought beside him."

To Emily Johnson's further surprise, he raised his voice slightly and called out. Soon they were surrounded by twenty warriors of the Seneca and the Cherokee. He spoke to them briefly, giving orders, and they scattered. Then he returned his attention to Emily. "If you please, Miss Johnson," he said, "we will start for your home now. We will stop about a half hour's march from here to make camp for the night and to provide you with a good supper. I am sure the Choctaw were not sufficiently considerate to give you adequate food." Allowing her no chance to reply, he began to steer her through the forest.

After a short walk they came to a large, swiftly moving river. Reaching a clearing on the curve of the stream, Renno halted, and within a few moments his braves had built a roaring fire. Then she saw it firsthand—the fabled resourcefulness of the Indians in the wilderness, as they produced a meal as if out of nowhere. One of the men shot a deer. Two brought

down a pair of large geese, and still others caught
some firm-fleshed fish with very white meat. The
food was expertly prepared for eating, and while it
cooked, still other braves appeared with a variety of
plant roots, which they threw into the coals. Two of
the warriors picked a considerable quantity of berries.

Emily was left to her own devices until it was
time to eat, and then Renno offered his own knife to
cut her venison and fowl. As she ate, she looked at
him occasionally. His behavior was like that of an
American gentleman. In spite of his heavy tan, his
skin was paler than that of other Indians, and she
observed, too, his eyes; he was the first blue-eyed
Indian she had ever encountered. His hair was brown,
rather than black, and she assumed that he had some
white ancestors. His austere manner made it seem
impossible to question him on such an intimate matter.

But Renno saw no reason to let his own curiosity
about this attractive young woman go unsatisfied. He
waited until they had eaten their fill and then rinsed
their faces and hands in the waters of the river.
"How did you fall into the hands of the Choctaw?"
he asked.

Emily wanted to retort that the answer was
strictly her own concern, but she reminded herself
that this man had saved her from a very unpleasant
fate, and she therefore owed him a civil and honest
reply.

"My father," she explained, "returned home after being away on war maneuvers. He had a skirmish
with the Choctaw and came home a week ago with a
considerable quantity of booty. He warned me not to

go beyond the town palisade because other Choctaw undoubtedly were in the vicinity. But I couldn't accept his word on a matter like that," she added, her voice becoming strident. "After all, I have been accustomed to going into the woods alone since I was a small child, and I saw no reason to change the habits of a lifetime." She became quieter and her smile was rueful. "You know the rest. My father was right and I was wrong. I was picked up by a Choctaw patrol, and although I don't know a word of their language, I assume they were taking me as a captive back to their own people. Certainly if they had known I was Colonel Johnson's daughter, they would have been in a position to hold me for a very large ransom."

"If they actually had elected to hold you for ransom, that is," Renno corrected. "The Choctaw are a strange and barbaric nation. They well might have chosen to enslave you and to put you to work for the rest of your life as a servant for one of their leaders. You are more fortunate than you apparently know that our paths crossed today."

Emily had no reason to doubt his word, and she was grateful to him. At the same time, she realized that her troubles were far from ended. She would be forced to face the wrath of her father, whose orders she had so blithely ignored, and she knew that he would be furious.

But she could not worry about something over which she had no real control. Her father would forgive her, she knew, so she successfully put the matter out of her mind.

When Renno went off to inspect the perimeter

of the camp that his men had established, Emily watched him curiously. If he had indeed served in the campaign against the Creek, her father would remember him. In that case, her curiosity about the Seneca and his background might be satisfied. Perhaps she could learn more about this unusual young man. She told herself that her interest was motivated only by the fact that he had saved her life.

The palisade of the fort had been extended twice. The town already had some five hundred inhabitants, quite sizable for the time and place. For the past several days, dozens of the men had been out in the wilderness, searching for clues to Emily Johnson's disappearance.

Captain Ben Whipple, a burly, outspoken man, whose many detractors claimed he had a permanent chip on his shoulder, peered through his enlarging glass at the small column making its way through the wilderness on the far side of the river. "There's a passel of Indian braves out there, and they've got Emily Johnson with them as a prisoner. Get the colonel here quick!"

By the time Roy Johnson reached the watchtower, a full company of infantry had been alerted and its men were taking their places along the palisade. The colonel picked up the enlarging glass and studied the Indians. "I'll have the hide of any man who fires a shot!" he called. "Go home, boys. You're dismissed!"

Captain Whipple stared at his superior in open-mouthed dismay.

"Those savages have Emily with them as a prisoner," he sputtered.

"Emily is with them, no two ways about it," Johnson replied coolly. "But she's no prisoner, and if you would bother to look at the war paint that the braves are wearing, they are not Choctaw. They're Seneca and Cherokee."

Whipple was apoplectic. "Dammit, Colonel, they're Indians!"

"If you jog your memory," the colonel said dryly, "you may recall that the Cherokee and the Seneca fought side by side with us when Jack Sevier's regiment battled the Creek to a standstill. These were our allies! And I am certain their leader, who is helping Emily to her seat in a canoe, is Renno, of the family of famous white Indians." He sighed, then said in exasperation, "Have the palisade gates opened wide, Captain! I'm going down to greet my daughter when she steps ashore!"

Ben Whipple reluctantly gave the necessary orders.

From her seat in the canoe, which had reached midriver, Emily saw the gates that faced the water swing open. She saw her father framed there. Taking a deep breath, she raised her hand in greeting.

Colonel Johnson's expression remained grim as he returned the wave. He had been greatly concerned when his daughter's disappearance became known. His worry had mounted hourly as teams of scouts continued to send back reports of failure to pick up her trail. Every day since her disappearance had been harrowing.

Emily felt a tingle of trepidation. Kidnapped after deliberately disobeying her father's orders, she knew how annoyed he rightly would be. Further, she recalled his distrust of Indians, and she hoped he would listen to the account of her rescue before condemning Renno.

She had little opportunity to dwell on the matter. As the canoe shot up onto the riverbank, her father reached down to lift her out with strong hands.

After embracing and kissing her, he held her at arm's length for a long moment. "If I were not so confounded glad to see you," he said, "I would spank you, even if you are too old to be spanked." He put her down on the ground again.

To Emily's amazement, he turned with his right hand extended and exclaimed, "Welcome, Renno!"

"I have been hoping to meet you one day, sir," Renno replied. "The circumstances, of course, might be more agreeable than these, but I believe that all is well now, in any event."

"Let me guess," Roy Johnson said. "A band of Choctaw or of some small, local tribe abducted this headstrong daughter of mine. And you rescued her. Right?"

"She *was* taken by the Choctaw," Renno agreed, "and fortunately, my escort happened to encounter them in the wilderness." He spoke with quiet modesty.

"Mrs. Johnson and I are grateful to you," the colonel told him warmly. "I know it could not have been as simple as you make it sound. And I hope you will be our guest at supper and spend the night with us. We have ample room for your men to make camp."

Emily was astonished to hear her father extending hospitality so freely to Indians.

Renno's response was equally unexpected. "I accept with pleasure, sir. We have just come from Mount Vernon, where I was so fortunate as to have an audience with General Washington. I believe you and Colonel Sevier will be interested in the opinions he expressed on our situation here in the West."

Emily's confusion was to become still greater. When they reached the Johnson dwelling, the warriors made themselves a bivouac in a wooded area behind it.

Her poise deserted her later when she saw her mother, with folded arms, her manner forbidding, her blond hair in a severe bun at the nape of her neck. Nora Johnson silently looked annoyed. Emily threw herself into her mother's arms and burst into tears. "I don't know why I had no more sense than to go off into the forest after Papa told me not to go," she said, sobbing.

"You've always been your father's daughter," Nora told her. "Forbid you something, and you immediately are determined to have it." She shook her head. "But I want you to know how terrible it has been for us to have you gone, and with no idea of what had happened to you."

Her father, who had come by during the exchange, stood watching them. "When I see the way you react to orders, Emily," he said, "I'm reminded of myself at your age. I console myself with the thought that in due time you will learn—provided you live that long. That was a very foolhardy and dangerous act. And it cost much unnecessary effort on the part of my scouts."

Emily started to answer, but Colonel Johnson gave her no opportunity. He changed the discussion abruptly, as if to put the harrowing experience behind them. "I'm sure you'll want to bathe and change before you help your mother prepare dinner," he said kindly.

As Emily started toward the main house, she paused abruptly. "Just who is this Renno?"

Her father now was enjoying himself. "Why, he's the great-grandson of the Seneca who was the most famous Indian of our century," he replied, turning away before she could question him further.

Three-quarters of an hour later, Emily, wearing an apron over a square-necked, full-skirted dress of pale linen, was in the kitchen cutting up vegetables. Her light conversation with her mother was suddenly interrupted by Renno's arrival at the entrance. She scarcely recognized him in a buckskin shirt and trousers. The war paint had been washed from his face, and save for his scalp lock he bore a striking, rugged resemblance to many American settlers of the area.

If Emily had not seen him fighting the Choctaw, beating them with their own weapons and tactics, she would have doubted that he was an Indian.

"Is there anything I can do to help, ma'am?" he asked after Nora Johnson had welcomed him.

Her reply was prompt. "Indeed there is. I will

be much obliged if you cut some wood for the cooking fires. You will find the axe in the woodpile."

He vanished, smiling in appreciation of his acceptance into the inviting domestic scene.

Further surprises were in store for Emily. When they sat down at the supper table, she saw again that Renno's manners—and her parents placed great store on such a detail—were perfect. He gave her father a complete account of his conference with General Washington. To her ear, he sounded much as Jack Sevier would have under like circumstances. By the time the meal ended and Nora Johnson had refused Renno's offer to help wash the dishes, Emily's confusion was complete.

After supper, while the women cleaned off the table and did kitchen chores, the men retired to Colonel Johnson's study to conclude their talk.

"I enjoyed a stroke of good fortune recently," the colonel said, as he took a seat by the fire. "When we were out on maneuvers, we happened to capture a supply train delivering arms, ammunition, and other goods to the Choctaw. It wasn't just that we got hold of the supplies, but we discovered a new link with the British." He fixed his gaze on Renno. "Have you ever heard of a Choctaw named Rattlesnake?" he inquired.

Renno shook his head.

"What does the name of David Simpson mean to you?" Roy Johnson persisted.

"It means nothing," Renno answered after a moment's thought. "Is he related, by chance, to the

Simpson I killed—the chief British agent west of the mountains?"

"David Simpson and Rattlesnake of the Choctaw are the same man," Johnson told him. "Evil flourishes just like the green bay tree, as the Scriptures remind us. You rid the world of one Simpson. But now his son has risen up to haunt us. Yes, David is the unfortunate offspring of Anthony. He chooses to pose as a Choctaw."

"My father and Wegowa of the Cherokee," Renno said, "will be very much concerned to learn that. If a Simpson is supplying British arms and ammunition to the Choctaw, then their threat must be taken with the greatest of seriousness."

Emily and her mother came into the room, and the men's conversation terminated abruptly.

"Tell me, Renno," Nora Johnson asked, "whether you see life here as very different from the land of the Cherokee."

"In our family," Renno said, "the differences are comparatively few. We, too, use candles and even oil lamps at night, and we often read, but I know of no other Indians who read. Our family is unique in that the members who had come from white settlements have taught us the English language and how to read it."

To Emily's questioning gaze, Renno continued.

"What my people might prefer is beside the point," he said with a shake of his head. "On the entire continent, not one Indian nation has a written language. Each generation learns its speech from the words spoken by the generation that went before it.

Therefore, we have no books, no accumulation of written wisdom, and no stories on paper. This, I think, is the single greatest difference between us. Our world is much simpler and less complicated than your world. Our homes and the way we dress are simpler, and even the foods that we eat are more simple."

"Which do you prefer?" Nora persisted.

The young Seneca regarded the question seriously and thought for a long time. "That is difficult to say. When I am in your world," he answered, "I think and try to live as you think and live. When I am in my own world, I think and live as do my brothers of the Seneca."

He opened new dimensions for Emily, and she was fascinated, but she warned herself not to become too interested in him. She would be wise, she realized, to put him out of her mind as soon as she could. Their ways were alien to each other, and even though he had accepted some of the more superficial ways of the colonists' civilization, he was still from a vastly different background, with ways and expectations very foreign to hers.

Chapter III

A messenger sadly hastened to bring word to the land of the Cherokee of Ja-gonh's passing. Ghonkaba accepted the news of his father's death with the calm of one who has spent a lifetime mastering his emotions. He was told, too, of the request made by Ah-wen-ga to join him and his family.

After conferring briefly with Toshabe, his de-

voted wife, Ghonkaba sent for Ena and Rusog, his
daughter and her Cherokee husband. They were
bickering over a few inconsequential matters, as they
so often did, and began to present their separate
arguments to him as soon as they arrived.

But Ghonkaba cut them off abruptly. "Ena," he
said, "the spirit of your grandfather has crossed the
Great River into the land of our ancestors. Your
grandmother has expressed the desire to join us and
spend the rest of her days with us. These are my
instructions now to you and Rusog. Without delay,
you will go and escort her here, taking with you as
many warriors as is necessary to assure a safe journey
for yourselves and for her."

Rusog accepted the charge without question.
"We will do as you have bidden us, my father."

Ena bowed her head in acceptance.

Ghonkaba appointed Rusog to command the
warriors. Knowing that Ena expected to have a suitable role, he named her as the head of the scouts
who would guide the party through the wilderness.
Having won her share of recognition as a scout for
General Washington's forces, she was rightly proud
of her exploits.

The young couple left early the following morning, accompanied by a hastily recruited band of Seneca and Cherokee warriors, forty strong. This company
was considered large and powerful enough to afford
Ah-wen-ga complete protection.

In the meantime, Ghonkaba and Toshabe built a
special fire to the memory of Ja-gonh. They kept it
burning night and day. Every morning for the next

twenty-one days, they would smear ashes from that fire on their foreheads.

In the weeks after word of his father's passing was received, Ghonkaba behaved with the calm that only a Seneca could achieve. When he grieved, he did it in private, going off alone into the woods and spending the better part of a day communing with the manitous. He implored them to guide Ja-gonh safely to the land of his ancestors, not knowing how quickly that journey would be accomplished.

On the seventeenth day, Renno and his escort returned. As was the custom of the Seneca, matters of national importance took precedence over personal affairs. In the presence of his father, Loramas, and Wegowa, with only the faithful dog Lyktaw as the single other witness, Renno forthwith reported on his conference with General Washington. To it, he added the disquieting news from Colonel Johnson to the effect that Anthony Simpson's son had become the go-between for British arms to reach the Choctaw.

At the end of the meeting, Renno accompanied his father to the home of his parents.

Having noted the mark of ashes on his father's forehead, and now observing that his mother's forehead was smeared, too, Renno was not surprised to learn of his grandfather's passing. Ghonkaba completed his recital of the melancholy news by stating that Rusog and Ena were on their way to the land of the Seneca to fetch Ah-wen-ga.

Renno prayed aloud to the manitous, asking them to give his grandfather safe conduct to the land of his ancestors.

Ghonkaba and Toshabe looked at one another. When Renno's brief but heartfelt prayer was concluded, Ghonkaba spoke. "My son," he said, "bad news often comes in clusters, you know."

"If you have more unhappy information for me, my father, I am prepared to hear it." Renno calmly folded his arms across his chest.

Ghonkaba looked at him approvingly; his son was truly a Seneca warrior. "On the very day that you departed to see General Washington," he said, "she whom you intended to take as your wife left also and has not been seen since."

Renno lost his poise and showed his astonishment. "*Dalnia disappeared?*" he asked, unable to believe what he had just heard.

His mother thought he should be told the full story. "On orders of your father," she said, "a great search was started. Her footsteps were found in the wilderness behind those made by you and your party."

Renno's amazement mounted. "Dalnia followed us?"

"Apparently she did for a number of days," Toshabe told him. "Then, the footprints of several males were found, mingling with those of Dalnia. And hers then vanished."

"I don't understand," Renno said indecisively.

"As nearly as we can make out," Ghonkaba explained, interrupting, "Dalnia probably intended to join you somewhere on the march. But she seems to have been captured by braves of some other nation before she was able to do so."

"Tell him the rest," Toshabe urged.

"I was coming to that," Ghonkaba told her. "Renno, it appears likely that your betrothed was taken by the Choctaw. On three separate occasions Cherokee warriors, passing near the border of the Choctaw hunting grounds, have heard it said by braves of local tribes in that vicinity that a young woman is being held as a prisoner by the Choctaw."

Renno became very calm, and his father recognized a strong family trait. The young warrior was now at his most dangerous.

"I cannot swear to it," Ghonkaba said, "that Dalnia is their captive, but nevertheless, I feel confident that it is she who is there."

Renno instantly recognized his responsibility. As a warrior whose betrothal had been publicly announced, he saw it as his duty—and only his—to invade the town of the Choctaw and bring Dalnia out—unharmed. No matter if this proved to be an exceptionally difficult and dangerous mission—the customs of the Seneca made no provision for difficulties. Nor did it matter that his ardor for Dalnia had cooled. His duty was plain.

"I request permission, my father, to go to the land of the Choctaw in order to liberate Dalnia."

"You are entitled to ask for help," Ghonkaba told him. "That is your right. How many warriors would you want to take with you to accomplish this task?"

"I seek the aid of no one," Renno replied flatly. "I do not see it as fitting that I ask any warrior to place his life at risk for this purpose. I will go alone." Hearing his tone, Lyktaw put his head mournfully down between his paws on the ground in front of him.

In Ghonkaba's own youth, he had sometimes engaged in foolhardy enterprises and later regretted his impulsiveness, even though he had succeeded. "You would carry too heavy a burden, my son," he advised now. "Think of all considerations before you commit yourself to such a course."

"I have no choice," Renno insisted firmly. "My conscience will not permit me to allow another warrior to accompany me. I must go for her alone. I will pray to the manitous for strength and guidance in the successful accomplishment of my mission. Our faith in them is so strong you need have no fear for me, my father. I will rescue her and I will return safely with her."

Ghonkaba was confident that if any man could accomplish the almost impossible feat single-handed, it would be his son. He felt gratified and reassured that Renno refused to admit even the possibility that he might fail.

To the untrained ear, the forests were silent. But to Renno they were bursting with life. He heard the stealthy movements of raccoons and foxes, of squirrels and weasels and possums as they made their way, by night as well as day. The rustling of wings overhead as birds lit on tree branches marked their observation of his steady progress. As one who had spent much of his life in the forest, he traveled without fear, yet he was ever-cautious, always on the lookout for human enemies who might try to halt him.

When he left the hunting grounds of the Chero-kee and entered the domain of the Choctaw, he needed no guide, but his caution increased. He knew that armed sentries of the Choctaw were keeping watch for possible intruders. If they encountered him, they were likely to shoot, then ask questions—if the intruder had survived. Consequently, he knew he had to outwit them and devoted all his efforts to that difficult enterprise. His travels took him through some rugged hills, and when he was only two and a half days' rapid journey from the Choctaw town, he came to a region dotted with limestone caves, their entrances concealed by the heavy foliage of the forest. An idea occurred to him, and he quickly inspected a number of caves until he found one to his liking. Its entrance was particularly hard to find because of heavy foliage. The interior was perfect for his purposes; it had a large chamber that eventually opened out from a narrow passageway. Convinced that the mani-tous were guiding him and watching over him, Renno was pleased with what he found.

Then, he initiated a cat-and-mouse game in which he demonstrated to his own satisfaction that the Choctaw were no match for a true Seneca.

Discovering a Choctaw sentinel in the vicinity, Renno adopted the simple ruse of leaving visible tracks. When he came to a particularly high, stout oak tree, he climbed high into it. As he anticipated, the sentry saw his tracks and followed them, then became uncertain when they disappeared abruptly.

Renno dropped from the tree to the Choctaw brave's shoulders, knocking him to the ground and stunning him. Before the sentinel could recover, his hands were securely bound behind his back, and a rawhide noose was around his neck.

Exchanging no words with his captive, Renno led him to the cave. After taking him into the inner chamber, he tied the man's ankles and forced him to lie down. He placed a gourd of water beside the captive's face, then took his leave.

Within the next day and night, Renno used the same tactics to capture two other Choctaw braves. After placing them with his first victim in the damp limestone cave, where he was confident they would be able to survive, he resumed his journey and soon boldly approached the town of the Choctaw.

Drums sounded an alarm as he made his way across the fields outside the palisade, but he made no attempt to conceal himself. A reception group of a half dozen armed braves awaited his approach. He amazed them by halting and raising his left arm, palm outward, in the universal form of Indian greeting.

"Tell the sachem of the Choctaw," he said, speaking first in the tongue of the Seneca and then translating his own words into the language of the Cherokee as he went along, "that a member of the Seneca nation has come to this place and desires to make words with the sachem."

One of the braves, a burly, thick-chested young man, looked him up and down slowly. "Why," he demanded roughly, "do you wish to see our sachem, Solomba, known as the Bird-Who-Eats-Flesh?"

The young Seneca returned his gaze calmly. "Renno," he said, "has business only with the sachem of the Choctaw."

"Did you say . . . Renno?"

In keeping with the impression he wished to establish, Renno merely nodded curtly.

In spite of his own belligerence, the heavyset Choctaw was impressed.

Renno fingered the handle of his tomahawk. "Renno of the Seneca does not enjoy being kept waiting until the sun disappears at the end of the day."

His prowess with a tomahawk, like that of his famous ancestor, had been enlarged each time the legend about him was retold. By this time, he was supposed to be endowed with magical qualities that guided his weapon unerringly to the heart of a target. The Choctaw brave had no desire to find out if the reports were exaggerated.

The eyes of the Seneca were blue. That much was undoubtedly true, and they held a cold menace that caused the brave to wince. His bravado deserted him, and he abruptly bolted, hurrying into the town.

Pleased that his playacting had been effective, Renno folded his arms as he waited, scowling for the benefit of the other braves who continued to stand near him, watching closely. After a short time, the brave returned and beckoned. He led Renno through the town while his comrades formed a phalanx behind.

It was impossible to retreat now, and no means of escape were conceivable. But Renno's actions made it clear that such concern was far from his mind. His success or failure depended in large part on his ability to carry himself with a menacing air, and he tried to look properly haughty, uncaring about his own safety, his manner positively regal.

The Choctaw peered at Renno as he moved past their houses. Women openly gaped and whispered to each other. The braves stared hard, some of them openly hostile, but all respectful to some degree. He seemed totally unaware of them and of their attitudes as he swept past.

His guide motioned him toward a hut somewhat larger than most others. Its door flap of animal skins was drawn aside.

Renno stepped inside and saw a Choctaw wearing an elaborate feathered headdress and a buffalo robe decorated with dyed porcupine quills.

Renno's voice was chilling as he declared, "You are Solomba, the Bird-Who-Eats-Flesh. Renno of the Seneca brings welcome to your nation from his nation."

Solomba refused to be outdone in courtesy. "The Choctaw rejoice," he said, "that you arrive in our midst as one who is famed in both song and story in every Indian nation."

"I have not yet achieved such renown," Renno told him. "The stories you have heard are of the ancestor whose name I am honored to bear." Realizing that he and Solomba could waste the rest of the day exchanging flowery compliments, he came to the point at once. "A female of the Seneca, one called Dalnia," he said curtly, "has been captured by braves of the Choctaw nation. At this very moment she is in this community as your prisoner."

Solomba made no reply, and Renno was relieved that he at least tacitly admitted the charge. Renno had consistently believed that if Dalnia was indeed here, he should find it a relatively simple matter to obtain her release.

"I have come here," he said, "to escort her to the town of the Cherokee."

"If it should be true," Solomba said, "that this female is in the possession of my people, surely you do not expect us to give her up without receiving something in payment for her."

"Ghonka, who was my great-great-grandfather," Renno said proudly, "halted the custom of paying tribute to other Indian nations. Since his day, the Seneca have paid no tribute to any nation for any Seneca who was unfortunate enough to be captured. Admittedly, that has been a rare occasion."

Solomba sighed regretfully. "In that case—"

"However," Renno continued, interrupting him, "the Seneca have no tradition that prevents the exchange of captives. You have Dalnia in your possession. I have three braves who were sentinels of your nation as my captives. If you release Dalnia to me, I will release your braves into your custody."

"How did these warriors come to be in your possession?" Solomba demanded, scoffing.

Renno remained calm. "I captured them, one by one."

Reaching into a pouch on his belt, he removed three feathered headdresses, each ornamented with

brightly colored beads sewn onto the leather background. "Seneca do not lie, but I nevertheless expected you to request proof."

Solomba examined the headdresses with great
care. In spite of his effort to retain his poise, he
became excited. "How many Seneca warriors came
with you into our land and committed these acts of
war against our people?"

Renno succeeded in looking faintly amused. "I
came alone into the land of the Choctaw," he said
succinctly. "In this time I have seen no Seneca warrior,
no Cherokee brave, no ally of any nation. I am
strictly alone."

The leader of the Choctaw swallowed hard. "And
you were alone when you captured my sentinels?"

"I was alone," Renno said, and lifted a shoulder
casually as though he had performed an ordinary feat
that required no further explanation.

Solomba stared hard at him for a long time.
Although such an idea was difficult to accept, he
realized that perhaps it was true that the Seneca—at
least those descended from the fabled Ghonka and
Renno—were unlike ordinary mortals. Perhaps, he
conceded, it could be true that the warriors of this
family bore a striking resemblance to the manitous to
whom they prayed and who acted as intermediaries
between gods and mortal men. It was inconceivable
to Solomba that without divine assistance Renno,
singlehanded, could have captured three tested
Choctaw warriors, the most accomplished fighting
men of the nation.

Solomba knew he could order his braves to seize

Renno and take him prisoner. But if the Seneca actually was related to the manitous or otherwise enjoyed their favor, he would make a mockery of any attempt to capture him. Thereby he would cause the sachem of the Choctaw to lose face. Solomba was unwilling to take such a risk.

Renno saw him hesitate. "Give her into my custody now," he urged. "Then let your most trusted brave come with us as far as the borders of your land. As we leave the land of the Choctaw, I will tell him where he can find your sentinels and set them free."

"I wish to send more than a single warrior to accompany you to the border," Solomba said, seeking to regain some part of the initiative he had sacrificed.

Renno's slow smile revealed his contempt for all foes of the invincible Seneca. "Send as many as you please," he said with a sneer.

The ruse was effective. Solomba went to the door. For the first time, Renno saw two braves stationed outside. When the sachem spoke briefly to one of them, the man immediately went off, quickly disappearing from sight.

"Before you leave, I wish you to tell me," Solomba said, returning, "how you effected the capture of three of my warriors."

Renno merely smiled. Each of the three Choctaw, he knew, would be reluctant to admit that one man had taken him captive in fair combat; they would be sure to exaggerate the circumstances. "I would prefer," he said, "that you learn the details from them."

A few moments later, Dalnia entered the hut; it was evident that she must have been very near.

She appeared to have been informed that Renno had come for her, because she showed no surprise on seeing him. He, however, was astonished at how well she looked. The stain of red berries brightened her lips, the residue of fire-charred sticks enhanced the size and beauty of her eyes, and she wore a spray of wild flowers entwined in her hair. Her simple dress was of doeskin and complimented her ripe figure. After a quick glance at the sachem of the Choctaw, she lowered herself to the ground in front of Renno and touched the ground with her forehead. Renno extended a hand and helped her to rise. That was the end of the simple reunion ceremony.

It was plain that Solomba intended to take no needless risks. He assigned four warriors under the command of a senior war chief to accompany the Seneca to the border.

Renno was soon on his way. Dalnia followed close behind, and on her heels came five representatives of the Choctaw. Renno made a point of abstaining from making intimate gestures to Dalnia or personal talk with her. He was aloof, keeping his distance from her. Although such remote conduct was alien to her nature, she seemed to understand. While the escort was with them, she responded appropriately to Renno's pattern of behavior.

Because of her presence, Renno was forced to proceed rather slowly. Not until late on their third day on the trail did they approach the commonly accepted border of the hunting grounds of the Choctaw and of the Cherokee.

At that point, he kept his promise and told the Choctaw war chief in detail about the location of the cave where he had hidden his three prisoners. The Choctaw party left at once, and only then were Renno and Dalnia finally alone.

She celebrated by throwing her arms around his neck, pressing close to him, and kissing him with all the passion she could command.

Renno, who had thought he had lost interest in her, immediately came to life.

"Is it true," he demanded, "that you were captured by the Choctaw while you were following me?"

Over a period of many days, Dalnia had had ample time to perfect her story. Sometimes she had thought she lacked any reasonable expectation that Renno or any other Seneca or Cherokee would come for her, but she had felt it most desirable to explain that although she appeared to have fared well at the hands of the enemy, she truly had not been favored. Now that the moment for explanations had arrived, she was able to launch into her version smoothly. "I cannot lie to you, Renno," she said. "It is true."

"Why were you trailing me?" he asked harshly.

"That is simple to explain," she replied, "if you recall what my life is like at home. The Seneca, especially the women of my own age and their mothers, all hate me. They made me feel like an alien. I not only wanted to be with you, I needed to be with you."

"Why should they hate one of their own?" he wondered, mystified.

"They grew jealous when you showed me your favors," she reminded him, coloring her answer with just enough truth to make it convincing. "After we became betrothed, the women of the Bear Clan seemed to want nothing more to do with me. From that time forward, they shunned me. I was lonely in a strange land, and I needed your company. That was why I followed you. You know the rest. I know I was foolish and that I caused you a great deal of trouble and anxiety. I can only apologize with all my heart." Her voice trembled as she spoke the words she had rehearsed in private with such care. She expertly told of the problems she had experienced as a captive, exaggerating to give an impression of conditions quite different from the facts. She breathed deeply with satisfaction and relief when it became apparent that Renno believed her account.

Knowing it was expected of her, Dalnia obediently built a small fire out of twigs and deadwood, and then went into the forest to forage for roots and plants, fruits and herbs.

Meanwhile, Renno brought down a duck with his bow. After preparing it for the fire, he placed the duck above the coals. While it cooked, he caught two fish in a nearby stream and put them over the fire.

They were too busy for conversation before they ate, and then Renno seemed content to remain silent while they consumed the fish and the duck, the vegetables that had been roasted in the coals, and fresh berries.

After glancing at him obliquely, Dalnia was satisfied to remain quiet, too, and to be alone with her tangled thoughts.

Renno was having an exceptionally difficult time with his own thoughts. He knew that his anger was justified, and that only her foolhardiness had caused him to travel into the realm of the Choctaw to save her. Yet, at the same time, her story of wishing to be with him made sense, and even more, he knew he wanted to be with her. Staring into the fire after they had finished eating, he told himself that he would sleep on the problem and perhaps would have a better idea by morning of how to react to her headstrong behavior that had caused so much trouble. Despite her appearance that revealed no sign of mistreatment, his faith in her was such that he saw no reason to doubt her story of Choctaw indignities and cruelties.

When night came, Renno cut down a number of small pine boughs and covered them with a blanket in order to make a bed for Dalnia. He gestured toward it and then went off into the forest to allow her privacy before she retired.

When he returned to the little fire, he saw that she had removed her doeskin dress and was using it as a blanket to partially cover herself. Her eyes were closed, and she appeared to be asleep. Saying nothing, he arranged his weapons so he could reach them instantly during the night, then stretched out on the grass.

Sleep took a long time in coming. Renno reviewed the events of recent days, and although most braves would have felt very proud of such accomplishments, he took no particular pride in them. In his opinion, he had achieved nothing noteworthy. His mind was fixed on the problem of how to deal with Dalnia. He was far from reaching a solution by the time he finally fell asleep.

Dalnia's proximity awakened him during the night. She had slid off the bed of pine boughs and had joined him on the grass. One soft yet firm thigh was pressing between his legs, her lips were fastened on his, and one hand was gently caressing him.

Had danger threatened, Renno would have been wide awake instantly, but under the circumstances, his awakening was slow and languorous. Scarcely aware of what he was doing, he pulled Dalnia closer.

She continued to take the initiative, quickening and intensifying her lovemaking.

Renno's mind refused to function. He knew he could not think clearly when he had become erotically aroused, and he wanted Dalnia with all of the passionate desire of a young male. She was skilled, tantalizing him until she knew he had reached a point of no return. Renno was far less experienced, and his lovemaking was direct, lacking in subtlety but making up in ardor for any absence of skill. No words were exchanged as they soared to climaxes and then drifted off into deep sleep.

When daylight awakened them, they made love again. By then, it was too late for Renno to think objectively. He discovered that he no longer resented Dalnia for causing him to follow her into the land of the Choctaw, and he knew that she had bound him to her with ties of erotic appeal as strong as bands of steel.

As for Dalnia, only the set of her mouth and the way she carried herself revealed her satisfaction with the way that events had turned the tide. From the outset, she had been confident of her ability to drain Renno of his hostilities and become sensitive to her wishes. She was pleased by her ability to handle him, and she reasoned that no real harm had resulted from her escapade. She was being returned safely, Renno's reputation was further enhanced, and no one had been injured. As to how she would deal now with the Seneca women—that was a matter for another day.

Before Rusog and Ena left for the land of the Seneca, Ghonkaba had unwittingly created a bone of contention between them. The trouble began on the evening of the second day on the trail.

Hunters had been successful in their search for food, cooking fires were burning brightly, and scouts had been called in. The entire company was resting before eating supper.

Rusog stretched on the ground, resting his considerable bulk on one elbow as he looked at his wife. "Ena," he said, frowning, "I hoped to confer with you at noon today. But you and your scouts were too far in advance of the main column for that to be possible. How far ahead of us were you?"

The slender Ena, who came up to his shoulder in height and was less than half his weight, considered the question. "I estimate the distance as two miles, sometimes as much as three," she replied.

Rusog shook his head. "I see no need to operate that far ahead when we have only a small number of warriors on the march. I realize you want to stay well in advance when you're scouting for an army, but it is unnecessary for a party as small as ours."

Ena interpreted his remark as a criticism and bridled. "I beg your pardon," she said coldly, "but are you attempting to instruct me in the command functions of a band of scouts?"

"That is not my intention," he answered. "I merely wanted to speak with you this noon. But, now that you mention it, your father placed me in overall command of this expedition. If you want to be technical, that command does include the scouts. I bear the responsibility for determining how far in advance you should march."

Ena's annoyance settled into anger. "Long before I knew you," she said, "long before I even heard of your existence, I enjoyed success as a scout. Not only was I a woman in a man's world, but I was working for warriors of great note—my father, General Washington, men of great distinction, men who have made their marks and will be remembered for all time as great warriors. Neither Washington nor my father ever told me where I was to operate in relation to the army. Not once was I directed to confine myself to a distance of a half mile or to extend it to five miles. They trusted my judgment!"

"That may be so," Rusog responded firmly, "but if so, it meant simply that they chose not to exercise the power that they held. They were satisfied that your conduct and that of your scouts met their needs of the moment. Well, the same is true for me—in reverse. I am not pleased with your conduct and that of your scouts. Therefore, I choose to exercise my authority, and I demand that you lessen the distance when you fan out ahead of the column."

Ena gestured impatiently and turned away.

Rusog stood up and caught her by the shoulders, and turned her toward him again. "Don't compel me to use force in order to get you to obey me," he urged. "Hereafter, the scouts will spread out at a distance of no more than one mile in advance of my main column. That is an order, and I expect it to be obeyed. If I must," he went on, his grip on her shoulders tightening, "I shall use any means at my disposal to ensure that my word is obeyed."

Ena wrenched free, massaging a shoulder where his grip had been too strong. "You're a brute and a bully!" she cried out.

"Call me whatever names you wish," he insisted, "but don't let your scouts venture more than what I permit."

"I shall do as you have bidden," Ena said coldly, "not because I am subordinate to you and not because I think you are correct. Only because of your superior physical strength."

That was the beginning of a disagreement that deepened as the journey went on. Their relationship had been marred by many such conflicts, but one or the other always capitulated fairly quickly, ending the crisis. Now, however, they were separated each day from sunrise until after sunset, and both were so headstrong, so stubborn, that the rift grew wider. By the time they reached the land of the Seneca, their marriage was badly strained.

Knowing nothing of the senseless dispute, Ah-wen-ga greeted the young couple joyously. They accompanied her to several farewell feasts in her honor, and in the presence of Ena's relatives and friends, they maintained an amicable facade.

On the afternoon before she was to depart from her lifelong home, Ah-wen-ga went to a little clearing in the forest that Renno the elder had discovered many years before. There she communed in silence and in private with the manitous. Feeling refreshed, she returned and ate supper at the home of No-da-vo and Goo-ga-ro-no.

"When your duties permit," Ah-wen-ga urged the couple, "come to us in the land of the Cherokee. They and all the Seneca who have taken up residence there will welcome you with open arms."

At dawn the following morning, Ah-wen-ga and her escort began the long march south. They had not gone very far when they were unexpectedly joined by one hundred men, women, and children who had changed their minds after deciding earlier to stay at home. The braves added their strength to those of the warriors who had been protecting the party.

The unpleasantness that marred the marriage of Ena and Rusog now inevitably called itself to Ah-wen-ga's attention. She gave no indication that she was aware anything was amiss, but biding her time, she kept the couple under close observation. The journey was uneventful, even when they skirted the edge of the hunting grounds of the Choctaw.

Finally, two nights before they were due to arrive home, Ah-wen-ga was eating supper on the trail with Ena and Rusog when she decided the time was right to speak. "I assume," she said to her granddaughter, "that you will have words with your father as soon as we arrive, and will ask him to dissolve your marriage?"

"Oh, no!" was the shocked response.

Ah-wen-ga's quiet calm was maintained. "I suppose it is just as well," she went on, "that as the Cherokee are the larger nation, to leave such matters in their hands. Rusog, I take it that you are going to speak to your grandfather about making a separation between you and Ena permanent?"

So upset that he could not speak, Rusog clenched his fists and shook his head vehemently.

"My husband and I were married for fifty summers," Ah-wen-ga said, "and except for those occasions when we were separated by war or by other duties, we slept together every one of those nights. I would be the last to deny that we had disagreements, but we never allowed a whole night to pass without discussing the matter and making an adjustment. From the time we were very young, we knew our love was a precious commodity and that it had to be preserved at all costs. You two are almost the equal in years to Ja-gonh and me when we were first married, but you do not seem to regard your relationship as something special, to be nurtured and protected at all cost. No such thing as a half marriage is conceivable. I have watched you closely for many nights. Not once have I seen you hug and kiss. Not once have I seen you exchange the normal confidences between husband and wife. Nor am I aware that you have slept together. That is wrong and unnatural. Your marriage is no real marriage, but a travesty of one. It is better to end the relationship now, before it is complicated by the advent of children. Therefore, I consider that I must recommend to your fathers that your marriage be terminated at once."

Ena was so shocked she could not speak. She tried, but no articulate sounds came out.

Rusog did slightly better. He made a rumbling noise that emanated from somewhere deep within him, and he finally found his voice. "I think you have erred in your assessment of Ena and me, honored grandmother," he said. "Your observations about us are accurate and I could not deny them, but your conclusions are mistaken. Ena has been a fool, but only because she has mimicked me. I have been the biggest of fools. I love my wife, but I have been too stubborn, too filled with pride to admit it."

Ena looked at Ah-wen-ga, then at Rusog. "We have quarreled like children," she said, "and like children, we have been unable to admit that we are sorry and that we repent of our wrongdoing."

"We would be awarded the misery we have earned," Rusog said, "if we were forcibly separated by my grandfather and by Ena's father, and were compelled to terminate our marriage. I could not rebel against the pronouncements of my sachem, even if he forces me to marry some other woman. I would obey him, even though my heart would be broken with unhappiness."

"If our marriage should be terminated," Ena said fiercely, "I will flee where the name of either nation is unknown. I will insist that Rusog come with me if he loves me—and I know he does—and he therefore will accompany me. We will be outcasts, but we will be together!"

Ah-wen-ga started to laugh. "Ena," she said, "you are truly the daughter of Ghonkaba. You are a rebel from the top of your head to the soles of your feet. If the worst befell you, you would do as you have threatened. But I assure you there shall be no need for either of you to defy the authority of those relatives who exercise command over you. I am curious, but I contain my curiosity. The cause of your disagreement is your own business, and it need go no farther than the two of you. I shall give you the opportunity to stop abusing the institution of marriage and start treating each other with the respect that you and it deserve. Behave in that manner, and I swear to you that I shall say nothing that would put your marriage in jeopardy."

Ena stood before her and lowered her head. "I thank you, my grandmother," she said softly.

Rusog joined his wife and placed an arm around her shoulders. "I add my thanks," he said, "to those that Ena has expressed."

Ah-wen-ga glared at them, her eyes suspiciously bright. "Have you nothing better to do," she demanded, "than to occupy the time of an old woman by chattering with her? Night has come and we have had a long day on the trail, so I am going to sleep in order to prepare for another long day tomorrow." She turned swiftly and retreated into the tent that had been set up for her.

Ah-wen-ga watched the young couple as they withdrew into Ena's tent. It was small, barely large enough to accommodate two persons, but she was confident they would manage.

Lowering the entrance flap of her own tent, Ah-wen-ga quietly hoped that Ja-gonh had been conscious of the scene that had just taken place. But she also hoped that he, like her, was no longer watching the young couple. At some moments in the life of a granddaughter it was not fitting to spy on her for even the most benevolent reasons.

Dalnia and Renno made love every night in the wilderness before they retired and every morning when they awakened. This activity became part of their routine. On their last night in the forest, Dalnia startled him by asking, "How well do you know Casno?"

"I have been well acquainted with him all my life," he replied. "I knew him first when I was a boy and he and my father were fellow war chiefs of the Seneca. Then I came to know him much better when he was second in command of my father's special unit during the American Revolution. He has withdrawn somewhat from our day-to-day existence in the land of the Cherokee since he became our principal medicine man. But I still feel I know him as well as I do anyone outside my immediate family. Why do you ask?"

She shrugged her shoulders. "It really does not matter," she said casually. "I was just curious, that is all." She forestalled further questioning by beckoning to him. Renno went to her, and that ended the matter for a time.

He was still wondering, however, about her unusual inquiry. Later, after they had made love, he brought up the question again as they were about to fall asleep.

"It isn't important," she said.

"I insist on knowing," he told her.

"I—I. No, never mind. It truly does not matter."

Though she was reluctant to speak, Renno persisted. "I demand that you tell me."

Dalnia moved closer into his embrace, her eyes troubled, her voice hesitant. "I—I do not want to cause any problems between your family and Casno," she murmured. "It is just that—well, I have been wondering whether he was the one who somehow secretly informed the Choctaw that I was following you and made it possible for them to find me and take me prisoner."

Renno was jolted as though struck in the forehead with a tomahawk. "Casno, of all people, could not be responsible for such a despicable act!" he protested. "I cannot imagine why he would stoop to doing anything of the sort."

"I know that there has been bad blood between my family and him," Dalnia replied, "but I do not want to dwell on such a matter. I have said more than enough, and I wish we could drop the subject."

She put an end to their conversation by again moving closer to him, raising her face to his, and initiating their new lovemaking. Eventually they fell asleep, and the subject appeared to be forgotten.

Renno continued to be troubled, however, and the next day he brought it up again. "I wish you would be frank with me," he said. "Tell me the real reason that you think Casno betrayed you."

Dalnia sucked in her breath and sighed gently, tremulously. "Very well," she murmured. "Age, apparently, does not determine the heat in a man's loins, nor does it have any bearing on his desire for a woman. I have seen and felt his eyes on me. He has wanted me, but I am betrothed to you. I have not been available for him. That has not curbed his yearning, nor has it stopped him from wanting me."

Renno was shocked.

"I cannot prove that what I have said is so," she went on, "but when I feel his eyes fastened on me, I know that my thoughts are true. Only a woman who is the object of a man's desires knows beyond all doubt when he wants her. And sometimes she knows, too, that he will stop at nothing to gain possession of her."

"How would Casno benefit," Renno asked, puzzled, "from your captivity by the Choctaw?"

"Had I been forced to remain with the Choctaw for an even longer time," Dalnia said, "my reputation for faithfulness to you could have been destroyed. You no longer would have wanted me as your wife.

Then, if I was returned to our people, it presumably would have been easy for Casno to arrange an affair with me—that, I am sure, was his thinking."

Renno pondered the significance of her words as they sank in. She presumably had suffered considerable embarrassment in satisfying his curiosity, but at least he could understand now why she maintained that Casno was responsible for her captivity. He would not forget her words, even though her suspicion seemed incredible. Ultimately, he was blinded to other possibilities by the strength of his physical need for her.

Later that same day, they arrived home, and Dalnia was restored to her parents briefly before going off to her own dwelling. Before they parted, however, a strange scene occurred. Lyktaw, overjoyed at seeing Renno at first, quickly turned away from him and, with ruff raised, snarled at Dalnia, ready to stalk her before Renno pulled him back.

Renno went at once to his father and Wegowa to report on his journey. In detail, he told them what had happened there. He saw nothing unusual in the method he had used to win Dalnia's release, but Wegowa was filled with admiration. The story of Renno's capture of three Choctaw braves soon was known to the whole community and added to the young warrior's stature.

Only when he and his father were alone did Renno reveal his belief that Casno might have been responsible for the capture of Dalnia.

Ghonkaba was incredulous. "You cannot realize what you are saying!" he declared. "Casno is incapable of such perfidy. During the long years of the war, he saved my life in battle, just as I saved his. I cannot and will not believe he is guilty!"

Renno let the matter drop. His loyalty to Dalnia was too great to permit him to reveal that Casno had felt lust for her and had been motivated by his desire to take her for himself.

Ghonkaba, however, saw no need to keep silent; on the contrary, he felt that fairness to his lifelong friend made it necessary to reveal the accusation to Casno. He went to the medicine man at the house where Casno lived. The two old friends adjourned to a wall outside the house and sat with their backs propped up against it as they smoked the clay pipes that were the invention of the Cherokee. They finally had found them superior to the pipes of wood or corncob that the Seneca customarily smoked.

Making clear his own refusal to believe anything untoward about his comrade in arms, Ghonkaba told Casno about Renno's charges against him.

The medicine man did not lose his temper but reacted with the calm typical of a Seneca warrior in a moment of crisis. "I refuse to dignify such rubbish by denying it," he said coolly. "If Renno were anyone but your son, I would challenge him to a hand-to-hand combat and I would kill him. But he is young, and he remains painfully gullible."

"Do you imply," Ghonkaba asked thoughtfully, puffing on his pipe, "that Dalnia is responsible for this lie against you, this throwing of dirt upon your integrity?"

"I do more than imply it," Casno said. "I state

flatly that she alone invented this untruth for what I assume to be her own purposes."

"What motive could she have, do you think?"

"I do not think, and I do not guess," Casno replied. "I know. Dalnia is the sort of woman who must build up the fire that cooks beneath the kettle of soup so it bubbles more furiously. She stirs it vigorously because she delights in the fumes that it gives off. She is happy only when she is the center of attention and is creating controversy."

"I have tried to show Renno that Dalnia is less than perfect," Ghonkaba said with a sigh, "but he is young and headstrong, and he is of an age when he will not listen to me. I am familiar with that stage of development toward maturity."

"He must see her for what she is—or expect to pay the consequences for his faulty vision," Casno said. "I see no alternative. Until such time as he comes to his senses, I cannot pretend that all is right between us, so I shall avoid him."

Ghonkaba could not blame his friend for feeling as he did, and was unhappy that Renno was responsible for the unfortunate rift in their relationship.

Chapter IV

When Ena and her scouts brought word that Ah-wen-ga was approaching, all the Seneca went out into the fields beyond the palisade to greet the widow of the Great Sachem of the Iroquois League. There, with Lyktaw bounding on ahead, they also had the unexpected pleasure of a reunion with their friends and relatives who had accompanied her on the long journey.

Ghonkaba and Toshabe were on hand, as were Renno and El-i-chi. Ghonkaba made a brief, extemporaneous address to the newcomers and presented them to Loramas, who welcomed them on behalf of the Cherokee. The Seneca community was now more than five hundred strong and unquestionably was the force to be reckoned with in the area.

With the necessary formal welcome concluded, Ah-wen-ga now had the opportunity for the private reunion with her son and his wife, those closest and dearest to her, Foregoing the strictures against displays of emotion, as soon as they were hidden from public view she demonstratively hugged Ghonkaba, before standing back to study his strong face with evident approval. Then she turned and embraced Toshabe, again taking time to admire the character and beauty of her features. It was one of the great moments of her life, this meeting after so many years of painful separation. Coming so soon after her husband's death, it assumed added emotional impact. Ghonkaba and Toshabe, themselves deeply touched and unusually stirred by the happy occasion, seemed close to tears for a few minutes. Tenderly and quietly, they spoke to Ah-wen-ga, seeking to tell her how pleased they were to have her join them, and how gratified they were to see her looking so well after her long journey. At last they escorted Ah-wen-ga to her new house, which had just been erected as an addition to their dwelling. She found it suitable for her needs, then made herself at home in Toshabe's kitchen, sitting on the ground before the stone cooking pit. While a container of herb tea brewed on the fire, she told her son and daughter-in-law about Ja-gonh's last hours on earth.

Ghonkaba rejoiced when he learned that his father had been trying to speak to those ancestors who had preceded him across the Great River. His admission to the cherished land of the ancestors seemed assured.

Toshabe poured gourds of the steaming tea. "I hope," she said, "you had an opportunity to become acquainted with the husband of your granddaughter on the journey south."

"Indeed I did," Ah-wen-ga replied enthusiastically. "Rusog is a fine young man and a fitting mate for our Ena. Together they are an impressive young couple." By no means would she reveal the quarrel that had threatened to separate Ena and Rusog, nor would she mention the part she had played in bringing them together again.

"Rusog shows promise of becoming a splendid warrior," Ghonkaba said, "but that does not necessarily mean he will also become a good husband. Only time can tell that."

"As for Ena," Toshabe added, "she won much glory for herself during the war as a scout, but whether she will become a good wife for Rusog remains to be seen."

"You need not worry about them," Ah-wen-ga said. "I spent several evenings talking at length with them on our journey. I find they are a sensible as well as a sensitive couple. I predict they will give us cause to be proud, even though they still have some problems to iron out over the years. Their temperaments are so much alike, as you know."

Ghonkaba was pleased. He recalled that ordinarily his mother had been sparing in her praise, and her admiration for Ena and Rusog was encouraging.

"It is my wish," she said, "to become better acquainted with El-i-chi. I scarcely could recognize him when I first set eyes on him today."

"You shall have ample opportunity to know him well," Toshabe told her. "He is the youngest of our children, so I have a soft spot for him forever within me. Even so, I can see his faults. I am afraid you will find him brash and inconsiderate of others and interested only in himself."

"You have given a perfect description of Ghonkaba when he was about the same age," Ah-wen-ga said with a laugh. "I see little wrong with El-i-chi, as you have described him, that the passage of time will not cure."

"For the sake of El-i-chi's future, we hope you are right," Toshabe murmured.

"We find it very confusing," Ghonkaba said. "One day El-i-chi is reasonable and straightforward, but the very next day he is so contrary that we can have no idea what he is thinking and where he stands."

"That is because his mind is a mixed-up muddle," An-wen-ga advised. "He is just discovering his own values. Give him time, be patient with him, and you will find he will straighten out and do you credit."

"I hope you are right, my mother," Ghonkaba exclaimed fervently.

"I am right," she replied. "You may take my word on it."

Ghonkaba sipped his tea and, relaxing, lighted his pipe.

Ah-wen-ga related briefly the words of Ja-gonh, imparted to her at his funeral pyre. She told of his admonishing her to bring her wisdom to her grandchildren. Then she went on to say that she had purposely saved mention of Renno until the last. "Because of the pleasant surprise he gave me when I saw him today," she explained with a smile. "When I last saw him, he looked exactly as Ja-gonh did at that age. And today, I am glad to say, he resembled him so much that I could have sworn his grandfather had come back to life." She smiled wistfully, shook her head, and said softly, "Such things are not to be." Then she brightened and added more forcibly, "At least Renno lives up to his famous name. Ena and Rusog regaled me with tales of his exploits in your war against the Creek and the Tuscarora. He sounded like the great Renno come to life again. When I was a young woman, and for many years after that, I was in awe of the great Renno. To me it sounds as though my grandson is cut from the same material. How I rejoiced when I was told how he had defeated the archvillain of the British, Anthony Simpson, in personal combat!"

"Such victories come easily to Renno," Ghonkaba said, and related to his mother how young Renno had successfully kidnapped three Choctaw braves.

"I have no doubt," she said, "that my grandson will win the special favor of the gods and be in the care of the manitous who would guide and guard him. But he must be especially diligent not to offend them, or they will turn on him and he will lose all that he has won."

She spoke with such solemn finality that Toshabe was frightened. "What do you mean?" she asked.

"Those who have been awarded the favor of the gods," Ah-wen-ga answered gravely, "are required to lead exemplary lives. They must be upstanding, not according to their own standards, but in accordance with the exacting standards of the manitous. They must demonstrate—every day of their stay upon this earth—that they are deserving of the favors and protection they are being given. If they fail to live up to this obligation, they are cast down and never rise again, no matter how long they live. Then they have cause to regret their indiscretions, but it is too late. With all this in mind, I still feel justified in having great confidence in Renno's future."

A dozen questions crowded into Ghonkaba's mind, but he refrained from asking them, realizing his mother would voluntarily tell all that she wished him to know.

"As for Dalnia, I have known her most of her life," Ah-wen-ga said. "I lived in the same town with her for years, after all, while she was growing up. I will not waste your time and patience by telling in detail the problems she caused for No-da-vo, your uncle, as the sachem of the Seneca. Let it suffice that he was repeatedly plagued by the same question, whether or not to expel Dalnia and her family from the Seneca nation. Even as a child, her behavior left much to be desired. Then her excuses were many and ingenious. Although No-da-vo was convinced she was lying, he found it difficult to prove her in error. She was infinitely clever and always remained a full step ahead of those who accused her of wrongdoing."

"Toshabe and I," Ghonkaba said, "were absent during the war years when Dalnia was becoming a woman. We know nothing about her at that time, and as Renno was already betrothed to her when she first appeared here, no one has been so indiscreet—or perhaps has had the courage—as to tell us the truth about her."

"I suspect that truth is harsh," Toshabe added. "I have never liked Dalnia since the first time I saw her. My woman's instincts repel me from her."

"The truth is indeed harsh," Ah-wen-ga said, "and your instincts are accurate."

Ghonkaba frowned and gestured impatiently. "This talk of instincts is irrelevant," he objected. "We have a practical problem that requires a practical solution. Renno seems to be in love with Dalnia. She has a strong hold over him, and the hold apparently grows still stronger, day by day. Toshabe and I tried to discourage the relationship, but Renno resented our interference so keenly that we fell silent. Since that time, we have said nothing. Any attempt on our part to discourage the relationship is bound to be violently resisted by both of them. We will accomplish nothing positive, and the result will be hatred toward us from Renno, and also from the woman who may become his wife."

"I will go a step further," Ah-wen-ga replied

calmly. "Dalnia is so clever that, if you openly oppose her now, she will bind Renno to her all the more tightly. They would be married before you know it."

Toshabe was deeply distressed, and her husband put a hand on her shoulder. "As we have already said, my mother," he declared, "you know Dalnia even better than we. What do you suggest that we do?"

"For the present," Ah-wen-ga said slowly, "I urge you strongly to do nothing. Under no circumstances criticize her. I was intending to speak to Renno, but I have changed my mind, and I will say nothing. Dalnia may be clever, but she is not wise, and she is certain to make mistakes. We can do nothing until she blunders. We must exercise patience and neither say nor do anything that will excite or otherwise change the present situation. We are to sit back and let Dalnia make her own mistakes, thereby defeating herself."

Ghonkaba was skeptical. "Do you imagine that Renno will refrain from marrying her while we do nothing?"

"Who can say?" His mother sighed. "His future must rest in the hands of the manitous. Beyond that, the gods will have to make their own determination."

A feast, attended by both Seneca and Cherokee, was held in Ah-wen-ga's honor on the night of her arrival. As the widow of the Great Sachem of the Iroquois, she was a personage of consequence, and virtually everyone attended.

Quarters of buffalo and venison were cooked, as were turkeys, ducks, and geese that had been brought down that same day. Venison was roasted, and women of both nations cooked large tureens of vegetables. The entire larder of the Cherokee nation was opened to honor Ah-wen-ga.

She sat with her son, Ghonkaba, on one side and with Loramas, as Grand Sachem of the Cherokee, on the other. Members of their families completed the circle.

Although she had always tried to avoid such events as a waste of time and energy, for this occasion Ah-wen-ga graciously consented to be the center of activities. "It is important," she told Loramas, "that the Seneca who came to make new lives so far from the home where they and their ancestors lived should develop a sense of continuity in their day-to-day existence."

As guest of honor, it was her duty to award the prizes at the games held before the banquet. She took great pleasure in handing awards to El-i-chi, for his prowess in foot races and wrestling matches. Renno and Rusog took advantage of their status as war chiefs to excuse themselves from participating in games of strength and skills for senior warriors, thus saving Ah-wen-ga from having to hand out prizes to other members of the family as well.

Enjoying herself thoroughly despite her misgivings, she ate with relish, finishing every dish that she was served. Those with her had no idea that meanwhile she was observing them, analyzing them, and weighing them.

Ghonkaba, she could see, had continued to grow into his responsibilities. Truly the leader of his people, he was guiding them wisely with a firm, sure hand. His mother was not surprised. Even when he was a rebellious youth, qualities that would enable him to develop into a sachem of distinction had been recognizable to her.

As Ah-wen-ga knew, Toshabe was unique. Even though she had been raised as an Erie, no woman in all the land of the Seneca better exemplified the nation's best characteristics. Believing devoutly in the principles that guided her in everything that she did, Toshabe was a rock of integrity, honest and sincere, completely reliable, and flawless as a wife and as a mother. She, too, had matured during the war and was strong and farsighted, a worthy companion to Ghonkaba.

Ena, the oldest grandchild, still brought a smile to her grandmother's lips, just as she had done all of her life. Enormously talented, she was mercurial and moody, subject to great swings in temperament. Unfortunately, she had married a man whose temperament was much like her own, and they had not yet reached an accommodation that would enable them to live in total harmony with each other. Ah-wen-ga doubted she would be able to help them make certain further desirable adjustments, despite her success as a peacemaker earlier. Ah-wen-ga wanted to help in any way possible but, at the same time, expected the initiatives to come from Ena and her husband. Whether they had the will, determination, and courage to work hard together toward the goal that would assure a happy future was yet to be seen. She remained optimistic that they would find their way.

El-i-chi was showing signs of the man he would become. His greatest qualities were rock-hard courage and unshakable loyalty. It was possible, certainly, to imagine him growing into a likeness of the first El-i-chi, who had been selfless in his devotion to his older brother and to the Seneca nation.

Ah-wen-ga left her contemplation of Renno till the last because he was by far the most complicated. Looking at him as he ate a dish of berries, she was struck anew by his startling similarity to his grandfather, so marked that she had to pinch herself in order to realize that she was not in the presence of her late husband. To be sure, her grandson was part Indian, and therein lay the only marked difference between them.

Even beyond the doubts she had raised in her conversation with Ghonkaba and Toshabe, she was very much worried about young Renno's future. That he faced a grave crisis, and that the attractive young woman beside him was responsible, could not be denied. Ah-wen-ga suspected that troubles awaiting Renno because of her could be far worse than any he had encountered.

Although she had dismissed thoughts of warning Renno of what might lie ahead, Ah-wen-ga was tempted to speak, even though she realized that she would be wasting her breath. She would be running the risk, too, of arousing her grandson's active opposition and forcing him into a still more intimate relationship with Dalnia. No good purpose would be served to arouse the active ire of a young man who thought himself to be in love. She remained determined to keep silent, as she had counseled Ghonkaba and Toshabe to do.

No matter what might happen or what danger threatened, Ah-wen-ga knew Renno would have to face his crisis alone. She could not interfere; neither could his parents nor any member of the Seneca hierarchy. She could only pray that he would have enough strength and mature common sense to fight his way out of the morass that threatened to envelop him.

Dalnia sat close beside him now, so close, in fact, that her left leg and his right leg touched, while his right hand hung down inside her thigh. He grasped and stroked her inner leg without even seeming to realize what he was doing. To his grandmother, it was evident that he was in physical bondage.

Renno was at a crossroads. Whether he went on to fulfill the destiny that lay in store for him, or if he floundered and fell by the wayside was largely up to him. His future would be shaped by his own resilience and valor.

As these thoughts passed through her mind, she was reminded again—as happened so frequently—of Ja-gonh's mandate to her to try to counsel these young people. This was her mission in whatever life was left to her.

She forced herself to listen to Loramas making short but rambling remarks welcoming her and wishing her a long and fruitful life.

At last she rose to her feet and smiled gently at her large audience.

Casting her troubles behind her, she said, "I thank the Grand Sachem for his warm and generous welcome. I cannot even begin to tell you how happy I am to be here. In fact, I feel at home here already."

Even as he sat at the celebration honoring Ah-wen-ga and extended his personal welcome to her, Loramas had not been feeling well. Despite the mounds of food put before him, he felt only revulsion and barely picked at dishes that ordinarily he would have devoured with gusto.

In fact, in recent weeks, in addition to losing his appetite, he had been sleeping poorly. His strength declined sharply, but because he felt no particular pain he had said nothing to anyone about his worsening condition.

When he became so haggard, however, that his condition could not be overlooked, Wegowa realized that his father's health was deteriorating. Greatly concerned, he went to Loramas and tried to insist that he talk about how he felt.

Loramas promptly rebuffed him. "I am free of pain," he said. "The Corn Mother has not decreed that I am ill or that I should suffer in any way. If I eat less food, it is because a man of my age does not require as much as younger, more active men. I pray to the Breath Holder, and he watches over me. I pray also to the Corn Mother. That is good enough for me, and I see no need to mention this topic again!"

He was so emphatic that Wegowa retreated in dismayed silence.

But Loramas's condition did not improve. The whole community soon was whispering about him. Word even spread to other Cherokee towns, which sent delegations of braves to call on him.

He told them he would respond to their concerns in a speech he intended to make in the council chamber. On the morning of the address, the chamber was crowded, not only with the delegates but with his own warriors, all seated cross-legged on the ground, awaiting his words.

When Loramas rose to speak, it was apparent that he was anything but his usual, robust self. His face was pale and drawn, one frail hand grasped the back of his chair to help support him, and his voice trembled slightly.

"For many weeks," he said haltingly, "I have repeatedly prayed to the Corn Mother, the great goddess who protects all of us, to look after me and to shield me, as your leader, so that I can continue to do my life's work in your behalf. She and her son, the Breath Holder, always have been kind to me, as they have been kind to our people for many generations."

He paused, coughed, and then struggled to regain his strength so he could continue. "At no time have I knowingly deceived our people. I have truly thought that I was in reasonably good health despite my weariness. But the Corn Mother apparently has willed otherwise. Little by little, my strength has ebbed. I have no idea of the reasons for my deteriorating state. But I have been forced to conclude that I have become too weak to continue as your Grand Sachem."

The entire assemblage began to shout, "No! No! No!"

Loramas held up a shrunken hand for quiet. "I am neither resigning nor abdicating," he declared. "I have full confidence that my health will be restored, and that I will once again lead you. Until I recover from the mysterious ailment that so severely hampers me, I designate my son, Wegowa, who has long since been elected as my successor, to act in my stead. But rest assured that as soon as I am able to do so, I shall return and shall take my seat upon this chair."

His audience cheered.

"I am pleased to say," Loramas continued, "that as I leave you for a time, our affairs are prospering. The Corn Mother has been generous in her bounty. Our larder is filled with the products of the field and with meat from the hunt. The Breath Holder has guided us with wisdom and compassion, and our relations with our cousins from the north, the Seneca who live in our midst, could not be improved upon. The only cloud on our horizon is caused by the Choctaw nation, which would destroy and enslave us, if it could. But our own arms, aided by the mighty arms of the Seneca, will oppose them and will prevail."

Suddenly, to the horror of the throng, he lost consciousness and slid to the floor.

The first to reach his side were Jejeno, his chief

medicine man, and Casno, medicine man of the Seneca.

Their frenzied incantations failed to arouse him. Finally, he stirred and opened his eyes when they burned pine needles beneath his nose.

He was too exhausted to speak, so Wegowa adjourned the meeting, and Loramas was carried to his own house and put to bed. There the two medicine men conferred, and decided to treat him by feeding him a preparation of grated sunflower seeds.

The old man was awake for the better part of the night, his mind remaining active as he stared off into space. In the morning, he ate a very small portion, with which he drank from a gourd filled with cool water. Then he sent for his son and Ghonkaba.

They went without delay to his room. Loramas spoke to them in such a soft voice that they were obliged to lean close in order to make out what he was saying.

"Some questions about the joint affairs of our two peoples remain to be settled," he whispered. "Do both of you understand that we Cherokee are free to select our own Grand Sachem in our own way, without interference from the Seneca? And that the Seneca are free to choose their own leader in any manner they wish, also without interference?"

Ghonkaba and Wegowa quickly agreed. Neither was in the least interested in the internal management of the other's affairs.

"Standing together," the old man said, "our two people complement and bolster each other. Divided, they are weaker and could perish. When war comes with the Choctaw—and come it will—Wegowa must relinquish the supreme command of our combined forces to Ghonkaba, who has greater experience in warfare and is better suited to hold that post. The same principle must be applied to all things pertaining to the relations between our two peoples."

Ghonkaba and Wegowa, separately and together, assured him that the conditions he had described would be followed at all times.

Only then was Loramas satisfied. Leaning back on his bed of young pine boughs, he closed his eyes for a few moments.

They thought he had fallen asleep and were about to leave when he opened his eyes and spoke again. "I am willing to admit," he said, "that I am stricken with a mysterious ailment that I cannot identify. I ignored it for too long, and now my life may be in jeopardy. I do not know if the Corn Mother will allow my life to continue, or whether the Breath Holder will come and take me away to the hunting grounds of the gods, where I shall reside for all time. That does not matter to me. I am indifferent to my own fate. What does concern me is that our people must live in harmony with each other, and with their new cousins, the Seneca, who also must live harmonious lives that mesh with those of the Cherokee."

Not until they went outside, where they found the two medicine men awaiting them, was it possible for Ghonkaba and Wegowa to speak freely. "Does either of you know the nature of the ailment that causes Loramas to be stricken?" Ghonkaba asked in a typical attempt to obtain a straight answer.

"It may be," Jejeno answered piously, "that the Corn Mother has decided that Loramas has spent enough time on this earth and she wishes him removed to the hunting grounds of immortality."

Casno was blunt, as usual. "Loramas has spent his whole life seeking harmony among men, as his religion has commanded him to do. That harmony has been achieved. The relations between our two peoples are best exemplified by Rusog and Ena, who have married each other and have united our people. Perhaps Loramas now has no further reason to live. His lack of interest in this life may be the root of the disease that saps his strength and seems to bring him closer to the end of his days."

The following morning, Jejeno and the younger medicine men of the Cherokee made a concerted effort to rid their leader of his ailments.

Allowing no one else to be present, they brought in scores of crickets that were to bring good fortune to whatever dwelling they infested.

The medicine men tacked up animal skins over the window openings. Then they built a roaring fire in the stone pit located in the central room of the dwelling, in order to smother the evil spirits in the house. The window coverings were to prevent the spirits' escape, since if they survived in that way they would be free to return later. The possibility that the patient might also smother apparently did not figure in the medicine men's reckoning.

The medicine men's next treatment was quite

different. They donned masks of leather glued to wooden frames. These were used as canvases on which were painted representations of the faces of wild animals. The hideous nature of these masks had been conceived and executed deliberately to frighten the evil spirits.

Each medicine man carried his own drum, which he beat steadily, providing his own rhythm. No two drums beat in unison, thus creating a noise harsh on the eardrums of any listener. What it might do to the sick man was hard to imagine.

Led by Jejeno, a single file moved through the house as the temperature rose steadily because of the fire. Dancing and cavorting as their drums throbbed, they occasionally raised their voices in strange wails also intended to frighten the evil spirits. Loramas raised himself to one elbow and watched, not at all surprised by their antics.

The heat was having an obvious effect on him. He had thrown off the blanket that covered him, and rivers of sweat ran down his forehead and face onto his buckskin shirt. In great discomfort, he made no complaint.

The medicine men continued their gyrations for several hours. Only when they were so weary that they found it difficult to stand did they then withdraw. No sooner were they gone than Wegowa entered, accompanied by two squaws who had been looking after Loramas, a widower, over a period of years. They removed the coverings from the windows, and Wegowa extinguished the fire burning in the pit. While one woman swept out the crickets, most of which had been killed by the smoke, the other gave Loramas gourds of cool water.

For the rest of the day and far into the evening, Wegowa kept a close watch on his father. Late that night, he reported to Jejeno.

"My father seemed very weak when we first went in to him," Wegowa said, "but several gourds of water seemed to revive him somewhat. As nearly as I can judge, he is no worse for his experience."

"Are you sure you could see no improvement in his condition?" Jejeno made no attempt to conceal his disappointment and surprise.

Wegowa shook his head. "None that I can see."

"The evil spirits are often quite stubborn," Jejeno said hopefully. "It may be they have waited until nightfall before they sneak away. We will be able to judge Loramas's condition far better by tomorrow morning."

When Jejeno returned in the morning, accompanied by Casno, he found the patient listless and uninterested in the state of his health. His appetite had not improved, and he had eaten very little.

Jejeno was forced to admit that his medicine, the most powerful he was capable of administering, had been ineffective.

After a moment's hesitation, Casno asked, "Would you object if I try?"

"I wish you would, my friend," Jejeno replied. "Perhaps the evil spirits that have entered Loramas's body are alien and will respond better to Seneca medicine."

During the long, difficult years of the American

Revolution, Casno had been no stranger to suffering and death. He had seen many men wounded and had watched in fascination as they had been treated by physicians who had saved the lives of many of their patients. These experiences drastically altered his views of Seneca medicine. After his release from the Continental Army, he became a medicine man and put his new ideas into practice.

No longer did he rely exclusively on the masks, incantations, and chants of the traditional Seneca medicine men. Continuing to utilize the ancient ways of his ancestors, at the same time he added the techniques of the physicians he had observed with the army.

First he sent El-i-chi into the forest with several young Cherokee, instructed to gather all the "red plants" that they could find.

The early English settlers had discovered, much to their surprise, that the plant—which they had called sassafras—indeed did have medicinal qualities. It had been used as a home remedy ever since that day.

El-i-chi and his companions returned with the root bark of a number of plants. Casno washed these, then put them into a container with a small quantity of water and boiled them. After allowing the sassafras liquor to cool, he poured it into a gourd and then gave it to Loramas.

"Drink all of this," he directed.

Loramas dutifully raised the gourd to his mouth and then lowered it again. The odor was unpleasant.

"Drink it, I say!" Casno thundered, and the

authority in his voice was so overwhelming that the Grand Sachem hastened to obey. He quickly drained the gourd. Casno took it from him and commanded, "Sleep!" Even though the sun was still high overhead, Loramas dutifully dropped off, not questioning the authority of the Seneca with the deep voice. He slept soundly for several hours. When he awakened, Casno was sitting nearby.

"How do you feel?" Casno asked.

Loramas replied by experimenting. First he sat up, then he threw off his blanket and climbed slowly to his feet. To his surprise, his dizziness had passed, and although he felt weak, he could discern nothing else wrong with him. "I—I think I am somewhat improved!" he exclaimed.

Casno immediately sent for more sassafras, which he treated in the same manner that he had the first batch. Then, instructing the squaws to give Loramas nothing but the sassafras liquor to drink and to allow no food to pass his lips, he prayed to the manitous before taking his leave for the night.

The next day, Wegowa could see a definite change for the better in his father's condition. Rusog was allowed to visit his grandfather, and Ena accompanied him.

When they arrived, Loramas appeared to be asleep, and they stood indecisively for a time in the entrance.

Without opening his eyes, he spoke. "Don't just stand there, shuffling your feet and gaping," he said irritably. "Come in and sit down!"

They obeyed with alacrity.

Loramas was in a foul mood. "Why have you come here?" he asked.

Rusog immediately got off on the wrong foot. "We are concerned about your health, my grandfather."

"Nothing is really wrong with me," the old man insisted. "I expect to walk out of here very soon, as strong as ever."

Ena threw a cautionary glance at her husband, warning him to leave the matter in her hands.

"You know far better than we do that the ways of people are strange, O Grandfather," she said. "Because you choose to rest and think for a while, some people misunderstand and think that you are still afflicted. We rejoice with you that you are enjoying good health. I must say," she added, pretending to study him critically, "you do look well."

Loramas, mollified, beamed at her.

Rusog, as usual, went too far. "You certainly don't look at all bad," he said, "for one who has taken very little solid food in almost a week."

The old man's temper flared. "Who says that I have not eaten?"

His grandson was trapped by his own words and could not find a way out. "I—I'm sorry," he muttered. "People say . . ." His voice dwindled away, and he started again. "Everyone has been worrying about you. . . ." Once more his voice petered out.

His wife came to his rescue for the second time. "Everyone in town," she said swiftly, "is eager to celebrate the coming changing of the seasons with you. I am delegated to ask whether you will wish to preside at a feast in honor of the occasion."

"If this is something that Wegowa can handle—"

"Oh, no," Ena interrupted. "The people insist that only you be in charge. You have supervised such feasts for so many years that people believe the seasons would not change unless you are present. And I must say, they do not speak falsely. Until I came to the land of the Cherokee and saw you in action, O Grandfather, I had no idea that the life of a nation could revolve so much around one man."

Loramas was pleased and smiled at her. "You do exaggerate," he said, "but I am beholden to you, all the same."

Ena returned his smile, then glowered openly at her husband, warning him not to speak again unless he had thought out in advance what he intended to say.

She spent the next quarter of an hour conversing with her husband's grandfather, and the time passed smoothly, largely because she lost no opportunity to flatter him.

When Ena and Rusog finally left, they found Wegowa anxiously awaiting them outside. He walked with them out of earshot, then demanded, "Well?"

"My grandfather," Rusog said, "is in a disagreeable mood. He challenged every word I spoke."

"On the other hand," Ena added, "he was amenable to the most obvious flattery."

"Provided it came from you," her father-in-law said with a laugh. "I see nothing new in that."

"The red medicine of the Seneca has made an

improvement in his condition," Ena said, "but he continues to have no appetite, and his inability to eat is a source of worry to him." She shook her head. "I cannot blame him. I told him how well he looks, but I doubt he was fooled. He actually looks ghastly, and it must reflect the way he is feeling."

"Casno, the medicine man of the Seneca," Wegowa said, "believes that my father has reduced every aspect of life to a predictable routine. Apparently, he cares little about anything. It is his indifference that is his greatest enemy."

"I have not lived long enough to know much about such matters," Ena replied, "yet a voice inside me says that Casno is right. When the day comes that Loramas cares deeply about something or someone—regardless of whether he loves or hates—that is the day his real improvement in health will begin!"

That day did not appear to be at hand. Loramas continued to drink regular potions of sassafras liquor, and they maintained his fragile health, but he did not improve beyond a limited point. Because the whole town knew of the Grand Sachem's indifference to food, everyone tried to arouse him from his lethargy. Women brought such delicacies as custards of turtle eggs and duck eggs. Braves appeared at his door with choice cuts of venison and buffalo, and he received so many steaks, so much stew, and so many cooked fish, that the squaws who took care of his household turned back most of the dishes. Loramas was unfailingly polite to those who came to see him, but their gifts failed to interest him.

One afternoon he was awakened from a nap

when he felt someone standing in the entrance to his room staring at him. He looked at her blankly for a long moment and recognized her as a Seneca. She was tall and willowy. Her mouth and cheeks were highlighted with red berry stain and she wore a substance around her eyes that seemed to enlarge them. He noted, too, that her voluptuous figure was encased in a snug-fitting dress of doeskin.

When she saw that he was awake, she smiled seductively and sank to the floor in a full curtsy that did not end until she had touched her forehead to the ground.

"I beg your pardon for this unseemly intrusion, O Loramas," she murmured.

Her husky voice was intriguing, and Loramas beckoned her into the room. "No need to apologize," he said. "Come in."

She sidled in with alacrity. "May I sit down?"

"By all means," he told her.

She gracefully seated herself on the ground, close enough to his bed for him to be able to reach out and touch her. Her tight-fitting skirt had ridden up when she had lowered herself to sit, and now rested high on her bare, firm thighs. Forcing himself to look elsewhere, Loramas noted for the first time that she carried a large ceramic pot covered with a loosely woven cloth.

"I am Dalnia of the Seneca," she informed him.

Now the Grand Sachem knew her. He smiled to encourage her.

"I bring you a small gift as a token of my esteem,"

she said, and removed the cloth that covered the bowl.

The bowl was filled with early-season berries that were ripe and bursting with juice. "I went out and picked these for you," Dalnia said.

"That was very kind of you," he replied, realizing it would be rude to point out his lack of interest in her gift.

Dalnia nonetheless sensed his lack of regard for it. "Here, let me feed you," she offered, and leaning forward, she giggled as she dropped a berry into his mouth.

Loramas, having no choice, ate the berry.

She fed him several more berries before the startled Loramas came to life and averted his face.

"Enough!" he exclaimed.

Dalnia's smile was tender. "What you need is someone who will look after you properly," she said. "You have been alone for far too long. I understand that more than ten summers have passed since your wife crossed into what you Cherokee call the eternal hunting grounds."

Loramas was uncomfortable as he returned her gaze. "Two squaws come here every day," he said, "to cook, clean my house, and attend to my needs."

Dalnia's smile was unwavering. "You fail to understand," she said. "I am certain they are competent housekeepers and that you lack for nothing in material care. What is missing from your life is the personal element. You need the warmth and the love of someone who really cares for you."

Loramas was stunned by the possibility that this

woman, young enough to be his granddaughter, might be seriously proposing herself as a candidate for marriage. He could not believe what he was hearing, particularly as he understood that she was betrothed to young Renno of the Seneca. Surely she could not think that he would make her his wife and knowingly steal her from Renno? The idea was absurd!

Dalnia still smiled steadily.

It occurred to him that she was confidently expecting him to make a move that would bind them close together and appropriately seal a union. Aside from her unwarranted optimism, he was irritated by the very idea that he would permit himself to come between a young ally and the woman he expected to marry.

Dalnia appeared to assume that the difference in their ages made him shy and reluctant to act. She inched closer, reached out, and slid a hand beneath the blanket that covered him.

Loramas was so shocked that for a long moment he froze and was unable to think or move. Then, as awareness returned to him, he swept her arm from beneath the blanket, and in a loud, deep voice that rose from within him, he commanded, "Get out! Leave at once!"

Dalnia's expression remained unchanged as, taking her time, she rose gracefully, bowed, and departed.

She had tried to reach beyond Renno in an attempt to better her lot in life swiftly and dramatically. Having failed, she shrugged off her failure and philosophically was prepared to go on from there, reasoning that she was none the worse off for her experience.

Loramas, enraged, was speechless and could only glare at her as she took her leave. Then, suddenly, his temper exploded.

Forgetting his physical weakness, he climbed out of bed, seized the bowl she had given him, and going to the nearest window, dumped the contents onto the ground outside. Then he deliberately threw the bowl with full force against the wall. It smashed into many small pieces.

Only after he had destroyed all signs of Dalnia's visit did he begin to relax, and then he realized that, for the first time in many weeks, he was ready to eat.

Going to the door, he bellowed for the squaws. One of them hurried to him, and to her surprised pleasure, he ordered her to prepare a substantial meal.

This she did and, to her further surprise, he ate much of it.

Loramas's complete recuperation began at that point. His appetite improved permanently, he began to sleep soundly again, and within another two weeks he was well enough to resume his responsibilities as Grand Sachem of the Cherokee.

Casno and Jejeno thought that their medicine was responsible for the restoration of Loramas's health. Neither ever knew, or even suspected, that what was responsible was his reaction to Dalnia's brashness. Shock and anger accomplished what the medicine men had been unable to do.

Chapter V

Reports steadily mounted to confirm that the Choctaw were preparing for a major military campaign.

Sir Nigel Durward was living up to his promise, with the result that every Choctaw warrior received a new British musket and ample ammunition for it. Reports from France by John Adams and other mem-

bers of the American peace commission intimated
that a treaty with Great Britain would be signed
soon. War in the West seemed inevitable, nonetheless.

Each day Loramas, now fully recovered, met
with Wegowa, as the nation's chief warrior, and with
Ghonkaba. Exchanging the scraps of information that
filtered in, the trio daily weighed the overall picture
anew.

"We are sure now that the Choctaw are determined to make war on us," Ghonkaba said. "I no
longer have the slightest doubt of it."

"They are waiting," Wegowa agreed, "only until
they succeed in building up their supplies still more.
Then they will strike."

"It is the policy of the Seneca to seize the initiative and strike first, once war becomes the necessary
course," Ghonkaba said. "We must take the war to
our foes, as General Washington advised. We shall
strike deep into their territory, confining the war to
their land rather than to our own. To that end, we
require specific information about the number of
braves they can put into the field and the armaments
they will carry. He wins battles who learns most
about his enemies. Therefore, I suggest we send
some scouts to learn what they can, and to return
with information we can use to decide on the moves
we should make."

Loramas and Wegowa agreed, and five of the
most accomplished scouts were assigned to leave
within the next few days to penetrate the land of the
Choctaw. Each would be responsible for covering a
difficult sector. Two of the scouts were Cherokee and

three were Seneca; in this latter group was Renno, who was assigned to the sector farthest from the village of the Cherokee. Like the other scouts, he prepared immediately for his journey, taking enough rations to avoid having to do any hunting that would delay him. After a farewell to Dalnia, he departed and traveled swiftly, jogging in the Seneca trot.

Utilizing his vast knowledge of the wilderness, he left no tracks. After he crossed into the land of the Choctaw, he slept in relatively secure places in order to avert capture by patrols of the enemy.

He followed the course of streams, knowing that large groups of men almost invariably marched near riverbeds, which would afford the least hazardous travel.

Covering as much as forty miles a day, he pressed on. After more than a week, his skill was finally rewarded.

He found tracks that led into the rugged hills beyond the river he had been following. He assumed that he had encountered the trail of an army. Proceeding with great caution, he soon looked down from the heights onto an encampment in a narrow valley between the hills. Making a quick count, he estimated that about four hundred Choctaw braves were in the force—information vital to his father and Wegowa.

Renno studied the scene, fixing its details firmly in mind as best he could determine it from his secluded vantage point. As dusk came, he turned and sped silently away, retracing his route. Hurrying northward along the riverbank, he called on his reserves of energy and did not halt all through the evening and the night. Occasionally, he paused to listen intently, one ear to the ground. His acute hearing came to his assistance, and he gradually was convinced that he was being followed.

This was a strange, totally unexpected development. To the best of Renno's almost positive knowledge, his path had not crossed that of any Choctaw sentinel or any brave from the main party of warriors. Nevertheless, the enemy must have picked up his trail in some mysterious way and were dogging his footsteps now.

Not until the early hours of the morning did he believe he had been successful in shaking off his pursuers, and only then did he pause to rest. He had slept for no more than an hour, however, when he was awakened by a sixth sense alerting him to danger. He scrambled into the high branches of an elm tree. From his vantage point, he eventually saw three heavily armed braves pass by. They surely were searching for him.

Wondering how they had learned of his presence in the area, he realized that understanding this question was hardly important now. All that mattered was that he be able to escape safely and return home with his information.

Renno stayed in the tree until the first streaks of dawn appeared. Then he abandoned the river route and struck out through the hills, heading due north. The terrain was unfamiliar, the hills were rugged, and the slopes were steep. But he pressed on doggedly, knowing that he had no alternative. If he hoped to escape, he had to keep moving.

Suddenly he heard a crashing sound directly ahead. His heart leaped to his mouth when a huge brown bear appeared in front of him and rose to its great height. At least a full head taller than Renno, the creature outweighed him by several hundred pounds. One mighty blow of a heavy forepaw would kill the young warrior instantly.

Renno reached for his tomahawk, the only weapon that would be effective at such close quarters, but stayed his hand before he could reach it. The animal looked familiar. On a trip to the land of the Seneca, he had rescued a bear from a man-made pit in Pennsylvania because it was his clan emblem. Intuitively, he realized this was the very same bear. It seemed inconceivable to him that the animal could have traveled hundreds of miles to these hills. But this was no ordinary bear.

Logic and reason were irrelevant. This bear was a creature of the manitous, and to the manitous, all things were possible. Events and happenings that mere man regarded as miraculous were everyday occurrences to the manitous, who could perform so-called miracles easily and at will.

Renno and the huge bear regarded each other soberly and at length. The Seneca raised his left arm in greeting and called, "Hail, my friend!"

The bear made no sound, and the expression in its dark eyes remained unchanged. But it raised one front paw and beckoned clumsily. The animal knew that this man had lost any sense of fear. Dropping to all fours, the beast started northward through the forest.

Doing as he had been bidden, Renno followed with no hesitation. The manitous had given him an order, and he was obeying their instructions without question.

The bear apparently knew where it was going. It moved rapidly for more than a mile before coming to an abrupt halt. As it again rose to its hind legs, Renno looked around him. The locale resembled that of any other ordinary part of the forest, with one notable exception.

A dead oak tree lay on the ground, and closer inspection revealed that it was hollow.

Renno now understood why the bear had brought him here and what was expected of him. "Thank you, my friend," he said huskily. "I am in your debt for all time." Taking a dead branch from the ground, Renno went back about one hundred feet and obliterated his footprints by sweeping the branch back and forth as he backed toward the hiding place. Then, lowering himself to the ground, he climbed into the hollow tree feet first, pulling his bow and quiver of arrows in after him. Finally, he drew some loose-lying brush toward him to cover the entrance to the log.

The bear stood silently, watching him. When the man had disappeared into the log, the animal dropped to all fours again and disappeared. Inside the hollow log, the smells of earth and wood were strong. Loose bits of damp, decayed wood clung to Renno's hair and buckskins, but he felt no discomfort and was surprised at how secure he felt. He lost all sense of time. While lying there, he recalled an old, often-told story of how his father had hidden his mother in a hollow log when they were fleeing pursuers outside Quebec.

He had become drowsy but was jerked wide awake by the sound of voices, very near. Two men were speaking in the language of the Choctaw.

"It is as Rattlesnake has suggested," one said. "The Seneca has entered into an alliance with the Evil One and employs black magic to do his bidding."

"Are you certain?" The second speaker sounded young and unsure of himself.

"Of course I am certain." The deeper voice registered annoyance. "One moment the signs in the forest are plain that Renno of the Seneca was traveling in this direction. But suddenly the signs stop, and all we see are bear tracks leading away."

"The moccasin prints were faint and difficult to read," the younger man said in a complaining voice.

"Difficult or easy, we saw signs and we could make them out. Now we see none. We have scouted in all directions, but have not found a single clue. It is as though the forest has swallowed up this Renno, or he has turned into a bear."

"Rattlesnake warned us that he is the most slippery of foes, that we would no sooner believe that we had him cornered than he would vanish. It has proved so, and Rattlesnake is an accurate prophet."

Knowing that Rattlesnake was the Choctaw name for David Simpson, Renno was interested to hear that the man knew of him, Renno, and had discussed him with other braves.

"Do you really think this Renno of the Seneca uses magic?"

"I hardly know what to think." The Choctaw was exasperated.

"We were warned, but the warning was not enough. We were not told what to do when Renno vanished."

The two Choctaw sounded closer still, and it occurred to Renno that they were now sitting on the log. They were separated from him only by the shell of wood above his head, but it held, and was still sufficient to provide perfect concealment. The bear had performed superbly his function of locating a safe hiding place.

The pair on the log called out, and a third brave answered, his voice growing louder as he joined them. "It is plain you have not found him."

One man on the log replied, "He has disappeared—again."

"But Rattlesnake swore that he would be headed in this direction, and Rattlesnake is never wrong!" the new arrival protested.

The pair on the log laughed. "You are free to search to your heart's content," the younger said. "We already have looked and looked, and we can find no trace of him."

"We have decided," the elder said, "that his magic is stronger than any magic that Rattlesnake may make."

Soon they began to speak of other matters, and

Renno's mind reverted to their previous conversation. Two questions were uppermost in his mind: how did Rattlesnake know that he was going to be in their territory? And what led Rattlesnake to conclude that he would be following a certain route?

He had no reply to either query, and this was not the time to search for the answers.

Ultimately, the three Choctaw decided to move on, and after a new, spirited discussion, they decided that Renno undoubtedly was following the river to the northwest. Therefore, they made up their minds to take that route, feeling hopeful that they would catch up with him.

After their voices faded in the distance, Renno waited for another hour before he crawled out of the log.

Blinking in the strong sunlight, he brushed bits of wood from his hair and clothes, then picked up his weapons and resumed his journey due north, taking care to leave no footprints or any other marks that might reveal that he had been in this neighborhood. His choice was between traveling at a high-speed Seneca trot or making his way more slowly while ensuring that he left no prints. He chose the latter course for several hours and felt sure that he was taking the right approach. He was deliberately increasing the belief of his foes that he was endowed with magical traits that enabled him to escape from them.

Actually, he reasoned, the Choctaw were not far wrong when they ascribed magical traits to him. He was under the protection of the manitous, provided that he obeyed them at all times and was sensitive to them. They gave him protection that could only be ascribed to supernatural sources.

Shortly after nightfall, he ate a little of his parched corn and jerked meat. Pausing briefly to drink clear water from a small stream, he felt refreshed. By now, he was far enough from the hollow log to be slightly less particular about leaving footprints. Therefore, he broke into a Seneca trot, and expending his energy freely, he maintained a very fast pace all through the night and the early hours of the following morning. Not until the sun was high overhead did he climb into the branches of a huge maple tree and fall asleep there. He slept for several hours, then waited until sundown to resume his journey, and did not pause again for more than a few moments at a time until thirty-six hours later. This time he slept in a glen that was protected on three sides. Only when he had entered the hunting grounds of the Cherokee did he revert to a normal schedule, traveling by day and resting at night.

Now he had an opportunity to dwell at length in his mind on the question of how the Choctaw had known in advance of his movements. He saw it as evidence that the enemy had been aware of his itinerary and had tried to intercept him.

To the best of his recollection, only two men had knowledge of the trails he would follow and the routes he would use. One was his own father, of whom perfidy of any sort was unthinkable. The other brave was Rusog, who had worked with each of the scouts before their departure and, with them, had laid out their rough itineraries.

Rusog was beyond suspicion, too. But as Renno thought of the narrow escape he had suffered, of the fact that he had been safe from capture only because of the intervention of the manitous, he began to realize that it was inevitable he should wonder about Rusog's loyalty.

Could Rusog possibly be jealous and afraid, too, that his own position as successor to his grandfather and father might be placed in jeopardy by Renno? In that event, how convenient he might find it to be rid of a rival by betraying him. . . .

Renno knew, of course, that he would have to use great caution. As the grandson of Loramas and the son of Wegowa, Rusog was no ordinary warrior. And his marriage to Ena gave him a prominent place in the Seneca hierarchy as well.

In following up on his suspicion, Renno would need to exercise extreme discretion lest he make himself his own victim. And he would be well advised to keep his eyes open.

Ghonkaba and Wegowa listened to Renno's report on the Choctaw column he had encountered. "I had no way of knowing," he told them, "whether these braves were the nucleus for the principal army of the Choctaw or were a special force."

"What would be your best guess?" his father inquired after a moment's contemplation.

"My supposition, without anything definite to substantiate it, is that they are the heart of their

army. They were about midway between what I
gather are the two principal towns of the nation.
That being the case, they can draw on men from
both places."

"Would you estimate that they were gathered
only for a training exercise?" Wegowa asked. "Or
that they were assembled in the first active step of a
campaign against us?"

Renno hesitated as he weighed his answer. "I
don't know that I can make an accurate assessment,"
he said. "I saw no targets set up for training purposes,
but that is not necessarily significant. They could
have designated various targets in the forest that I
couldn't see. I was unaware of the movement of any
large body of men in the immediate vicinity. But,
again, that does not mean much. They could have
been joined the next day by equally strong forces.
For all I know, they might be marching toward our
border at this very moment. On the other hand, if
they were together for training, their attack could be
delayed for days. Even for weeks."

"I think we would be wise," Ghonkaba said, "to
increase the sentries at our border."

"So do I," his Cherokee counterpart agreed. "I
will instruct Rusog to increase the border patrols
immediately. The entire area should be covered, to
eliminate any chance that we could be surprised."

He took his leave, and father and son were
alone. "I trust that Rusog can be counted on to carry
out that assignment," Renno said in a low voice that
suggested doubt.

His father looked at him sharply. "What are you saying?"

Choosing his words carefully, Renno told his father of his experience and of his reason for suspecting betrayal by his brother-in-law.

Ghonkaba was stunned. "Surely you realize the gravity of such an accusation?"

Renno, who had thought of little else for days, held firm in his charge.

"You understand, of course," Ghonkaba said, "that in bringing your suspicion to the fore you are actually charging him with treason? And you are speaking of a member of our family?"

"That is regrettable but cannot be helped," Renno answered. "I would be derelict in my duty if I failed to speak what I fear is the truth."

"Would you be able to prove your charge?" Ghonkaba demanded skeptically. "Think well on this because I know of no accusation more serious. Nothing can influence more significantly the relations of the Seneca and the Cherokee."

"As you rightly assume," Renno said, "I do lack proof that would convict Rusog if he were to appear, say, before a court-martial board of the Continental Army. More pertinently, I do not have the evidence at hand, either, that would cause a council of our war chiefs to find him guilty. Yet I have sadly become convinced in my own heart and mind that he is acting as a traitor."

His father remained unpersuaded. "What possible motive could he have? His grandfather is the head of the Cherokee nation, and his father is the principal war chief. In due time, if he continues to conduct himself with valor, he is certain to follow in their footsteps."

"Can it not be," Renno conjectured, "that the pace of his advancement is too slow to suit the demands of his ambition? Or that he is jealous of your high place in the councils of his nation—and of the favors shown to me? I am younger than he is by at least five summers, but my rank is as great as his."

Ghonkaba shook his head. "His advancement in the hierarchy of his people seems assured," he objected, "and as the husband of your sister, he should be glad that you, too, are rising in the ranks. I can see no reason he would be jealous of you."

"You may be right, my father, but nevertheless, I am not making the accusation lightly," Renno insisted. "I regret to say I feel confident that I can find proof Rusog is guilty of treachery."

His father stared into space for a long time before he replied.

"I do not doubt your sincerity, my son," he said at last, "but in all justice, I must see that proof before I can accept your theory and act on it. Until you provide me with such evidence, I must ask that you keep your charges to yourself. Unless you can credibly support them, the warriors of the Cherokee would be unanimously behind Rusog. The warriors of the Seneca would retaliate by supporting you. Then the dissension in our camp would give an undue advantage to all our enemies, whoever they may be. For the sake of fairness and also of preserving a united front, I insist that you say nothing until you can present that missing proof."

Renno saw that he had no choice, no matter what his impulse might be. His father had spoken emphatically and it was his place to obey without question. If he had his own way, he would cast caution aside without delay, bring his charges into the open, and challenge Rusog.

Dalnia, having caught three fish, had succeeded in trading them for a large buffalo steak. Part of this was smoking over a low fire, and she had broiled the remainder for supper. She expected Renno to join her, as he usually did when he was not away. With the meat she roasted potatoes in the fire and prepared some edible leafy vegetables on which she sprinkled a variety of herbs. She timed the meal so it was ready when Renno arrived after his conference with his father. Although his behavior disclosed that he felt upset when he came into her house, the odor from the steak cheered him. Dalnia's greeting was especially warm as she hugged and kissed him.

Renno was silent when they sat down to eat, his attitude dour because of what he regarded as an unsatisfactory talk with his father. But, thanks to Dalnia's skilled ministrations, his outlook gradually became better. By the time they were through with their supper, he was relaxed and laughing. As always, she had succeeded in improving his mood.

"I suppose," Dalnia mentioned casually, "you will be home for only a limited period of time and soon will be going on another expedition."

"I imagine that's right," Renno said. He saw no need to point out that the actual departure of Seneca braves in a military campaign invariably was kept secret by the high command. The warriors who were to be participating were never notified until the evening before the march was to begin.

Dalnia sighed plaintively.

"I doubt," Renno went on, "that we will be absent from home on a long campaign. We are evenly matched with the Choctaw, but our Seneca warriors hold the true balance of power and we should be able to force their surrender rather quickly after we teach them a lesson they will not forget."

"From the time I was a little girl," Dalnia said, "I can remember my father telling my mother he would be away from home for only a short time, whenever he went marching off on a military campaign. But something always seemed to happen, delaying his return. He never came home until long after my mother expected him."

"I must be honest and agree with what you are saying," Renno admitted with a smile. "Delays do occur, and although they do not seem like anything of significance to us in the field, I can see that must be very hard on those at home who are counting the days until we return."

Dalnia was sober and unsmiling as she returned his gaze. Her eyes looked enormous in the light of the small cooking fire. "I am glad you know about the delays," she murmured. "Then you surely understand the way I feel."

He looked at her blankly.

She took a deep breath and faced him squarely. "I want to be married at once," she said. "Before you go off to war."

Renno had been assuming that they would marry soon after the campaign ended. The unexpectedness of her request startled him.

He immediately wondered if she was going to have a child. "Is there a special reason you want to be married now?"

"My parents are unhappy," Dalnia told him, "because we are so close all the time without the benefit of a ceremony performed by a medicine man. Then, too, many of my 'friends' regard you as a special catch. They are very jealous. Once you go off to war, I want to avoid a lonely, unpleasant time."

"I wish you had mentioned this idea weeks ago," he said, frowning. His voice was troubled.

"Until very recently, I didn't believe war was so near," she said.

"And until recently," Renno said, "my father was the head of our family. I needed only his approval in order to marry you. He has always believed that affairs of the heart are a man's own business, any problems to be solved by him alone. I cannot imagine his objecting to our being married."

"Neither can I," Dalnia concurred quickly.

Renno's frown deepened. "But as you undoubtedly recall," he said, "my grandmother arrived recently. She is not only the widow of the Great Sachem of the Iroquois, but as my father's mother she replaced him as the head of our family upon her arrival here. I am obliged, therefore, to apply to her for permission to marry."

"I have been known to Ah-wen-ga since I was a child," Dalnia assured him, "and she always has seemed a kind and gracious lady. I would not expect that she would stand in the way of our marriage."

"When my grandmother first arrived," Renno went on, "and learned that we are so intimate, she looked at me with eyes that cut into me like sharp knives. She has not mentioned the subject to me but her views are well known. Before she and my grandfather were married, King Louis of France wanted to have an affair with her, but she successfully eluded him. I doubt that she would even sleep with my grandfather until they had been married. I fear she does not have too high an opinion of us just now."

"Then she should be pleased," Dalnia said with a smug smile, "that we have decided to marry. That is proof that we are accepting the moral standards of her generation."

"I cannot promise that I know how she will respond," Renno said. "But I do give you my word that I shall speak to her this very night. I will present our case, and then we shall see what she has to say."

After eating supper with Ghonkaba and Toshabe, Ah-wen-ga returned to her own dwelling. She found Renno squatting before the fire he had kindled in her stone pit. He jumped to his feet to greet her. She smiled at him. "You are here," she said, "to obtain advice for which you find it necessary to come to me. A warrior of your age seldom voluntarily seeks the company of a woman who has as many summers in her life as I."

Renno grinned in return. "I seek something far more important than your advice, my grandmother. I come to you as the head of our family to seek your permission to be married without delay to Dalnia of our nation."

Ah-wen-ga was dismayed, but her expression remained unchanged. She offered no clue to her feelings, making her response noncommittal. "I have watched Dalnia grow from a small child to womanhood," she said. She refrained from adding that on at least one occasion it was her own appeal that had prevented No-da-vo and Ja-gonh from expelling Dalnia's entire family from the community because of her behavior. She had intervened because she felt sorry for Dalnia's parents, who lacked control over her.

"Then you will grant permission for our marriage, as Dalnia wishes? And as I do," he added hastily.

Ah-wen-ga chose her words carefully. She knew that if she revealed the extent of her dislike for Dalnia, she would arouse her grandson's determined opposition. He might even try to find a way to marry immediately, in defiance of her authority. "I have gleaned from what your father has told me," she said, "that you and the other warriors of our people will be departing shortly for a campaign against the Choctaw. Is that correct?"

"Yes, my grandmother, it is my understanding that we and the Cherokee soon will be summoned to defend our freedom in combat with the Choctaw. They have engaged in a secret alliance with the British to deprive us of our liberty."

Ah-wen-ga knew of only one way to handle the problem. "You will say that I am hopelessly old-fashioned," she said, "but I am opposed to the marriage of any warrior in the days immediately prior to his departure for war. Both partners should ponder their agreement to wed in peace and tranquillity. No one can achieve such a state of mind immediately before a warrior goes off to battle."

Renno made a valiant effort to justify his case. "As Dalnia says, she and I are hardly typical of a couple who seek to be married," he objected. "We could remain single for many months to come, but it would give her great satisfaction if we marry before I go off to war."

"I will not pretend to be unaware of the intimacy of your relationship with Dalnia. Nor can I say that I either understand or condone it. You who have come of age recently seem determined to go against the traditions of the Seneca. At your age, I was afraid of arousing the ire of the manitous by the mere thought of compromising my moral codes. But young people today seem to defy the manitous when it pleases them, and they remain unchastised. All the same, you cannot expect me to change my thinking of a long lifetime. If you still seek my approval for your marriage when you return from the wars, come to me again. I will give the matter due consideration then. Do not expect me to think in such terms until that time."

Hearing her speak, Renno could have no knowledge of the fact that Ah-wen-ga herself, in her youth, had enjoyed one tryst with Ja-gonh before their marriage. It was a fact that Ah-wen-ga had always concealed from her family and, at last, even from herself. Instead, all that Renno heard was the same note of harsh finality in her voice that he had recognized since earliest childhood. His grandmother had made up her mind, and nothing would change it. He knew it was useless to cajole or argue. Only if he openly defied his grandmother could he tell Dalnia that he was free to marry her now. To go that far, and incur Ah-wen-ga's active displeasure if not her wrath, was more than he was capable of doing. Bowing his head to show that he accepted her decision, he took his leave.

Looking after him as he stalked away, Ah-wen-ga knew that she had postponed a crisis for only a short time. She would need to warn Ghonkaba and Toshabe that their son had lost his sense of judgment and that in all probability Dalnia would now strengthen her hold over him.

As Renno walked back toward Dalnia's dwelling, he tried his hardest to accept the realities. He knew he would be wise to put the entire matter out of his mind, no matter how displeased Dalnia would be.

For his own sake, he was not sorry that the decision had been postponed. Although he was frank enough with himself to admit Dalnia's strong influence on him, he was actually none too certain that he wanted to spend the rest of his days with her. She seemed to lack the respect for the gods and manitous of the Seneca that was instinctive to him. She was sometimes too ready to break the rules that held the nation together. Certainly it would do no harm to have extra time to contemplate the idea of marriage and face realistically the step he would be taking when Dalnia became his wife and the mother of his children. Though earlier in his life he had rebelled against authority, that phase belonged to the past. His attitude had changed. Promotion to war chief had given him a new sense of responsibility. Ignoring the wishes of his grandmother would not be a genuine possibility.

On the other hand, he knew that Dalnia would be vastly disappointed that Ah-wen-ga had refused to give permission for an immediate marriage. She would create a scene, weeping and giving vent to her explosive temper. He could expect her to try to persuade him to disregard the need to have the approval of the head of his family. A very unpleasant session awaited him, and he unconsciously slowed his footsteps. He knew, however, he would hold firm and would not back down in his resolve.

When he arrived in the area where young married couples made their homes, Renno caught sight of a hulking warrior outside a house directly ahead. He realized too late that it was Rusog, and he could not avoid his brother-in-law. If he turned away now, he would be insulting him, which his father had ordered him to refrain from doing, even unintentionally. He braced himself and held to his course.

What he could not know was that Rusog had become involved in another senseless squabble with

Ena. When an argument had threatened to become too intense, they recalled their session with Ah-wen-ga, and her counsel. With Ena's hearty approval, Rusog had come out into the night to cool off.

Renno, as his wife's brother, was about the last person Rusog wanted to see. He did his best to be polite, not realizing that he sounded surly as he called, "Hail, Renno!"

Renno had no wish for small talk with the man he considered responsible for having betrayed him to the Choctaw. He lifted his left arm and, not slowing his steps, replied, "Hail, Rusog!" His tone was as lacking in warmth as Rusog's.

Rusog thought Renno was mocking him by mimicking his own greeting. He stared hard, his temper flaring. Reaching out, he caught hold of Renno's upper arm in a viselike grip. "In the name of the great goddess of the Cherokee, what do you think you're doing?"

His touch made Renno's flesh crawl. Worried about his coming confrontation with Dalnia, he lost control of himself. "Get your hand off me, you damned traitor!" he ordered coldly.

Rusog glowered, his face stiffening in shocked anger. *"What did you call me?"* he demanded.

Too late, Renno realized he had gone further than he had intended. He had disobeyed his father's instructions. Now he could hardly afford to make matters worse by explaining why he had used the word "traitor." All he could do would be to try to be evasive enough that the moment would pass harmlessly.

But Rusog continued to grip his arm, a hamlike hand digging into his skin. Renno's anger flared anew. "I told you to take your hand off me!" he said angrily, and knocked Rusog's heavy arm aside.

Rusog bridled, leaning forward until his face was only inches from Renno's. *"What did you call me?"* he repeated.

"You have the manners of a wild boar, Cherokee," Renno told him. "Let me pass."

"You bear a marked resemblance to a wild boar, Seneca," Rusog responded.

They glared at each other, their mutual fury mounting.

"Be warned, Cherokee," Renno rasped. "If necessary, I shall remove you from my path."

"Try to move me, Seneca," Rusog replied violently. "Come ahead—try!"

Both were heading swiftly toward a point where their senseless dispute could be settled only by violent means. Lyktaw was nearby, growling and barking in an effort to show his displeasure at this turn of events.

Having already lost his temper, Rusog plunged even further into his self-created morass.

"I challenge you," he roared, "to a free-for-all contest—to the death."

Renno became icily calm, a sure sign that he, like men in his family for generations, was at his deadliest. "I accept with pleasure," he said, "provided we carry knives."

"That's fine with me," Rusog answered disdainfully. "I will dispose of you that much more rapidly."

At the same moment, they became aware that the buffalo-hide flap over the entrance of the house had been pushed aside. Ena stood on the threshold, looking first at her husband, and then at her brother. She was a study in controlled outrage. "I thought at first when I heard your voices that you were joking, but apparently you were not. What is the meaning of this disturbance?"

They spoke simultaneously, each trying to tell his version.

At last, she raised a hand to silence them. "Enough!" she commanded. "Let it suffice that you took umbrage at each other's tone of voice or found some other imagined slight that started this feud. It doesn't really matter how it began. Rusog, you are a war chief of the Cherokee. And you, Renno, wear three feathers in your scalp lock that show you are a war chief of the Seneca."

A note of stinging contempt crept into her voice. "Both of you should be devoting your thoughts and your time to considering ways that you can defeat the Choctaw. Instead, you are doing everything to make certain that we lose."

Her expression indicating disbelief, Ena shook her head. "Your fathers," she said, "spend all their waking hours trying to devise strategies and tactics that will ensure victory over the Choctaw. Little do they realize that their sons seem determined to undermine all that they are trying to accomplish. Has it occurred to you how braves of both nations will react when they learn that the sons of Ghonkaba and Wegowa are engaged in a personal feud? And that

you care so little about our campaign that you place
it in jeopardy? You are like two young bulls of the
buffalo, great shaggy creatures, endowed with tremendous physical strength, but lacking even the small-
est brain. Like those young buffalo, you start to fight
with each other for no reason. While you do, you
leave unprotected the families who are in your charge."

Rusog hung his head in shame.

Renno, too, knew his sister was right and could
not meet her contemptuous gaze.

"I will not allow you to place our entire expedition in jeopardy because of your own stupidities,"
Ena declared. "Rather than permit you to engage in
combat against each other, I insist that you fight me.
You may choose whatever weapons you wish. You
intended to arm yourselves with knives. I urge you
to select tomahawks in your fight with me. They are
a far deadlier weapon than a simple knife at short
range."

"No Cherokee has ever engaged in free-for-all
combat with his own wife," Rusog said miserably. "I
shall be the laughingstock of our nation."

Renno nodded glumly. "No warrior of the mighty
Seneca has ever deigned to meet a woman in combat,"
he said. "If I fought my sister, I would be a disgrace,
not only to my father, but to all my distinguished
ancestors. I cannot do it."

"Nor can I," Rusog agreed.

Ena had difficulty in keeping a straight face.
"You cannot fight each other unless you first fight
me. If you refuse, then I insist that you clasp hands
in friendship."

The "young bulls" looked at each other, then reached out tentatively and grasped each other's wrist in the Indian sign of comradeship. Lyktaw jumped up happily, his paws resting on the chest of each man in turn, his tongue lolling out one side of his mouth, making him look as if he were grinning.

Ena had accomplished her goal, preventing her husband and brother from shedding each other's blood. Although their feud might be ended only temporarily, at least they would now be able to put the coming war ahead of all other considerations.

Ah-wen-ga's soup was a simple dish, but its recipe was a closely guarded secret that Seneca women handed down to their daughters or the wives of their sons. The stock was made up of deer bones and a small quantity of deer meat, boiled for hours. To them a number of vegetables were added. For the final minutes of cooking, a variety of herbs were dropped into the brew. Her youngest grandchild, a sinewy and stalwart young man developing rapidly from the slender stripling that he had been in his midteens, was her special guest. For her own purposes, growing out of her recent discussion with his parents, Ah-wen-ga had made a particular point of inviting him to join her without other, distracting company.

"This soup is good, my grandmother," El-i-chi exclaimed enthusiastically. "You make it better than anybody else in the world!"

Ah-wen-ga smiled gently. "Your mother also

makes a splendid soup," she replied. "I have enjoyed it at your house many times."

"It is good," he declared judicially, "but not as excellent as this. You really know how to tickle the appetite of a Seneca."

"I have been a Seneca for more than seventy years," she said. "Is it any wonder that I do things in the Seneca way?"

"You must have known all the great Seneca about whom we have learned! Did you actually know Ghonka?"

"He was the grandfather of my husband," she said, "but by the time we were married, he had gone to the land of the ancestors. My father served under him as a warrior when I was a child, but unfortunately I cannot recall him from that time."

"But you must have known Renno, after whom my brother was named," he persisted.

"Of course," she replied. "The white Indian was my husband's father. I knew him well for many years."

"Was he as great a man as the legends say?" El-i-chi asked eagerly.

His grandmother's eyes glistened. "The stories told about him do not exaggerate. He was the perfect warrior in all ways. He was a wise and generous leader, and he was all things to the people of our nation."

"Then he was a Seneca beyond all else."

Ah-wen-ga looked at him curiously. "Of course," she replied. "Why do you make a point of the obvious?"

"He could not have been a Mohawk, let us say, or a—a Cherokee."

"I cannot imagine the great Renno being anything other than a Seneca," Ah-wen-ga said flatly. "Does that satisfy your curiosity?"

El-i-chi grinned broadly. "Yes, ma'am," he said with evident satisfaction, "it does. It most certainly does."

Ah-wen-ga thought that she possibly had detected a clue to his frequent quarrels with his Cherokee friends.

"You take pride in your Seneca heritage," she suggested tentatively.

"How could I not be proud?" he replied fiercely. "I am directly descended from Ghonka, from Renno, and from Ja-gonh. The greatness that has been the heritage of the Seneca for more than one hundred years is in my blood."

She felt increasingly certain that her instinct was right. "The junior warriors of the Cherokee with whom you associate," she said, "do not share your enthusiasm for your ancestors."

"May the bodies of the junior warriors of the Cherokee rot," he declared scornfully, his eyes flashing. "And may their bones bleach white before they are transported to the land of their ancestors."

"You dislike them," his grandmother murmured, trying to encourage him to keep talking but without causing him to become further aroused.

"They are like the worms," he said, "that rise up out of the earth when it rains and lie wriggling upon the ground."

"Your father," Ah-wen-ga pointed out, "does not regard them with contempt. He has made them his allies and they and our people share in all things."

"My father, like his ancestors before him, is a great leader of our people in both war and in peace. But he lacks the perfection of the manitous. He is human, and he makes mistakes. Certainly he made a serious error when he judged the Cherokee to be his friends."

Ah-wen-ga's guess was confirmed. "Why do you hate the Cherokee?"

"Those whom I know best, their junior warriors," El-i-chi said, "are stupid and ignorant. They lack the talents of the Seneca for making war. Their abilities as hunters are inferior to ours. Their knowledge of the wilderness is adequate, but it is no match for that of the Seneca. As trackers, they cause us to laugh at their failures."

"Let us assume that you are right," Ah-wen-ga conceded diplomatically as she served him two ears of freshly roasted corn. "It seems to me that we should feel sorry for them because of their inadequacies."

Between bites of his corn, "It is difficult," he said, "to feel any sympathy for those who display only arrogance."

The picture was becoming clearer in his grandmother's mind. "You are the only Seneca in your group. Am I correct? All the others are Cherokee."

Busily devouring his corn, El-i-chi could only grunt and move his head vigorously.

"There are ten or twenty junior warriors of the

Cherokee in your group," Ah-wen-ga said, "and you are the only Seneca. When an instructor is present, the others are quiet and mind their manners. They treat you with respect. When you are alone with them, however, they torment and try to degrade you."

Still eating his corn, he bobbed his head even more vehemently.

"You refuse to accept such treatment," she continued, "so you respond with harsh words about the Cherokee. Soon blows are being exchanged, and since they outnumber you so greatly, you always lose."

"I may lose to them, my grandmother, but they always know they have been in a fight. It takes at least four or five to beat me."

Ah-wen-ga stroked her chin thoughtfully. The portrait was now complete.

"Ghonka and the great Renno would have been pleased to acknowledge me as their descendant. So would Ja-gonh, my grandfather."

"Ja-gonh would have been disgusted by your conduct," Ah-wen-ga said quietly. "As for Ghonka and Renno, they would have shared Ja-gonh's feelings, I am sure."

El-i-chi was so stunned he could only gape.

"Only one excuse can be made for you," she said. "You are young and lack experience."

El-i-chi was horror-stricken. "What do I do that is wrong, my grandmother?" he asked. "How do I err?"

"When a Seneca faces adversity of any kind,"

she said, "he is always to display calm forbearance. Do you remain calm when the junior warriors of the Cherokee lash out at you? And do you respond to them in a calm tone? Hardly! Are you forbearing? You are not!"

El-i-chi began to understand.

"When the Cherokee tease and torment you," Ah-wen-ga said, "display the calm that your father and your grandfather and your other ancestors back through the generations would have demonstrated. Never let them see that they have succeeded in annoying you. When you have failed to become wildly angry, their sport will soon lose its flavor. They will then abandon the game."

Ah-wen-ga was not yet finished. "When peace has been restored," she added, "it may be that you and they will find qualities in each other that you admire—just as your father and Wegowa of the Cherokee discover such qualities in each other."

"It may be that you are right, my grandmother."

Convinced that at least one immediate crisis had been surmounted, Ah-wen-ga rewarded him with a dessert of blueberries and maple syrup.

Chapter VI

Renno was still asleep when, early in the morning, a messenger arrived, summoning him to the house of his father. He hastened his preparations for the day but took care to apply his war paint. Ghonkaba was a stickler for appearances, and any war chief who was careless in such matters was sure to receive a sharply worded lecture.

Renno's parents were ready for the morning meal when he arrived, and his mother insisted that he join them. She had prepared a dish of corn meal with berries and a fried fish. They spoke first of personal and inconsequential matters, and only when Toshabe went off to clean up the gourds did Ghonkaba refer to the reason he had sent for his son. "I have written a letter," he said. "In English. Read it, please."

Renno took a small parchment scroll from him and, unrolling it, read a brief communication addressed to Lieutenant Colonel Roy Johnson, as commander of the militia battalion. He read that Ghonkaba and Wegowa invited the battalion to join in their campaign against the Choctaw. Although no date was mentioned for the start of the campaign, the letter stated that if such an arrangement was agreeable to the colonel, Renno would guide the battalion to the land of the Cherokee.

"I want you to take that letter to him without delay," Ghonkaba instructed. "There you will wait for a reply. You will inform Colonel Johnson that the campaign will begin as soon as he is able to lead his battalion here. If you find that you are about to be captured by the enemy, destroy the letter if you can. If necessary, eat it." With a wry smile, he added, "Let us trust that does not prove necessary, my son."

Renno put the communication into a pouch, along with a supply of emergency rations, which his mother gave him. Quietly bidding his parents farewell, he stopped to see Dalnia. She was still asleep and was irritated when he awakened her. But she quickly regained her poise and exhibited a lively curiosity. "Where is your father sending you?" she asked.

Renno shook his head. "I am not allowed to reveal my destination," he told her. "This is one of those secret trips for which messengers are needed to carry out orders of the heads of military operations."

"I am always amused," she said, "when grown men devise secrets, like little boys." She raised her head for a kiss and slid her arms around his neck. Clinging for a long moment, she released him reluctantly. "May the manitous watch over you and bring you back to me safely," she said mechanically as he prepared to take his leave.

"I will be quite all right," he told her. Without thinking, he added, "After all, it is for only a few days, to see Colonel Johnson."

Renno knew it was important that he reach Colonel Johnson as soon as he could. He set a grueling pace, pausing to rest for an hour or two only when absolutely necessary. After spending slightly more than two days and nights on the trail, he reached his destination. There he found that the sentry detail again was under Captain Ben Whipple. In a gesture typical of him, Whipple tried to prevent or postpone Renno's admittance to the fort.

Renno was in no mood for a needless delay, however. A confrontation with Whipple was avoided only when a major of militia, who was making an inspection of the fortress palisade at the time, overruled the captain. He admitted the young Seneca without any more waiting. A military escort was, in fact, provided.

Renno was conducted to the building where Johnson, engaging in his civilian activity as a justice of the peace, was conducting a trial.

Recognizing his visitor instantly, he adjourned the trial and received Renno in an anteroom.

After reading Ghonkaba's message, Johnson listened while Renno delivered the oral instruction that accompanied it.

"How soon does your father want me to act?" he asked.

"The sooner the better would sum up his thoughts, I believe. I know that he didn't give you any more advance notice than he thought absolutely necessary because he is aware that word could leak out to the Choctaw that you will take part in the campaign. He prefers to surprise them with that fact, if at all possible."

"This is Tuesday noon," Colonel Johnson said. "I think we can be ready to march by early Thursday morning. Would that be soon enough to suit you?"

"That would be fine, sir!"

"You look as though you need a few hours' rest," Johnson said. "I am going to provide you with an escort to my house. I will be there as soon as possible. We will of course put you up."

Walking with the colonel's principal aide, Renno realized that he was about to see Emily Johnson again. The prospect filled him with a suppressed excitement that he could not analyze.

Nora Johnson, genuinely glad to see Renno, made him welcome. Emily was apparently not at home, for her mother made no mention of her whereabouts. Renno wanted to inquire about her but felt too shy. Inexplicably, he reacted much as he had when he had first begun to develop an interest in girls. Though he wanted to know all about her, at the same time he could not bring himself to ask.

The feather bed in his small room looked inviting, and Renno soon dropped off to sleep. He did not awaken for several hours, until a hired man brought a small tub of hot water and lighted the oil lamps.

Refreshed after washing up, Renno was pleased to discover that Mrs. Johnson had provided trousers and a shirt of fringed buckskin. Attired now in the typical clothing of a frontier settler, he went downstairs.

As he reached the lower hall, he unexpectedly came face to face with Emily Johnson.

Both were startled and, temporarily unable to speak, stared at each other.

Emily broke the silence. "Well . . . hello!"

Renno, equally embarrassed, felt awkward. "I—I hope I am not disturbing you?"

"Not at all," she replied, smiling with an evident effort. "Mama told me you were here and that you could be expected to come down soon. May I offer you a glass of sack before we eat?"

"That would be very nice." The roof of his mouth was painfully dry. Only because of his fascination with Emily, however, did he agree to try the beverage, which he ordinarily would have shunned.

Emily went promptly to the sideboard and poured two small glasses of sack, handing one to him. "Mama will join us shortly, and Papa will be here before long. He always seems to be delayed these days on government affairs."

"I know," Renno said, accepting a glass from her and bowing.

"This militia activity—would it have something to do with you?"

"Unfortunately, I am not permitted to discuss such things," he said shortly.

"I understand," Emily replied, and after a pause she added, "Won't you sit down?"

"Thank you very much, ma'am," he answered formally, lowering himself to the edge of a straight-backed chair.

Emily raised her glass demurely, Renno did the same, and both sipped self-consciously.

"This is very good sack," Renno said after several moments. Actually, he had tasted sack so infrequently that he had no idea whether or not the wine was particularly good.

"I wouldn't know," Emily replied. "Papa brought it home last year from a trip to Spanish Florida."

That seemed to exhaust the subject, and Renno searched his mind desperately for something else to discuss. "You look well," he offered at last. "Frontier life must agree with you."

"It should," Emily told him. "I never have known any other that I found so stimulating. My parents like the atmosphere of the frontier, and I must admit that I do, too. It is so much freer here than it could be in more settled communities."

"I can't say I really am familiar with frontier towns," Renno admitted, but added, "They do remind me of the Indian towns that I love. Their atmosphere is similar, possibly because both are surrounded by wilderness."

"I never thought in those terms," Emily said, "but I am quite sure you are right. The influence of the wilderness is very strong. You find it everywhere."

Renno peered at her. "You are not afraid of the wilderness?"

"To speak in terms of fear is to put the wrong emphasis on frontier living, at least in my opinion. The way of life in a place like this is like no other on earth. I lived for short periods of time when I was small in cities—Philadelphia and Boston—and they cannot compare with the day-to-day life here. At the same time, I realize we need to observe certain cautions. The forces of nature are very near and must be respected. We need to keep watch for unfriendly Indians and for wild animals that can overpower and kill us. All in all, the benefits of wilderness living far outweigh the dangers."

"Because—as you put it—you enjoy a greater sense of freedom here?"

"I expressed myself rather clumsily," she said. "I am not sure I can explain what I really mean."

"Let me try for you," Renno said, and paused, collecting his thoughts. "People who live in the small towns enjoy no greater freedoms, really, than do those in the cities, but they do bear a greater responsibility for the way they live. The cities have constabularies to make certain that laws are obeyed. Here, it is the duty of every citizen. Not only do you have a voice in determining the laws, but you must see to it that you and your family obey them. You have more direct control over your own destiny, so freedom is more keenly appreciated."

"You really do understand," Emily murmured, a note of wonder in her voice.

"I do not find that strange in the least," Renno told her. "The forest that feeds and clothes and nourishes me also sustains you. We speak different languages and worship different gods. But the customs that bind us together are far more common and more important than those that separate us."

Emily shook her head, and her blond curls danced up and down in the light cast by the oil lamps burning in the room. "How wrong I was," she said, "to think that the ways of Indians were so alien to my own ways."

"The thinking of the Iroquois nations and that of the colonists is similar because they are shaped by the same wilderness forces," Renno continued. "Their ways of life are like those of brothers. The resemblance between you settlers and the Cherokee is less close. But, nevertheless, they are like cousins. Only the more primitive nations such as the Choctaw have far less in common with you. And you will find almost no resemblance exists with outlaw tribes like the Seminole."

Emily had become so engrossed that she neglected her duties as a hostess. When Colonel Johnson arrived, he greeted Renno, then took one look at his empty glass and promptly refilled it.

The truth was that Renno had not even known that he had drunk all of his sack. He and Emily had

struck a surprising rapport as their lack of ease had
dissipated. She was the first young colonial woman
with whom he had become well acquainted, and he
was struck by her willingness to accept him completely at face value. This was the Indian way of
regarding new acquaintances. He was first of all a
Seneca, although he was part white, but Emily, like
her parents, made no attempt to keep him at arm's
length. He felt completely at home with the Johnson
family and enjoyed himself thoroughly at supper.

After the hearty meal, Nora Johnson led a lively
conversation. Renno was pleased by his ability to
participate, but he soon realized how lacking he was
in one facet of civilization. The Johnsons made frequent references to books they had read but of which
he had no knowledge. Perhaps, he thought, he could
have various volumes sent to the town of the Cherokee, if Emily would select them for him.

The evening was uneventful, but it proved memorable to Renno because of Emily's presence. Later,
he found himself remembering many of her remarks
and the way she looked when animated or subdued,
excited or playful.

Renno slept well in the feather bed, and in the
morning he found Emily waiting to share breakfast
with him. He discovered it was very pleasant to start
his day at a meal with her.

"Papa said this morning that you will have nothing special to occupy your time today, so I wonder if
you have anything that you would like to do. He
asked me to . . . look after you."

"Thank you for the offer," he said, "but I am not

altogether helpless, after all. I am sure I can find some way to keep busy."

"I don't mind in the least," she assured him, "and I would enjoy showing you around. Women and children are not permitted now beyond the palisade; too many Choctaw are abroad. But my father said that he would leave it to your judgment as to whether you and I might venture out farther."

He was flattered by Colonel Johnson's faith in his judgment, but at the same time he knew he would need to exercise great caution. Both Emily and he would be a great prize for the Choctaw to capture, and if the enemy became aware that they were in the forest, their scouts would make every effort to locate and seize them. Taking no needless risks, he armed himself with his bow, a quiver of arrows, and his tomahawk.

Captain Whipple was again on duty at the palisade. He tried to make an issue of their departure.

"You are free to come and go when you choose, Seneca," he said. "You can enter and leave any time you please. But according to Colonel Johnson's orders, Emily must stay inside. No two ways about it. She absolutely cannot go out."

"I knew you would be a stickler about this, Ben," Emily retorted. "As it happens, I have my father's permission to go with Renno."

"I need that in writing," the captain told her.

"Here!" She thrust a small, folded sheet of parchment at him. It bore the signature of Colonel Johnson and granted her the right to leave, provided she was escorted by Renno.

Whipple took the paper, shook his head, and glowered at Renno, making clear his disapproval of the young Seneca and of Colonel Johnson's decision to make Renno responsible for his daughter's safety.

Emily flushed, but Renno remained inscrutable, his expression registering nothing.

Reluctantly, Whipple opened the big wooden gate. After they had passed through it, Emily said, "Pay no attention to Ben."

"I was surprised when he would not accept your word."

"He doesn't like it when I spend time with anybody else," she explained. "I understand he has even told other people that he's . . . 'sweet on me.' But I am not beholden to him, and I have tried to make it clear that I am not interested in marrying him," she said, with a toss of her head. "I frankly don't care what he thinks!"

Renno was relieved, but he decided to say nothing.

Renno and Emily plunged into the forest, where he took every precaution to assure they were alone. He examined the ground to see whether other humans had passed that way. Then, putting his ear to the ground, he listened for footsteps. Only after reassuring himself that they would be unmolested did he consent to go on.

"I would like you to see a favorite place of mine here in the woods," Emily said, becoming shy.

"How far is it?"

"No more than a mile."

He considered briefly and decided the excursion

ought to be safe enough. "All right," he told her, "but take your time, and make as little noise as possible."

Emily started off into the forest. She lacked the instincts and the training of an Indian, but she moved with a natural grace and had an affinity for the wilderness that made her completely at home there.

He followed her for about a mile until they came to an open area. Branches of the big trees nearly formed an interlocking, vaulted roof overhead. Through this the sunlight filtered. Three boulders dotted the clearing, the knee-high grass was sweet, and the only sound was the gurgling of a small brook that ran at one side.

It was a lovely place, tranquil and isolated, and Renno could understand at once why Emily liked it.

"There is a place in the land of the Seneca," Renno recalled, "where my ancestors have gone for generations to pray to the manitous for help and guidance. The atmosphere must be much the same."

"I was still a child," Emily said, "when I found this place. I was out walking in the woods one day. Ever since that time, I have been coming over occasionally. I never have spoken of its existence to anyone, so of course I never have brought anyone else here."

"I am honored," Renno said, and meant it. "I feel . . . at home here."

"I knew you would understand and appreciate this place," Emily said, then suddenly whispered, "Listen!"

He heard no sound but the gentle gurgling of the stream.

"As a girl," Emily went on, "I played a strange and wonderful game. I pretended to myself that the sound of the brook was the voice of the spirit of the forest and was speaking to me alone. We confided many secrets to each other. Those times were precious to me."

"It well may be," Renno told her, much impressed, "that you were in indirect communion with the manitous that rule the wilderness."

"That could not be," Emily replied. "I never have worshiped the manitous."

"On the other hand," Renno told her, "I doubt if you ever have denied their existence, either."

"How could I?" she asked. "The longer I stay in a secluded place like this, the more I realize that the forces of nature are as strange as they are basic. Above all, they are powerful beyond belief. Who am I to deny the existence of the manitous simply because I was not taught about them in my religion? Those you call manitous may be the angels who stand watch over us who worship Almighty God."

She was an extraordinary young woman, a thinker whose fundamental ideas Renno could not deny.

She sat on a boulder and made herself comfortable, drawing up her knees and hugging them.

Leaning against another boulder, Renno looked at her hair and profile as a shaft of sunlight illuminated her. He had not thought much previously of how exceptionally attractive she was. Her beauty was not like that of Dalnia, whose features were regular and chiseled, but she depended more on the character that shone from her being and was such an integral part of her nature.

It was amazing, he thought, that he had not become entranced by Emily's beauty the first time he saw her.

She became aware of his close scrutiny and, deeply embarrassed, averted her face.

"Do I offend you by looking at you?" he asked quietly.

Her color became more deeply ruddy, but he could see she was not offended and, in all honesty, hardly could object. She shook her head, and the wind rustled through her hair.

Renno would realize much later that it was on this day he lost his heart to her. As for his commitment to Dalnia, he had been conscious of Dalnia's faults for a long time. But now he knew he had lost interest in her. He recognized that he did not really love her and had never loved her. What he had felt had been no more than a passing physical infatuation, and now that it seemed to have been satiated, he no longer entertained even these feelings. Her attempts to incite him, he could see now, were deliberate provocations in a vain attempt to hold his interest and to manipulate him. Seeing through her efforts, he wanted nothing more to do with her.

Emily was a woman of stature, suitable to join the pantheon that included Toshabe, Ah-wen-ga, Betsy, and Ena. As he worked to emulate his ancestors' deeds and accomplishments, he needed Emily as his mate. It was a very disturbing thought to realize how mercurial his emotions and affections were. He was surprised at himself and his infidelity of spirit toward the woman to whom he had pledged himself. He tried now to turn his thoughts elsewhere. What was most important in his life, he told himself, was making his position secure in the ranks of the Seneca and the land of the Cherokee. Rather than rely on the luster of his ancestors, he had to try to accomplish enough to win increased renown as a war chief and as a man.

Because he had obligated himself to Dalnia, he could not allow himself to think in terms of another romance. His honor was continuing to bind him to her, and he assumed he never would be able to escape. Even though he had made a grave error, he would have to live his life in keeping with the promise he had made. That would mean abandoning all thoughts of finding happiness with Emily, though his instinct told him they could have achieved a warm and lasting relationship.

Emily, too, was in turmoil, which she tried to the best of her ability to conceal. Her femininity came to her rescue, and she succeeded in hiding her true feelings. Aware for some time of her growing interest in Renno, she knew a crisis was approaching as he watched her with an expression of open adoration in his eyes. No doubt was in her mind that she could fall in love with such a man. But one very large question remained: whether she had the strength to live as an Indian. It was a question she could not even think about now.

Independent-minded all her life, Emily was de-

termined that she would make her own decision
when the time came, without taking her parents'
preferences and prejudices into consideration. Such
a time seemed remote, at best. When her father's
battalion marched out in the morning, Renno would
be leaving with it. The campaign against the Choctaw
might require many weeks and perhaps months. Possibly he might not return; she might never see him
again. She saw it as useless to speculate on what
might or might not happen. The whole future was
too riddled with question marks for that.

The glade expertly cast its spell. They dreamed
their separate dreams, thought their individual
thoughts. Finally, when their eyes met, they knew
that it was time to return. With Renno in the lead,
they began their walk back to the fort. Oddly, their
sojourn had drawn them much closer together, and
although they had had no physical contact, a sense of
intimacy suffused them.

The battalion assembled at dawn. Families and
friends of the troops were on hand to bid the militia
farewell, and it seemed that the entire town had
gathered to see the men off to war.

Among those present was Emily, who was pre-
sumed to have come to bid farewell to her father,
but Colonel Johnson was everywhere, supervising
the mustering of the battalion. Those with sharp eyes
and inquisitive noses saw that she drifted near Renno,
who was ready to act as a guide on the initial march
to the land of the Cherokee.

No longer could Renno be mistaken for a settler.

Full war paint was daubed on his face and torso, and three hawk feathers denoting his rank as a war chief protruded from his scalp lock. Wearing only his loincloth and moccasins, he stood alone in splendid isolation, paying no attention to the bustle around him.

Then Emily approached and extended a hand. "I want to wish you the best of good fortune in the campaign," she said. "May you succeed quickly in your endeavors."

Her hand felt warm and small in his. Renno smiled self-consciously. "Thank you very much," he managed.

"Keep watch over my father for me," she said. "He sometimes forgets that he no longer is young. He takes needless risks."

"I shall do what I can," Renno promised.

"And be careful yourself," she went on. "I have heard that in the heat of battle you often forget yourself and take terrible chances."

"Oh, I will be cautious enough," he told her, finding it impossible to explain that he was under the protection of the manitous. He doubted that she would understand that, thanks to the umbrella of safety they provided, he was able to take risks denied to ordinary mortals. That was a matter, in fact, between him and the gods. He knew that he must reveal the secret to no one.

Emily withdrew her hand from his grasp. He thought he could detect a lingering expression of regret in her eyes that she had to break off contact with him. He warned himself, however, not to read too much significance into it. And before he had an opportunity to think more about her behavior, several young officers standing at the head of their gathering troops hailed her. She turned away toward them, pausing to smile warmly once more at Renno.

He watched her as she moved off, and felt a pang of deep regret for what might have been. He knew that he could have developed a deep and abiding affection for Emily.

As Colonel Johnson gave the order to form into ranks, Renno dismissed such thoughts from his mind and immediately started off through the town gate and headed toward the wilderness. He was advancing ahead of the battalion, and he had started his duties.

Within minutes, the frontier battalion of long rifles followed. Trained by Colonel John Sevier, these were seasoned Indian fighters, men worth three times their number in wilderness warfare. The long-pending campaign against the Choctaw at last was under way.

Chapter VII

Three days later, after a rapid, uneventful march, Renno led the battalion into the town of the Cherokee, arriving early in the afternoon. Colonel Johnson promptly went into conference with Ghonkaba, Loramas, and Wegowa.

Preparations were started at once for a feast in honor of the battalion. The entire army would begin its march toward the land of the Choctaw within two or three days.

After reporting briefly to his father and paying his respects to his mother and grandmother, Renno went to Dalnia's dwelling, feeling that he had no alternative but to do what would be expected despite his heavy heart.

Dalnia greeted him warmly. Instead of going off with the other women to prepare for the feast, she chose instead to spend the time with Renno and had received grudging permission to do so.

Renno could not object, and he had to admire her appearance; her beauty was enhanced by the red berry stain on her lips and the dark circle of ashes applied around her eyes to make them look larger and deeper.

Her conduct at the feast was exemplary. Devoting her attention exclusively to Renno, she seemed oblivious to any other brave, much less the visiting settlers.

After the feast, Ghonkaba promptly called a council of war, attended by war chiefs and all officers of the battalion with the rank of captain and above. Renno was present as head of the little company of scouts.

Loramas sat on his thronelike chair surrounded by the medicine men of the Cherokee and Seneca. At his feet were Wegowa, Ghonkaba, and Colonel Johnson. They continued to confer privately until the chamber was filled. Then Ghonkaba asked for silence.

"Your high command," he said, "has devised very effective tactics, which we intend to carry out in

the days ahead. We will appear to drive straight at
the main town of the Choctaw. A special troop from
each of our three separate units—the militia, the
Cherokee, and the Seneca—will be aimed at its heart.
In this way, we hope to entice the enemy to make a
stand with his entire force in front of the town to
protect it from what will appear to be a concerted
drive. But that will be only a feint—not our principal
thrust. At a late hour, a most important part of our
force will sweep around to the rear and carry out the
key part of the attack. This will be our advance
guard, and the success of their maneuver will spell
the success of the entire expedition. We expect not
only to surprise the Choctaw in this way, but to
make use of our greater mobility, made possible by
operating with a smaller force." He smiled, refraining from mentioning the Choctaw's natural advantage in outnumbering the attackers.

"And," he added, "if we can defeat them, the
Choctaw will be eliminated as a threat to our
existence."

Only a few of the junior leaders offered objections to the plan. These were quickly overcome by
the high command. The leaders were instructed to
be ready to begin their long march promptly at
daybreak. As for Renno's scouts, they were told that
when they left they would head straight for the town;
they would be informed when they were to change
direction.

When the hour for departure approached, Renno
went to his mother and his grandmother, exchanging
quick, unemotional farewells. Out of no more than a

sense of duty, he walked on to Dalnia's house. She
was awake and waiting for him. She offered herself to
him silently, and he took her, feeling stirrings of the
passion that had once bound him to her.

After his yearnings were satisfied, Dalnia surprised him by producing a refreshing beverage of
fruit juices. While they drank, they talked at length
in an amity unusual for them. Renno monopolized
the conversation, thanks to Dalnia's clever manipula-
tion. He spoke mostly of the subject uppermost in
his mind, the campaign—and she was shrewd enough
to make no objection. Eventually, they dropped off
to sleep locked in an embrace. Renno could not help
wondering when, if ever, he would be intimate with
Dalnia again. She presented him with an impossible
problem. He resolved to leave to the gods a solution
to his dilemma.

The morning was still dark when he awakened.
He daubed himself with war paint, then went to
meet his scouts, all of them amply experienced in
the wilderness. They promptly started off, scattering
as they moved into the forest. Other than Renno, the
band included several Seneca, as well as numerous
Cherokee, and a few frontier dwellers. Each had his
appointed lane, and they spread out before the main
column was prepared to march.

Despite the ancient custom among virtually all
nations for the leader of a military force to march at
the head of its units, the allies were employing a
different arrangement. Behind the advance guard,
made up of one company each of militiamen, Cherokee, and Seneca, the high command stayed together

as a unit. They reasoned that they could arrive at
joint decisions far more effectively and thus give the
army a greater malleability as a striking force. Time
alone would confirm whether their reasoning was
accurate.

The tempo of the march depended a great deal
on the speed achieved by the scouts, and Renno saw
no reason to tarry. He knew that sooner or later—
probably before reaching the land of the Choctaw—
the advance of the column would become known to
the enemy. No matter how expert the individuals
might be in travel through the wilderness, a thou-
sand men could not avoid detection for very long.

In any event, the less notice given the enemy,
the better the attackers' chances were. The scouts
scoured the countryside, and at the end of each day,
they rejoiced because they had seen no sign of the
enemy.

About seventy-two hours after reaching the land
of the Choctaw, Renno found evidence of enemy
warriors. Traveling two miles in advance of the main
column, he came across signs that suggested a party
of three or four warriors had camped there. He
promptly reported his find to the high command,
and they lost no time inspecting the site.

Wegowa and Colonel Johnson were quick to
agree with Ghonkaba, who said, "We have to assume
the enemy has sighted us and is now keeping track of
our movements." All three were unanimous, too, in
determining that the time had come to put their
tactical scheme into operation.

The scouts were drawn in and ordered to advance no more than one mile ahead of the column. The pace of the advance guard was contained, too. These shock troops were ordered to keep within a couple of hundred yards of the main force, which was aimed straight at the main town of the Choctaw, advancing as rapidly as possible.

The army halted and prepared for battle after reaching a point not far from the town. At sundown, scouts were dispatched to find out what disposition the Choctaw were making of their units. They found out abruptly. After advancing about three quarters of a mile, each scout was met by several dozen Choctaw armed with muskets and with bows and arrows. Renno, like the other scouts, was halted by heavy firing, which was maintained while he retreated to his own lines, taking the lives of some Seneca and Cherokee. To the surprise of the strategists, the enemy had refused to respond as it had been expected to do.

"The Choctaw have reacted a little too soon for my taste in establishing a defense sector," Colonel Johnson commented when Renno reported the situation.

"We have only two alternatives," Wegowa declared. "We can try to smash through their defenses and make our drive at their town. Or our advance force can turn now and make its move without our attacking first."

"Would you say, Renno, they are prepared," the colonel asked, "to offer us serious resistance if we try to push any closer on this front?"

"Yes, sir, I don't see any question about that.

They have entrenched themselves and have erected a long, solid line of breastworks. To dislodge them, we would need to exert a tremendous effort. Already, we have paid more heavily than we would have liked."

"In the course of that effort," Ghonkaba said thoughtfully, "the Choctaw will hold every advantage. As we expected, they will outnumber us, and they may also have superior firepower. I fail to see how we could successfully attack their present line without exceptionally heavy losses."

"You are right," Wegowa agreed. "An attack would be a reckless waste of our men."

"Move on to the second part of our plan," Roy Johnson advised. "Our advance guard, led by Renno and his scouts, will strike out on a tangent and go around their town to the rear, from where it can attack without expecting to encounter any fixed enemy positions."

The scouts were drawn in, and following directions by the high command, they started on a wide swing to the south.

As they reached a point due west of the town without opposition, Renno was encouraged. It was possible the move could result in placing the attackers in a position to achieve victory at small expense.

A little later, however, he was stunned by the intensity of enemy fire that greeted the scouts. Although his men were spread out over a wide area, each was subjected to a heavy barrage. Two more scouts fell to the enemy fire. To attempt to advance farther would have been suicidal.

Renno waited until the three companies of the advance guard arrived and bolstered the scouts' position. While they burrowed into the ground and hid behind tree trunks, boulders, and other obstacles, he made his way back to the high command post.

His report alarmed and perplexed the commanders.

"They knew exactly what we were going to do. They were lying in wait for you!" Colonel Johnson was explosively angry.

Wegowa had listened attentively. "They've outfoxed us!" he exclaimed. "We've been so busy trying to deceive them that we could not see them fooling us."

Ghonkaba remained calm. "The Choctaw have robbed us of any choice," he said. "We are outnumbered by perhaps two to one. We have lost any advantage, the element of surprise that was in our favor. If we want to survive, we must fight like hell!"

Roy Johnson pulled himself together. "Renno," he said, "you have shown that you know what you are doing. Take command of the entire advance guard, as well as your scouts. Have them open fire, making every shot count. We must not yield as much as one inch of territory." He scrawled the order authorizing Renno's new responsibility and handed him the scrap of paper.

"Yes, sir!" Renno replied, bringing his right hand to his forehead and saluting in the fashion of the Continental Army rather than Indian style. He returned to his unit of advance guard, which was still located on the far side of the town. The going was

difficult, especially in the last seventy-five yards as
bullets and arrows whistled overhead. Reaching the
sanctuary of a large boulder, he summoned the leaders of the advance guard and his own deputy leader
of the scouts.

He found it unsettling to realize anew that the
leader of the Cherokee advance guard was Rusog,
with whom he was still on bad terms. Rusog, however,
quietly demonstrated his own self-discipline and
loyalty. Recognizing the need for unity, he accepted
the high-command decision placing him under Renno's
orders, as did the other leaders when they heard
Colonel Johnson's instructions.

"Return the enemy fire," Renno said. "Make
every bullet and every arrow count. The battle may
be a long and difficult one. We will need all our
courage and stamina and character to carry out this
assignment. We must not even consider retreat. No
matter what the cost, we must not only hold firm,
but force the enemy to go back. It will not be easy,
but we will do it!"

The subordinate commanders passed the word,
and when Renno gave the signal, a thin ripple of rifle
and arrow fire broke out behind him. Miraculously,
almost every bullet and every arrow found its mark.
Rifles and bows were used sparingly but continued
to take a toll on the Choctaw.

Stung by the precise fire of their foes, the
Choctaw increased their own fire and laid down a
very heavy barrage. The Seneca and the militia dug
in, and the Cherokee followed their example until
the barrage ended. Then, again responding to Renno's

order, they sent another shower of bullets and arrows at their foes.

Renno concluded that he must now assume a
more active role in the combat as more of his subordi-
nates fell. Fitting an arrow into his bow, he took aim
at a Choctaw war chief who was leading the enemy's
response. The shot was a difficult one, since the chief
had stationed himself behind a large tree. Only partly
visible from Renno's vantage point, he repeatedly
disappeared from view for a few moments before
coming into sight again. To put him out of action
would require deft timing and a delicate hand, but
Renno eagerly accepted the challenge. Drawing back
the bow, he waited until the chief could be seen, and
then before the Choctaw could pull back, he released his arrow.

It buzzed with a soft, high-pitched hum as it
sped toward its target.

The Choctaw screamed, clutched his throat, and
staggering into the open, collapsed.

Robbed of their leader's guidance and example,
the braves under his command faltered. More of
them appeared in the open, as they sought to compensate for his loss, and were shot down as they
tried to fire in the direction of their enemies.

The advance guard of the Cherokee gradually
took the lead in the attack, sustaining numerous
losses. This was Rusog's first opportunity to prove
himself since Renno had accused him as a traitor. He
more than demonstrated his loyalty and worth to the
allied cause. Setting an awesome example for his
men, he alternately fired his rifle and his bow, rising

to one knee in the tall grass to discharge his weapon before dropping to the ground again.

Rusog became a natural target for the Choctaw, and the ground surrounding his place of concealment was constantly disturbed by enemy bullets and arrows.

But Rusog led a charmed life, and the Cherokee began to believe that the gods of the Seneca were giving him special protection. According to their own beliefs, their gods did not intervene in human battles, but now it was clear to all that Rusog was enjoying protection of a very special sort.

He seemed indifferent to his own safety. He rose up within plain view of the enemy again and again, not only firing his own weapons, but directing the fire of his warriors.

When the Choctaw found themselves unable to silence his weapons, they deliberately avoided him. Given a free hand, he was able to double his efforts and succeeded in cleaning out the entire sector in front of the position where his embattled Cherokee were holding firm despite the toll the enemy had taken on their ranks.

Rusog's instinct was to push forward into territory nominally occupied by the enemy, but Renno refused permission to advance. The more experienced men among the Seneca and the militia were able only to hold their own. They could not be driven from the ground they occupied but lacked the strength to advance into the territory held by their Choctaw opponents. Consequently, Renno realized that if Rusog managed to push forward, his relatively small unit soon would be completely surrounded, and he would suffer crippling losses. He would be lucky if he proved able to keep his unit intact.

Unable to push ahead, the Cherokee concentrated on the ground opposite their left flank. These Choctaw were engaged in a deadly struggle with the Seneca advance guard. Renno was surprised and gratified when Rusog, unbidden, came to his aid.

Together, they and their braves pounded their foes. The two leaders knelt together and fought shoulder to shoulder. What Rusog lacked in Renno's cool expertise, he compensated for in the wealth of emotion he displayed. It was a rallying challenge for everyone. Between them, Renno and Rusog succeeded in removing a dozen Choctaw from combat, efforts that would later be the inspiration for stories and songs about their miraculous exploits.

United in their determination to rid the sector of their enemies, they so disorganized the enemy that its fire dwindled and became only a slight hazard.

Rusog was still less than satisfied, however, and Renno was inspired by the giant's example.

They continued to fight until the Choctaw fire dropped off almost completely, and then they transferred their attention to the sector still farther to their left, opposite the militia. Armed with their long rifles, the soldiers were facing the majority of the Choctaw advance guard. They had held off repeated attacks only because of the accuracy of their own fire. But they had suffered unexpectedly heavy casualties, as had the Seneca and the Cherokee. As the fighting wore on, their reduced ranks were threatened by a force that could prove overwhelming. The support provided by the Cherokee and the Seneca steadied them and gave them the strength needed to repel the Choctaw, who were firing both bows and muskets.

"I'm sure glad to see you, lads," Captain Amos Winston of the militia said when Renno and Rusog crawled up beside him. "We can use some help right now."

Quickly surveying the situation, Renno decided against dividing the area into sectors and assigning each to a separate unit. The front that separated his men from the enemy was crowded, so he made up his mind to use all his effectives in a concentrated push. The cost might be additionally heavy, but it had to be risked.

This would use up a lot of valuable ammunition, perhaps, but it had a chance of guaranteeing a fairly rapid victory.

He called out his orders and then, alternately firing a rifle and then reaching for his bow, he took part in the new surge.

The reinforcements heightened the pace of the battle dramatically. The rifle fire increased, and the air seemed filled with arrows. Taken aback, the Choctaw retreated a dozen paces, then halted and made a stand. They used their tomahawks for the first time and, unable to meet their foes in hand-to-hand combat, resorted to the desperate measure of throwing their axes.

"Heads up, men," Renno called, first in English, then in the tongue of the Seneca.

Avoiding the flying tomahawks was relatively easy. Then the Choctaw, having exhausted these weapons, were forced to rely again on their unreliable British muskets and their bows. Also, they seemed to have lost the will to fight, and their efforts seemed halfhearted. They fell back swiftly, and Renno was forced to caution his men not to follow.

"Hold steady!" he called repeatedly. "Hold steady, do not advance!" Rusog and Captain Winston echoed his cry. The allied troops and warriors, consolidating their positions, obeyed and resisted the temptation to move forward.

Nightfall was imminent. The Choctaw had disappeared from sight, the entire sector became quiet, and the allies rested on their arms.

The high command appeared and made a thorough inspection of the position. They paused occasionally to confer in low tones. Wegowa beckoned to Renno.

"As the commander of the sector," Colonel Johnson said to him, "you have done exceedingly well. We are pleased that you succeeded in holding a vastly superior enemy force at bay. And you wisely refrained from following them. That could have been catastrophic."

Renno felt it was wrong to accept praise for achievements other than his own. "I cannot claim credit," he protested, "for things I did not do. Full credit belongs to Rusog of the Cherokee, who fought with the ferocity and determination of a bobcat. If any one person is responsible for turning back the Choctaw and clearing out the sector in front of us, it is Rusog."

Captain Winston was quick to add his own

corroboration. "Renno is right, gentlemen," he said. "Rusog fought like a madman, and any soldier, any brave on our side who did well today undoubtedly was influenced by his example."

Rusog was pleased, but he, too, wanted to be fair.

"As for our decision not to advance," he said, "I was so filled with the glory of our exploits that I would have raced after the Choctaw and thereby would have exposed the advance guard to the enemy. But Renno had the good sense to halt us before it was too late."

Wegowa laughed. "One way and another," he said, "you managed, between you, to put us in a splendid position when the battle resumes. For that we are grateful, and we shall not forget your contributions.

"Meanwhile, we must try to understand why the toll on our men has been so great, and try to prevent it from happening again."

The high command studied the terrain ahead until it became impossible to see clearly. They withdrew then, issuing no fresh instructions. Renno was still under orders to obey the last commands that he had received.

The advance units settled down for the long night ahead. Strong sentry outposts were established, to be relieved on a staggered schedule that was fair to every man. Renno forbade a fire for any purpose.

After assuring himself that the advance guard was distributed evenly throughout the area, he sat down beside a large oak near the front of the occupied area. Opening his pouches of emergency rations, he prepared to eat a few handfuls of parched corn and several strips of dried meat.

The bulky figure of Rusog loomed up beside him. He lowered himself to the ground. "It is too quiet tonight," Rusog said. "After all the noise and excitement, I wish we had some way to keep fighting and resolve the battle before we rest." He began to munch his own parched corn.

"Even the most proficient marksmen need a respite," Renno said. "And unless they have extraordinary vision, they are handicapped by an inability to see at night."

"I know," Rusog said with a sigh. "It's just that when my heart is pumping and I am filled with the spirit of battle, I prefer not to stop." He selected a strip of dried venison from his pouch and, biting off a piece, began to chew it slowly.

Renno was silent for some moments, until, out of an inner turmoil, he blurted, "I tried in the presence of the high command to right a grievous wrong that I have done you, Rusog, but I succeeded only in part. I owe you an apology."

His brother-in-law was nonplussed. "We do not need to go into that," he muttered.

Renno was reluctant to drop the matter until he had cleared the air. "Due to mysterious forces and the interplay of circumstances that I do not yet understand," he said, "I mistakenly thought of you as possibly a traitor who had placed me in a terrible position.

"You proved me wrong in today's battle," he

continued, "and my father knew from my statement
this evening that I withdraw my absurd charges. I do
not understand the perfidy that was involved, and I
cannot ferret out the truth now. I know for certain
that you could not have been responsible, and I am
sorry that I ever was so mistaken as to suspect you,
and thus cause bad blood between us."

Rusog laughed unexpectedly. "My wife is a wise
woman," he said at last. "Before we left, she pre-
dicted that you and I would emerge from this campaign as good friends—if we did not kill each other."
He extended his hand and grasped Renno's wrist in a
circle of friendship.

Renno promptly returned the gesture.

Again Rusog laughed, and the sound rumbled
up from deep within him. "When I see Ena," he
declared, "I must convince her that the Choctaw are
so ornery that I could not afford to waste a bullet on
you."

Renno joined in the laugh, and the breach that
had separated them was healed.

They finished their unappetizing meal in friendly
silence. The Seneca were accustomed to living on
such fare for long periods during a campaign, but to
the braves of other nations such meager food for two
or three days was all they cared to tolerate.

"What do you suppose the high command has in
store for us tomorrow?" Renno asked at last.

"The battle will pick up where we left off today,
I suppose."

"It cannot work that way," Renno said. "We
emptied our sector of enemies. But as I hardly need

remind you, the main bodies of the two forces have yet to join the battle. So far, it has been strictly an encounter between our advance unit and theirs. But the real test will come only when the principal armies engage in direct combat."

The night passed slowly. At regular intervals, Renno and Rusog toured their sentry outposts, which remained undisturbed, as did those under Captain Winston. If the Choctaw were intending to wage a large-scale battle, they gave no sign of it.

Renno rested when he could, sleeping intermittently. Finally, in the night's waning hours, he prayed to the manitous for strength, courage, and assistance in destroying the enemy. Then he applied fresh war paint and was ready to resume the combat. When the day finally broke, he stood and, with Rusog beside him, peered off into the forest for signs of the enemy.

"Here they come!" Renno shouted.

Choctaw braves by the hundreds were advancing, lightly camouflaged by tree branches and other foliage.

A messenger was dispatched to the rear to notify the high command. In almost no time, Ghonkaba and Casno, who was once more acting as his deputy leader, appeared on the scene.

Casno had temporarily put aside his duties as medicine man to resume his old place as a war leader.

Ghonkaba did not waste a moment. "Bring up our main body of Seneca," he ordered, "and throw them into the line that our advance guard has estab-

lished on this side of the town. They are to hold the
Choctaw at all costs!"

"Yes, sir!" Casno replied, and hastened to do his
chief's bidding.

The appearance of the Seneca veterans filled
Renno with pride. Here were the finest fighters in
all of North America, men so accustomed to combat
that they required few orders. Not only were these
braves wholly self-reliant, but they had learned the
extent to which each could depend on his comrades
in battle. Each knew that those comrades would
never panic, never give in to unreasoning fear, but
would remain steady no matter what the provocation.

More than two hundred came forward in battle
formation, prepared to use their bows initially to halt
the drive of a Choctaw force that outnumbered them
by at least two to one.

"Hold the advance guard aside until you get
word from me to join us in battle," Ghonkaba said,
and crept silently forward to join his lieutenant at the
head of his elite band.

Cast in the unusual role of an observer for a
time, Renno alertly watched, as did his compatriots.

The Choctaw warriors continued to advance. To
Renno's consternation, they approached close to the
allied line. When they were ten yards away from the
nearest braves in the defending sector, Ghonkaba
gave silent signals. The braves promptly went into
equally silent action. The air was filled with arrows
as the Seneca veterans hammered at their foe.

A number of enemy braves were killed or

wounded, and the Choctaw advance halted, abruptly resorting to their British muskets.

But the Seneca, prepared for the violent reaction, were arrayed in a triple row. Those who had not found concealment behind trees, boulders, and bushes were artfully hiding in the tall grass. The musket fire passed overhead and left them unscathed.

The Choctaw fired for several minutes, with a prodigal waste of ammunition. Each of their warriors fired at least six shots during that time, but not one even wounded a Seneca. Gradually, the barrage faltered.

"Now!" Renno muttered.

Reacting as though responding to his order, the Seneca marksmen let loose another flight of arrows. The havoc they created was even more intense and widespread than had resulted from their initial firing. So many Choctaw fell that their efforts were severely hampered, and a large number of replacements had to be moved forward into the line.

The Seneca greeted the new arrivals in the enemy line with a fresh barrage of arrows. Then, acting on an unspoken command, they switched to their long rifles.

Again the muskets of the Choctaw blasted. Their weapons aimed so high that it was impossible for them to cause any real damage.

The Seneca responded with an accurately aimed round of rifle fire that took its toll. The Choctaw moved more reinforcements forward, but the Seneca did not wait for them to take part in the combat.

Instead, they greeted them with a second, fierce round of rifle fire.

Ghonkaba withheld the order for the Seneca warriors to take a sharp initiative. The move from defensive to offensive customarily was accomplished gradually, step by step. The great Seneca war machine, not yet in motion, was getting ready to roll.

The scouts in the advance guard were taking no part in this phase of the operation, but Renno determined to participate individually. His particular skills would be handy in the coming drive. Quietly, he joined a group of young warriors with whom he had undergone rigorous training. Subordinating himself to the authority of the war chief in command of the unit, he fitted an arrow into his bow and awaited the signal to move forward.

He did not have long to wait. A sweeping movement of the war chief's arm set the entire unit in motion. Crouching low, Renno ran forward, a fellow warrior at either side. They advanced some twenty paces, then halted, dropped to their knees, and searched the terrain ahead. Seneca procedure forbade firing blindly; warriors always chose a specific target and directed fire at it before continuing an advance.

Renno caught a glimpse of a Choctaw warrior partially concealed by foliage. That glimpse was all he needed. Extending his bow, he let fly, and his arrow found its target, penetrating one eye of its victim and killing him instantly. Other Seneca marksmen quickly followed his lead, and six Choctaw were felled.

Renno waited for the signal he knew would be given, the jabbing of the war chief's forefinger. As soon as he saw it, he led the charge, again bending low and sprinting forward about twenty paces.

The Choctaw, stunned by the rapid advance of their foes, were unprepared for the vicious attack that followed. Renno swung his tomahawk in a wide arc, first to the left and then to the right. He made contact with any enemy within reach, as did his comrades. The surviving Choctaw, frightened by the brutal efficiency, fell back.

Trained to take advantage of every break, the Seneca moved forward again. When they strengthened their line, they solidified their advance.

Another shower of arrows flew in the direction of the Choctaw, who were trying desperately to reorganize their forces. Again they fell back. The Seneca advanced into the void left by their retreating foe. They took no additional ground, however. Ghonkaba and Casno conferred briefly, and the deputy leader ordered the advance halted. Renno could see valid reasons for the caution. Their allies were less fortunate in their own phases of the battle. The militia battalion, pitted against by far the largest number of Choctaw braves, was having difficulty in dislodging the stubborn enemy. The battalion's frontier marksmen took a heavy toll, but every time they killed or wounded a Choctaw warrior, another stepped forward. The capacity of the Choctaw for providing replacements appeared endless.

As anticipated, the Cherokee were encountering the greatest difficulties. Their braves were inclined

to fight somewhat tentatively, with the result that
the Choctaw were more successful in holding them
off. Wegowa provided adequate leadership, and the
tactical spark supplied by Rusog and some other war
chiefs was effective. But a handful of leaders could
not compensate for the relative inexperience of the
unit. Instead of inching forward when they gained an
advantage, the warriors hesitated. By waiting for an
order, they missed numerous chances to take the
lead.

Another lull in the fighting developed, and while
men on both sides rested for the climactic phase,
Ghonkaba summoned officers and leaders to another
council of war. Colonel Johnson opened the discussion,
speaking succinctly.

"We can win the day, I believe. But only if we
reverse our tactics. I say that even though they have
enabled us to be partly successful on our front. In
this next phase, the men there must hold firm. *Give
up no territory!*—that's all that is required of them."

"In the meantime," Ghonkaba said, picking up
the burden, "the advance units will attack the enemy
in our rear, with no holds barred. You have your
work cut out for you, Renno."

"Yes, sir!" the young war chief replied.

"What greatly concerns me," Roy Johnson said,
"is that we have had to revise all our plans, step by
step. The Choctaw act as though they have second
sight, or are mind readers. They know every move
we have intended, even before we make it!"

"It is true," Wegowa said, "that at the very least

they have had the assistance of a medicine man whose prowess is great."

Renno had no right to interrupt the conversation of his superiors. But, at the same time, he could not refrain from speaking up. "Either they have the help of a medicine man who is in miraculously close touch with the gods of war," he said, "or they have had help from an extremely clever spy."

All three of his seniors stared at him.

"This is not the first time you have made such a charge," Ghonkaba said. "In the past I disagreed completely with you about those you suspected of spying. But I am willing to admit at last that it looks as though the Choctaw have had the advantage of placing a spy in our camp. Do you happen to have any new guesses as to his identity?"

Renno felt foolish. "No, sir," he admitted.

"Our first requirement," Ghonkaba said, "is to drive the enemy from the field and win the battle. Only when we are victorious can we afford the luxury of searching for the traitor who has forced us to alter our entire battle plan."

The meeting ended, and the high command split, with each member going off to join the fighting men of his own nation. Renno still headed the advance units of all three major forces; his mind was full as he started toward the rear, accompanied by his lieutenants, who trotted eagerly behind.

He knew that, at the very least, an exceptionally difficult task awaited, but he nevertheless had no idea of its scope. Not until he reached the area where the battle would take place did it fully dawn on him that he faced a problem of the first magnitude.

The vast field that stretched out ahead of him was flat and barren. Trees and bushes were scarce, and not a single boulder that could be used for cover was within sight. The area plainly had been chosen, not by the Seneca, but by the enemy, which would have a preferred position.

Determined to make the best of the difficult situation, Renno ordered his men to spread out. He was dismayed to see as much as six feet appear between any two members of his unit. As he did his best to absorb the dismal picture, he felt someone approach and stand beside him. Turning, he saw his father's deputy, Casno.

The grizzled older man's eyes were hooded as he studied the field. After several moments, he spoke, addressing Renno for the first time since being accused of being a spy for the Choctaw. "As a medicine man," he said, "I have unlimited faith in the power of the manitous. But it would be asking for too great a miracle to give your little advance guard victory over a force as numerous as the enemy you will face. You cannot possibly win, Renno. The odds against you are overwhelming."

"I have no choice," Renno replied grimly, "I have been ordered to clear the Choctaw out of this sector so that our own men may occupy it. I am obliged to do as I am instructed."

"Ghonkaba is not aware of the size of the problem you face," Casno said. "He is not an unreasonable man, and he does not expect you to do the impossible. No two ways about it—I shall have to come to your help, with about half of my effective force. I will lend you the services of one hundred of the finest Indian fighters on earth. I shall command them myself."

Renno was overwhelmed. Tongue-tied, he did not know what to reply.

Casno expected no comment and appeared to understand the awkward silence. "I think that between us we can demonstrate what the warriors of the Seneca are able to do when the need arises," he said quietly.

Still unable to speak, Renno reached out and grasped the older man's wrist in a show of friendship.

Casno plainly harbored no grudge over the injustice that had been done. Saying nothing, his face immobile, he returned Renno's gesture, then went off at the familiar Seneca trot. His mission was to fetch the warriors who would assist in the maneuver that promised to be the most memorable event in the prolonged battle.

The advance units moved silently into place. Warriors and militiamen alike knew they had a formidable task; nevertheless, they were in high spirits, grinning at each other, exchanging jokes, without hesitation taking up their battle stands. On their heels came Casno's hand-picked unit, one hundred of the most seasoned and resilient warriors on the continent. Included in the unit were all veterans of the American Revolution who had served in battle under him and Ghonkaba for years. All were as much at home with the long rifle as with the bows of their ancestors. All knew the odds against them were overwhelming. They would be going into battle against a greatly superior force, and they had very little protection in the way of natural cover.

Nominally, Renno was in charge of this sector, but he deferred to Casno.

"Do you think we should assume the initiative from the beginning?" he asked as Casno rejoined him.

Casno looked at him for a long moment. "How do you react to that idea?"

"I am very much inclined to do it," Renno replied. "If we take the offensive at the beginning, they will find it much harder to stop us."

Casno shook his head. "We could be suffering greater casualties that way than we need to," he said. "Remember how badly we are outnumbered. In my opinion, we should wait to see the enemy's actual strength, allow it to commit itself inflexibly to its positions, and only then strike with our full force. We would sustain fewer losses, and our chance of achieving victory would be better. This fight will not be won or lost in the opening minutes—if we conduct ourselves with the proper mixture of patience and daring."

"I have placed myself and my entire command under your orders, sir," Renno reminded him.

Casno acknowledged the gesture by inclining his head slightly.

The lack of natural cover on the front facing the enemy made it necessary for the advance guard to improvise. Men in the small unit that comprised a portion of the militia carried short iron spades. They used their tools to throw up crude chest-high breastworks facing across the fields. As soon as they completed the chore, they passed their shovels to the Indians, who for the first time in their lives also erected breastworks. Every man was assigned a specific place in the line, and Casno gave the same instructions to each unit.

"Use your rifles," he told the soldiers and the Seneca, while the Cherokee were directed to rely on their bows and arrows. "But hold your fire until I give you the order, personally, to shoot. Until then, do not give in to temptation, but let the enemy come so close that you can count his eyelashes. When you do open fire, lay down a heavy barrage, as heavy as you can manage, and do not let up until the enemy begins to move in reserves. I am not advocating your squandering ammunition, however. Make every shot count, and take aim as though you were at the end of your ammunition."

Only when a militiaman or a warrior appeared to understand thoroughly what was expected of him did Casno move on to the next man.

Renno marveled at his patience and the precision of his planning. For the first time, he understood why Casno was successful as his father's deputy. No detail was too small to engage his complete attention. He was willing to take the time to make certain that every member of his command understood what he was to do when the moment of crisis arrived. Renno grasped anew the significance of painstaking planning.

Renno's hearing, more acute than that of the ordinary warrior, enabled him to give the first warning of the enemy's approach. "They're coming!" he called softly, and the word was passed rapidly up and down the line.

Hammers clicked on rifles, arrows were nocked onto bowstrings, and the defenders braced themselves as they made ready to protect their position, an unusual role for most of them.

Kneeling, Renno placed the butt end of his rifle down to the ground and rested his weight against the upright weapon as he peered ahead. The enemy was crawling into the open from the forest at the far side of the extensive clearing. Their distinctive war paint was clearly visible against the green background of the foliage as the braves crawled through the tall grass. All were carrying British muskets and awaited the order to use them.

More of them came, and still more followed. Renno tried to keep count, but the numbers soon overwhelmed him. Even with Casno's reinforcements, the advance guard was outnumbered by at least two to one.

He raised his rifle to his shoulder and peered down its length. He caught a war chief in its sights, and his trigger finger itched.

A swift look at Casno, who crouched beside him, revealed that he had no intention as yet of giving an order to open the battle. His lean face immobile, Casno stared with unblinking eyes at the Choctaw, who continued to pour onto the field in ever-increasing numbers.

Renno began to feel uneasy. The unfavorable odds were rising rapidly, and no end appeared in sight.

He was sorely tempted to give the order to open fire, but he could not, having passed up the command to Casno. He had to wait in mounting anxiety, wanting to urge Casno to put their men into action, but refraining because he realized his superior's greater experience in battle made him aware of many vital factors.

More and still more Choctaw appeared, and their tactics became plain to Renno. Their leaders would seek to overpower their foes with as strong a force as they were capable of mustering.

A single glance at the veteran Seneca warriors of the defending force at least partially reassured Renno. They were viewing the increase in their enemy's numbers with amazing calm and did not seem bothered by becoming seriously outnumbered. Suddenly, however, the veterans reacted as one man to unspoken orders. A difference in mood swept through the ranks. Each man picked up his rifle, checked it, then raised it to his shoulder and waited calmly.

Casno himself reacted to a sixth sense he had developed in scores of battles. "Now!" he called.

Almost simultaneously, one hundred veteran Seneca warriors squeezed the triggers of their rifles. The militiamen and braves of the advance units quickly followed, and the entire line seemed to erupt. Bullets and arrows began to pour toward the enemy in steady streams. The marksmen seemed to ignore the fact that some of their own number were falling at their side.

Renno took an active part, firing and reloading his rifle repeatedly. At last he understood the point of Casno's tactics. So many Choctaw were on the field that it was virtually impossible to miss a target. The carnage was unbelievable, unprecedented.

Seeing the enemy hesitate, then begin to falter, Renno exuberantly gave a Seneca war whoop.

His fellow Seneca responded by redoubling their efforts.

The Choctaw were not yet finished, however. A less valiant tribe might have retreated, reasoning that its honor was intact and that its braves had suffered no disgrace. But that was not the Choctaw way. Their pride was great, their determination to emerge victorious from every battle was overwhelming. They absorbed their losses, regrouped, and again swept forward.

The only way to combat such spirit was to meet fire with fire. Just as the Choctaw were reluctant to stay on the defensive, it was all but unthinkable for the Seneca to give up ground, despite the cost already sustained in human life.

Renno braced himself. "Hold firm, my brothers!" he called. Suiting deeds to words, he pumped shot after shot at the enemy, pausing momentarily, just long enough to reload his long rifle.

But by the time the other Seneca rallied, they had been forced back a dozen paces. This maneuver had no effect on the tactical balance the Seneca had achieved, but it did have one unfortunate result:

Renno was left isolated. In almost no time at all, he was surrounded by Choctaw, who surged around him. With his rifle useless against so many foes, he resorted to his tomahawk, which he swung wide, then effectively chopped with it viciously between the longer sweeps.

In this way, he temporarily held his enemies at bay. But in the long run, he would be doomed. No one man could stand up against a dozen determined foes.

Renno was fighting for his life; a single error could mean the end of everything. His actions now resembled a whirlwind.

Casno busily steadied the wavering Seneca line. As he did, he became aware of Renno's predicament. Not hesitating, he moved forward again, accurately swinging his tomahawk with abandon. His assault was so strong, so vicious, that he felled two Choctaw braves before they had the opportunity to defend themselves. Fighting with agility and cunning, he made his way to Renno's side.

Belatedly realizing that someone had come to his assistance, Renno was amazed when he finally recognized that it was Casno. The senior warrior, whom he had accused of treason, was risking his life to save Renno's. Casno's prompt and courageous intervention vastly reduced the peril to Renno, who became more daring, pressing his opponents still harder.

They stood back to back, in the classic position that Seneca were taught to adopt under such circumstances. Both were chopping and flailing incessantly with their tomahawks. The enemy was too close to permit effective use of firearms and bows, but the Choctaw who opposed them were similarly handicapped. In that sense only was the combat equal.

The Choctaw soon realized that the two Seneca had an identical attitude. The pair went about repelling their foes with cool efficiency, neither revealing emotion, both of them very calm. They had practiced just such a maneuver, and now they were spontaneously putting it into effect. It was the first time that Renno and Casno had ever fought together in close combat.

Tomahawks wielded by the Choctaw were no match for the two Seneca. Hacking relentlessly, Renno and Casno gradually succeeded in cutting an ever-enlarging space around themselves. Their tempo of battle remained even, unchanging.

At last they gained an advantage, and when they did, they reacted in unison, increasing the tempo of the combat.

After a time, they found themselves engaging in a friendly rivalry—at the expense of the Choctaw— and they began to enjoy themselves thoroughly.

Together, they achieved the goal of every Seneca warrior in combat: harmonious joy in battle, for its own sake.

As their ranks thinned, the Choctaw became discouraged. They retreated singly and in pairs until the circle that had formed around Renno and Casno vanished.

Other Seneca now began to move forward again to fill the vacuum that the daring of Casno had created. Soon the entire Seneca line began to inch ahead, and the militiamen under Amos Winston followed, as did Rusog's Cherokee. The retreat of the Choctaw became a rout.

At last Renno and Casno were free to take their places at the head of their commands, and they began to drive forward through the ranks of the foe, not pausing, not hesitating, but constantly on the move.

The Choctaw had lost all appetite for combat and began to disappear from the field.

The first to go were their younger, least experienced warriors. Then the veterans became as discouraged and frightened. It was too late for their leaders to halt a retreat that had become a panicked flight. The battle quickly became one-sided.

The ranks of the Seneca remained intact as they maintained their drive. Virtually all of those who still stood were engaged in combat. Ghonkaba ordered the main body of the militia to enter the fray. On their heels, he sent in Wegowa's Cherokee. The momentum established by the dauntless Seneca was not lost.

The entire allied force smelled victory in the air and acted to assure it. As if indifferent to the losses they had sustained, and overrunning pockets of stubborn Choctaw resistance, the militia and the braves swept forward together, forming an irresistible combination.

Only now that victory was assured did the Seneca pause to take the scalps of their fallen foes. Now they drove the last remnants of the once-proud Choctaw legions from the field.

Renno paused and looked at Casno, the man who had saved his life. With a sense of great, crushing shame, he realized that when he accused Casno of treason never had he been so badly mistaken. He found it impossible to express his gratitude in words.

"Thank you, my friend," he said simply, and could find no way to elaborate.

Now that the battle was ended, Casno reverted in spirit to his chosen profession, that of the medicine man. His expression was benign, and he spoke softly, without rancor.

"May the manitous bless you," he said, "and may they keep you from harm for all time and protect you from the foes of the Seneca." He touched the younger man gently on both shoulders before turning away.

After the battle, Renno performed one last function. Responding to his father's directive, he commanded the special detail that scoured the battlefield, gathering the bodies of the many Seneca dead for honorable burial, and removing their wounded for further treatment and care. The allies were notified promptly of any Cherokee and militia injured who were found on the battlefield. All these men were removed quickly, in time to receive medical assistance.

As to the Choctaw dead, they were ignored. Those of their wounded who were unfortunate enough to be still sprawled on the field of combat met a rough fate. First a Seneca tomahawk dispatched them promptly, and then, like their comrades who had died earlier, they were scalped.

Finally Renno's work was done. He sent his men back to camp, while he went off to report at headquarters. Then he went to his own bivouac area, where he drank greedily from a running stream, splashed cold water on his face, and stretched out on a makeshift bed of pine boughs. He was very tired after his long, unremitting exertions, and without difficulty he fell asleep.

Renno had no idea how long he slept, but he gathered it was only a short time. Someone was shaking his shoulder insistently, and he woke to find anxious Seneca braves surrounding him. Night had not yet come and no cooking fires had been lighted. Renno waved his comrades-in-arms away impatiently, but no one moved.

"You are needed," they told him. "You have been elected as chief of our kick-ball team."

Kick-ball, a Cherokee game, used twenty players on each of two opposing teams. They fought for control of a ball of soft wood, several inches in diameter, that had to be kicked with the side of a foot. The team to score the most goals in a determined time was judged the winner. Renno, who normally enjoyed all sports, played the game well, but he looked now at his comrades in consternation. "Have all of you gone mad?" he demanded. "In case you have forgotten, we just played a very major role in an exhausting battle. I think we are a bit too tired now for stupid games."

Several of the braves started answering simultaneously, but one, appointing himself as spokesman, silenced his colleagues and stepped forward.

"The Cherokee," he said, "have insisted to us that since the beginning of time they have celebrated their military victories with games of kick-ball. If we refuse to accept their challenge, they will become unbearable. When we return home they will claim that they were largely responsible for the victory that we won, when the truth is the opposite."

Renno shrugged and laughed. "Let them boast all they please," he said. "Who will believe them?"

"Our own people will be tricked by their words, just as the Cherokee at home will be fooled. None of them were present during the battle. We who were present will not be believed because the glib liars will prevail."

Renno shook his head gently in an attempt to clear the fog from his mind. "If I understand correctly, you intend to prevent this untruth from being fostered by meeting the Cherokee in a game of kick-ball, which you intend to win."

"That's right!" the spokesman declared flatly, as though defending unassailable logic.

Renno wanted nothing less than to take part in a strenuous sporting event that well might drain away his last, reserves of energy. But, cornered, he no longer had a choice. "All right," he conceded wearily, "we shall go play their game of kick-ball."

Surrounded by his jubilant fellow Seneca, he accompanied them to a nearby cleared field. There, to his astonishment, the entire high command was gathered. His arrival was cheered lustily by the Seneca who had taken part in the battle. Rest was far from the minds of virtually everyone present.

Leading his teammates onto the field, Renno saw that the Cherokee team was practicing under the leadership of Rusog, who was racing up and down the field, kicking the ball with such strength that it rose into the air and, spinning madly, continued its rapid flight. He was good, Renno admitted to himself, a foe to be respected.

Reminding himself to use only the side of his foot, he kicked hard at the ball and sent it spinning high into the air and down the field. The kick surpassed the best effort of Rusog, and the Seneca onlookers went wild. Leaping up and down, pounding one another on the back, they unleashed their ferocious war cry. Ghonkaba and Casno were no more restrained than the youngest and most volatile warriors.

Wegowa agreed to referee the match, even though the Cherokee team was led by his son. Younger men boosted the Cherokee chief to the lowest fork of a maple tree overlooking the grounds. When he was handed a drum and a stick with which to beat it, the match was ready to start.

Colonel Johnson flipped a coin, the Cherokee elected to receive the ball, and the Seneca spread out on the field.

Renno launched a hearty kick, then ran down the field after it, closely followed by his teammates.

No player other than the two goaltenders was allowed to touch the ball with his hands. As the ball began to descend, one of the Cherokee courageously placed himself in its path and allowed it to hit his chest, where it left an ugly bruise. He had, however, succeeded in halting the flight of the wooden ball. Rusog, charging forward, began to kick the ball up the field, alternately striking it with the inside of a foot, running and dodging forward several paces, then repeating the kick. In spite of his bulk, he proved to be nimble. Familiar with kick-ball since boyhood, he was an exceptionally clever player. Feinting and kicking the ball with force only when it was under his control to regain it, he nursed it past the entire team of defenders until only Renno and the goaltender stood between him and the score.

Pretending to move to his left, Rusog ducked to his right, and the ball passed Renno. Rusog also slipped past him and a moment later landed a solid kick that sent the ball flying toward the goal. The Seneca goaltender made a valiant effort to halt it but could not. With the match barely started, the first score had been made.

Only a few minutes later Rusog scored again. Sneaking behind the Seneca defenders, he took the ball, passed to him by a teammate, and drove it unopposed into the goal.

Drawing equally on his reserves of strength and on the will to win that his ancestors had made famous, Renno refused to concede what was beginning to appear as certain defeat.

He soon succeeded in scoring a goal, when two of his teammates blocked Rusog long enough to give Renno the opportunity. Shortly thereafter, he duplicated Rusog's feat by maneuvering the ball with his feet almost the entire length of the field to even the score.

Rusog retaliated with a series of false starts and stops, head feints, and other clever moves that enabled him to break free and to score a third goal.

The two principal players spent the rest of the game thundering up and down the field, kicking and then chasing the elusive ball, until even the spectators grew weary of watching them. Neither was able to score again, and the victory went to the Cherokee by the narrow margin of one point. The Seneca had missed the cherished opportunity to gain the upper hand when the recounting of the victory over the Choctaw began at home.

In remarks to Renno after the game, Wegowa summed up the general feeling of those who had watched the match. "You are truly remarkable," he said. "You have played kick-ball for only a short time, but your proficiency equals that of Rusog, who has played the game all his life. I wonder: is there anything you cannot do?"

Chapter VIII

The women of the Seneca were noted for their long memories, an unwillingness to forget slights, and a refusal to forgive insults. So far, their move into new homes had failed to bring about any marked changes in these qualities or in their dispositions otherwise.

Consequently, Dalnia remained thoroughly unpopular among them. They made it clear that they wanted as little as possible to do with her. The older women were shocked and nettled by her lack of moral standards and disregard for expected behavior patterns. The younger women bitterly recalled the many occasions when she had flirted with their husbands, and some carried grudges that dated back several years to her affairs with betrothed warriors in a brazen attempt to win them away from their fiancées. They laughed as they passed around the story of how Dalnia had been backed into a corner at her own dwelling by Lyktaw, who had invaded her area in an unprecedented display of canine dislike and distrust. Neighbors had to pull him away, snarling and snapping.

The fact that she was to be married to Renno influenced their attitudes not at all. Saying with sneers that it was only typical of her to aim so high, they felt sorry for Renno and sympathized with what they understood his family to feel.

Largely cut off from the mainstream of Seneca life because of her unwillingness to live in the long-house of the unmarried women, she ate and slept alone in her own dwelling. The exception to this isolation, of course, occurred when Renno was in the town and she was able to lure him to share a meal or even to enter her quarters during the night.

She was not excused, however, from the chores every Seneca woman was required to perform. In the fields where her presence was obligatory, she worked in surly silence, snubbed by all and virtually ignored by many. Her few attempts to establish even casual relations with one or two young women failed miserably.

Afraid of punishment if she showed up late, she appeared on time for work every morning, and at the end of each day she returned home alone. She never appeared to let the isolation bother her; she refrained from complaining aloud.

Ah-wen-ga, who insisted on doing her own share of work, was in the gardens daily and had become aware of Dalnia's situation quickly. She chose to observe the younger woman for several weeks, gradually forming a grudging admiration for her. She particularly liked her stoicism. One day she stopped near Dalnia's place of work. "If you are not otherwise engaged this evening," she said quietly, "perhaps I might persuade you to come to my house and keep me company at supper."

Dalnia gracefully concealed her surprise. "Thank you," she answered. "I would like very much to join you."

After she finished her day's work, she went for a swim in the lake, changed into fresh clothes suitable for a visit, and set out for Ah-wen-ga's house. She carried a dish of dandelion greens, to which she had applied her favorite dressing of herbs.

Impressed by Dalnia's display of manners, Ah-wen-ga thought that it might be a sign that the rebel was beginning to be ready to grow up.

The principal dish at supper was a rich buffalo stew with corn and broad beans. Ah-wen-ga served it with slabs of fresh corn bread and Dalnia's greens.

"This is delicious!" her guest exclaimed.

"Let me refill your gourd?"

"It is tempting, but I must decline, thank you. When Renno comes back from the war, I wish to be as slender as he likes me to be."

"I am pleased that you put Renno first in your consideration," his grandmother said, struck by the thought that perhaps the reputation for single-minded selfishness was somewhat exaggerated.

Dalnia was not forgetting for a moment that she was speaking with the highly influential head of Renno's family. "That is the very least I can try to do for him," she said modestly. Long convinced that she was far more attractive to all men when she was as thin as she could be, Dalnia ate so sparingly that she stopped little short of starvation for days on end.

"I want to tell you that I admire the way you deal with other young women," Ah-wen-ga went on, intent on putting her guest at ease. "They treat you unpleasantly, I observe, but you seem to take no notice of them."

"I am pleased that you respond in that way to their attitude. They are very jealous, as you probably know."

"Jealous?"

"After all," Dalnia said with a note of triumph in her voice, "I have won Renno! Everyone is envious— that is why they snub me." She hoped that Ah-wen-ga had not heard the other reasons—those directly relating to her conduct—that were behind the snubs.

Ah-wen-ga's apparent sympathy made Dalnia abandon her customary caution. "Let them enjoy themselves," she said with almost a snarl, "while they can. My turn will come!"

"I fail to understand," Ah-wen-ga murmured.

"The day cannot be far off when Renno will replace his father as the leader of the Seneca who live here. When that day comes, may the manitous take pity on these women! I will not forget a single one, nor what any one of them has done to me. I will outrank all of them, and I will make their lives so miserable that they will wish they had never been born."

Ah-wen-ga, nonplussed, remained silent.

"I shall use my influence with Renno to deny advancement to their husbands. Before I am finished with them, they will regret the day they crossed me!" Her attitude softened, and she smiled at Ah-wen-ga. "But I need not tell *you* all the tricks I will be able to employ. Your husband, after all, was the Great Sachem for many years."

Ah-wen-ga knew it would be useless to protest that not once had she ever used her influence with Ja-gonh to settle a personal problem. Never would it have occurred to her to employ her husband's power in such a way.

"I have in mind," Dalnia went on, "every slight, every insult, every unpleasantness. Each night, I think of how I will make them all pay!"

Ah-wen-ga was dismayed to see the glee with which Dalnia anticipated her revenge. Putting aside her willingness to be open-minded, she realized that nothing whatsoever admirable could be found in Dalnia's view of those who showed their dislike. She was simply biding her time, waiting for a chance to even the score, and looking forward to that day with sufficient relish to sustain her through a difficult period. Completely lacking in humility, she had no sense of charity toward others. Worst of all, as Renno's wife, she would be in a position to cause great dissension and unhappiness. Instead of doing everything in her power to help the Seneca to stand united, she would be dividing them, uncaring whether such divisiveness would eat away the strength of even as strong a minority as the Seneca. Her vitriolic demand for vengeance could destroy that branch of the Seneca nation.

She was, Ah-wen-ga decided sadly, dangerous and deserved to be eliminated from Renno's life. But Ah-wen-ga faced the same dilemma that had long confronted her. Prying open her grandson's eyes sufficiently to see Dalnia in her true light would be virtually impossible. Any attempt to persuade him to be reasonable was likely to backfire.

Ah-wen-ga could only hope that when he returned from the present military campaign Renno might prove to have matured enough to see Dalnia for what she really was. On that forlorn hope, she realized, the entire future of the Seneca might well hinge.

Panic among the Choctaw was short-lived. They recovered their sense of proportion soon after they had fled from the battlefield. Singly and in small groups, they prepared to return, shamefaced, to their homes. The battle was lost, and they could not compensate for their failure to win the day. Their war chiefs neither lectured nor punished; the loss of face was more than enough punishment. In their usual unit formation, they quietly began the march home. Hunters were assigned to procure meat for the defeated army, and other braves were designated to forage for edible plants and berries.

Without doubt, they had suffered severe losses. Their count of dead and wounded was high, and the survivors limped slowly homeward, no longer glorying in their reputation for ferocity.

Sentry outposts were established at night. As soon as they had eaten, the other exhausted warriors threw themselves on the ground and slept.

Only in the tent of Solomba was there any activity. His key lieutenants appeared to give an up-to-date report on casualties and to discuss reorganization of their battered units. Planning was essential if the Choctaw hoped to retain their present boundaries and continue to exert dominion over less powerful neighbors.

After all the war chiefs had reported, a very tired half-breed, who also wore Choctaw war paint, dragged himself to the tent.

In spite of his exhaustion, Rattlesnake's mood was defiant. "I suppose," he muttered bitterly, "that we are to lick our wounds like a dog that has been whipped."

"That happens to be necessary, in my opinion," Solomba replied angrily. "What would you have us do? Should we launch another expedition and lose the remainder of our fighting force? We have no choice."

Rattlesnake growled inarticulately.

"I deeply regret our inability to wage war right now," Solomba continued, "but I am compelled to withdraw until we are able to even consider fighting once more."

"You cannot allow a setback to destroy the nation," Rattlesnake answered, his voice seething with bitterness.

"On the contrary," Solomba countered, "this respite will make it possible for us to fight again in the future and to hold the territory and influence we possess. We have learned lessons from this battle, I hope, and I do not intend that they will be ignored or forgotten!"

"What lessons?"

"If we had faced the Cherokee alone," Solomba said, "we would have won handily. But they were strengthened by the Seneca. We missed an opportunity that we will not have again. Like so many nations humiliated by the Seneca, we lack the strength and cunning to defeat them. They are too strong and too shrewd. After what we have experienced, I am forced to admit that I am no match for Ghonkaba. And his son already is a field leader without an equal. We will need to prepare long and hard if we hope ever to win a campaign against them."

"Then you will bow to the dictates of the Cherokee," Rattlesnake said with a sneer, "and place our people under their authority?"

Solomba shook his head. "No. But neither will I

challenge them in battle again so long as they have the Seneca and the militia as their allies."

"If we withdraw now from the war," Rattlesnake objected passionately, "then we lose the chance to ally ourselves with the British. Their ability to gain possession of the country west of the Appalachian Mountains will vanish."

"I have no intention of abandoning the British," Solomba retorted. "As you know—better than anyone—they have supplied us with arms, ammunition, and many other items. We are in their debt, and I shall see that debt repaid. But we cannot hope to accomplish that in a day, or in a month. We must be patient. First, we must regain our strength. And then we will find the way to catch the Cherokee unaware and attack them—and them alone—when they least expect it. Only in that way will we clear out their lands and prepare the way for the British to march in and take possession of part of this territory. I am assured that they will divide it with us suitably."

With great effort, Rattlesnake was able to control himself. "I hear the commands of my war leader, and I obey him now, as I always have obeyed him in all things," he said. "But surely Solomba does not object if I quietly probe for weaknesses in the Cherokee alliances with the Seneca and the settlers. We must be prepared to exploit any such holes. If we find none, then it will be up to me to create some. Like you, I have no intention of seeing our dignity as a nation sacrificed. I have no desire to bow my head and my back to the Cherokee, the Seneca, or the settlers. The day will come when the Choctaw will rise triumphant over the prostrate forms of their enemies. To do all in my power to hasten the arrival of that day will be my constant goal!"

The leaders of the allied force gathered before an open fire outside Ghonkaba's tent. While they ate supper, they discussed the battle they had just won. Their casualties were too high to permit anything approaching a celebration, and they weighed their words soberly.

"The Choctaw," Lieutenant Colonel Johnson said, "still will have an enormous nuisance value. But I think their power as a major force is destroyed. No longer will they have the strength, either alone or in collaboration with the British, to occupy the lands west of the Appalachians other than those they now control. The way is open for further American settlement of the frontier lands—without disturbing the territory of our allies, of course."

"I am wondering," Wegowa said, "whether we would be wise, despite our losses, to attack the main town of the Choctaw. We could so cripple them that they would have no power again for at least a generation."

"As I see it," Ghonkaba countered, "we would be taking a needless precaution. And we also would be guaranteeing their future enmity. I say, leave them in peace. Make no demands on them. By the time they sufficiently recover their strength and their dignity to become a threat, many months will have passed. The prospect of a new alliance with Great Britain will be long past."

The other commanders agreed, and then Colonel Johnson advanced a suggestion. "We can assure ourselves," he said, "that the Choctaw are planning no new uprising and are making no plans for future invasions. All that is required is for a patrol of scouts to be sent into their territory to inspect their towns and their hinterlands."

"That is good," Wegowa said. "I would recommend further that we dispatch our missions openly, making no particular secret of their goals and their intentions."

They left the details to be settled the following day, then scattered to their respective headquarters.

Ghonkaba, alone now, sent for his son. When Renno appeared at the tent, Ghonkaba told him that the high command had agreed that the ability of the Choctaw to make war had been destroyed. "Do you agree?" he inquired.

Renno thought for a time. "No question about it," he said at last. "If the Choctaw were to be attacked, I daresay they would be capable of defending themselves. But they lack the ability to launch an offensive against us. It may be years before they recover enough to undertake one." He smiled faintly, then grew somber. "But before we rejoice prematurely, let me say that we and our allies are in no shape to launch offensives, either. We suffered surprisingly heavy casualties. Some months must pass before the wounded men recover and we can try to regain our full strength. But, we have gaps in our own ranks that cannot easily be filled."

"As you can imagine, I have been devoting much

thought to our wounded and our dead," Ghonkaba replied, "and to the cause of our regrettable losses." He sighed. "When you came to me with accusations, first against Casno, and then against Rusog, I laughed at the idea. I was right, and you were gravely mistaken. But now I am agreed that it is probably true that a traitor is somewhere in our camp."

Renno stiffened, awaiting his father's thoughts.

"Look back at the battle. Live it again in your mind once more, step by step," Ghonkaba said. "See if you agree with me that the enemy knew in advance what we intended to do, what tactics we planned to employ. The Choctaw were not engaging in guesswork. They had their own responses prepared."

"You are completely right, my father. It is no accident that the enemy divined our intentions. They did not engage in lucky guesswork. They actually *knew* our most intimate plans."

"How could they discover them?"

Renno grimaced. "I made a terrible error when I accused Casno of being a traitor. Then I compounded my mistake when I pointed at Rusog. Both are innocent. Both are loyal patriots, and I was totally wrong in casting doubt on their integrity. I have apologized to them. I have no desire now to make a similar mistake by accusing someone of whose guilt I have no proof. I learned my lesson."

"I approve of your caution, my son," Ghonkaba told him, "but at the same time, I rely heavily on you to help me solve this mystery. Devote further thought to it, and let me know the result of your thinking."

Relieved that he had not been reprimanded, Renno returned to the bivouac area of the advance guard and scouts, an outpost that continued to supply sentries for the entire camp. There he ate a late supper of warmed-over buffalo stew. After his meal, he made the rounds of the sentries' positions to assure himself that all was well. Finding nothing amiss, he returned to his headquarters. For the first time in two days and nights, he stretched out on the grass. The rest his body craved was a luxury he had denied it for too long, and he soon drifted off into sleep. In spite of his physical and mental exhaustion, he began to dream, and to his surprise, the images that he saw and heard were as real as though they were actually taking place. . . .

. . . Somewhat to Renno's surprise, he found himself once again on the battlefield littered with the bodies of the dead of both armies. All was quiet, and he smelled the stench of death in his nostrils.

As he stood looking around uneasily, he was horrified when the dead began to rise and to form a circle around him. Some were fellow Seneca, and as he stared at them, he realized that he knew them well. They were friends who had been junior warriors with him; they had learned their craft as warriors together. Some were gaunt militiamen, and still others were warriors of the Cherokee, men with whom he had lately become acquainted.

One by one, they took their places in a solid phalanx that surrounded him on all sides. His uneasiness increased, but the dead refused to step aside for him when he would have chosen to go elsewhere.

They closed ranks and completely cut off his escape. In hostile silence, they stared at him, raising their weapons to block his exit. His flesh crawled.

Suddenly, a voice, hollow and echoing, spoke up from somewhere in the ranks of the dead. "Warriors of the Seneca, warriors of the Cherokee, and militiamen of the regiment, hear my voice. There in your midst stands Renno, the son of Ghonkaba, a warrior who bears the most noted and distinguished name in the entire history of his people. I accuse him of killing us. He might as well have pulled the trigger of his rifle as he pointed at each of us in turn."

"We accuse you, Renno, of murder," the other ghostly figures said in hollow voices.

Renno's blood ran cold in his veins, and a shiver crept slowly along his spine.

"You are directly responsible for our deaths," another ghostly voice charged.

A sea of pale forefingers pointed at Renno. "You killed us," voices murmured. "You are a murderer, and you killed us!"

All the dead were whispering now, their fingers still pointed at him. "You killed us," they insisted. "You are the murderer who killed us!"

Sweat, clammy and cold, ran down Renno's forehead, blinding him.

But no escape was possible. "You are the murderer who killed us," the dead chanted.

Renno wanted desperately to put his fingers in his ears in order to shut out the sounds of the accusing voices, but he was unable to move.

"Murderer! Murderer! Murderer!" the chant echoed relentlessly.

The young Seneca opened his mouth and screamed, but he could make no sound.

Then, suddenly, he heard his own voice, as though coming from a great distance. As he listened, he could hear himself, speaking clearly, explaining to an unseen listener the tactics that the Seneca and their allies intended to employ in the campaign against the Choctaw.

All that he said was true. Within himself, he now suspected that he had truly spoken such words at some time in the past. They had an uncannily familiar ring.

The accusing stares of the dead assailed him from every direction. Their expressionless eyes burned in their sockets and shone strangely from their blank, pale faces. "You killed us, murderer!" they shouted over and over. "You killed us, murderer!"

. . . Suddenly, Renno was awake. The members of the advance unit stretched out on the ground beside and around him. All were sleeping. But the echo of the ghostly voices still sounded hollowly in his ears. He shook his head vigorously in an effort to rid himself of the sound.

His physical torment eventually ended, and the night was very still.

Shuddering, bathed in sweat, Renno struggled for composure. As he grew calmer, he knew beyond all doubt that his dream was no figment of his imagination. It was true. He had talked out of turn, and his comrades had died in battle because the enemy had been prepared. Taking a sacred vow to the manitous to learn the whole truth, he made up his mind to say nothing to anyone until he understood better what was to be required of him. At the same time, he felt crushed by the burden of the unwitting role he had played in the treachery.

The drums throbbed incessantly at the village of the Cherokee and Seneca. Their insidious beat filled the air and seemed to crawl beneath the skin of the participants in the victory celebration honoring their battlefield warriors.

The medicine men of the Cherokee, having engaged in a friendly contest among themselves and with Casno, danced to the point of exhaustion. They were joined now by scores of warriors and women. They all stomped and whirled incessantly, never pausing for breath. Elders sat in the shade provided by canopies of woven leaves and branches, watching the spectacle. The old men were smoking pipes, the old women murmuring to each other as they concentrated on their sons and daughters, grandsons and granddaughters.

Small children ran wildly about the field, accompanied by their excited, barking dogs. This was a special occasion, when boys and girls were allowed to roam freely without supervision, doing as they pleased. Their shrieks of delight echoed across the hills and occasionally competed with the beat of the drums.

Those in charge of preparations for the feast worked indefatigably. Quartered buffalo turned slowly on spits erected above smoking fires of hickory wood, and smaller sides of venison were being similarly prepared. Squash and beans were bubbling in large vats. Corn, still in its husks, was roasting in the coals of huge fires. The meal promised to be memorable.

Ghonkaba and Toshabe danced together, then joined his mother to exchange visits with Loramas and Wegowa. Returning to their proper places, they received the Seneca who were obliged by custom to greet them upon arriving at the festivities.

Ah-wen-ga looked with approval at her granddaughter, Ena, dancing with Rusog. Joyously reunited after the battle, they were inseparable now. Displays of affection were forbidden by custom, but Ah-wen-ga smiled when Rusog and Ena stopped dancing and fell into conversation with several other couples. Their arms touched frequently as they chatted, their hands sought each other briefly, and after making contact, withdrew again. As she watched the young couple gain assurance from one another, Ah-wen-ga was reminded of the early years of her own marriage, when she and Ja-gonh had established the roots that served them so well in the half century that had followed.

Her gaze straying, Ah-wen-ga caught sight of her youngest grandchild, El-i-chi, who had been assigned the chore of providing wood to maintain the cooking fires. All four of his companions were Cherokee, and she concentrated her full attention on them. They seemed indifferent to being from two different tribes. Their arms loaded with wood, they quietly fed the fires, then exchanged comments and jokes as they went off to fetch more wood.

Ah-wen-ga could see no difference in the way the young Cherokee treated each other and the way they behaved with El-i-chi. She could see that he was as much at home with the Cherokee as they were at ease with him. It was evident to her that, since her talk with him, he had reached an understanding with his contemporaries. Yes, he had made his peace with the Cherokee, and by the same token, they accepted him. No animosity separated them now, and his future seemed assured in the land where the two nations were becoming one.

Several new arrivals interrupted Ah-wen-ga's reverie, and she turned to greet them. Among them, she saw Renno, still looking tired and worn. With him was Dalnia, whose smiling, proprietary air caused Ah-wen-ga to stiffen in involuntary protest.

Renno bowed to his parents. Dalnia did the same, and they engaged in conversation for several minutes. Then it was Ah-wen-ga's turn.

"Greetings, my grandmother," Renno said, and lowered his head in tribute.

"Hail, Ah-wen-ga," said Dalnia, inclining her head slightly.

Ah-wen-ga's wave commanded the young couple to sit.

They obediently lowered themselves to the ground, and if Dalnia was reluctant, she concealed her feelings well.

"I have learned what you are being too modest

to tell about yourself, Renno," Ah-wen-ga said. "Namely, you once again fought with great distinction."

"I did only what was necessary in battle, my grandmother," Renno answered.

She laughed. "You remind me of your grandfather. He performed feats in battle beyond the capacity of ordinary warriors. Yet he always claimed that he was merely doing his duty."

"I know how he felt," Renno muttered in embarrassment.

Ah-wen-ga glanced obliquely at Dalnia and saw that she seemed bored by the conversation.

"You must be proud of Renno," she prompted.

Dalnia's response was mechanical. "Oh, I am," she concurred. "Very proud."

Ah-wen-ga knew that her suspicions were accurate. Dalnia's interest was aroused only if she was the center of attention. The sooner that Renno parted company with her, the better it would be for him, his grandmother thought helplessly, still believing that no one in the family could advise him. He would need to make any such decision himself, without assistance. Only in that way would it be effective.

Neither Ah-wen-ga nor anyone else could realize it, but Renno was in a worse turmoil than ever over Dalnia. He had discovered when he had returned home from the war that she still had a magnetic physical appeal, and that as soon as he looked at her, he wanted to be with her.

At the same time, however, he felt a permanent, deep debt of honor to his comrades who had lost their lives in battle with the Choctaw. He had to place them first.

His fears had become so awful, so stomach-turning, that he hated to admit them, even to himself.

Forced to face reality, he was compelled to concede that he now suspected Dalnia of being the traitor who had betrayed him and his fellow warriors. It was she, he reluctantly realized, who had received the vital information he had unthinkingly passed on. He knew he had spoken freely to her—as he had spoken to no one else—about various military plans of the Seneca and their allies. Those plans had been mysteriously transmitted to the enemy, who then prepared to counter them at a cost to the Seneca and their allies of many lives. The dead, who had called Renno a murderer in his dream, were not mistaken.

He knew that he had erred twice when he had tried to identify the traitor. He could hardly afford another mistake. To make certain that his accusation was accurate, he had to put Dalnia to the test.

If she was innocent, he realized that he would remain obliged to marry her at the earliest opportunity. If she was guilty, however . . . His mind refused to function. That eventuality was one he would be required to face when the time came. Until then, he could not bring himself to dwell on it.

Concealing his feelings, he managed to get through the evening of celebration. He danced frequently with Dalnia, pretended to eat large quantities of food, and laughed too loudly and too long at the coarse jokes of other braves.

One of the evening's events surprised Renno.

Cited by Casno for valor in combat, he was authorized to wear an additional hawk feather in his war chief's headdress. Even this reward struck him as false, however, and he felt undeserving of the honor. He would not add the fourth feather to his headgear until he felt that he had earned it.

He and Dalnia returned to her home late that night. No sooner had they reached it than she threw herself at him. He allowed himself to be persuaded to make love to her and felt surprised that he carried off his role with as much zeal as he did. His whole reaction, he knew, was simply a part of a plan he had worked out in his mind.

With Dalnia warm and drowsy beside him, he made a point of sighing loudly.

She stirred slightly. "Surely you are not unhappy?" she whispered.

"But I am," he said. "If I had my way, I would stay right here with you forever."

She laughed sleepily. "Where do you think you are going now?"

Renno replied with great deliberateness. "In five days," he told her, "I am being sent by Ghonkaba on another mission, a secret mission."

He thought he felt her becoming tense. "What sort of mission?"

"It's confidential."

Dalnia snuggled closer. "You can tell me," she murmured. "After all, you have confided many secrets to me."

"So I have." He hesitated, and then went on, seemingly reluctant to speak. "In five days' time," he said, "I will go to the land of the Choctaw. They will not expect me so soon after the campaign, and I know they are not anticipating another attack."

"An attack?" She sounded casual.

"I have been directed by Ghonkaba and the members of his council," he said, speaking slowly and distinctly, "to enter their town on the fourth night after I leave this place. I am to kill Solomba while he sleeps, and if at all possible, I am to do away with Rattlesnake. I am ordered to flee as soon as I have committed these murders and to return here by the fastest route I can devise. I am to follow the river when I go, reaching the great bend on the third day of travel. But I am free to choose my own route of return."

"Why have you been directed to kill these Choctaw?"

"The council," Renno improvised quickly, "believes that we and the Cherokee will not be safe from attack until the pair who are responsible for Choctaw military activity are removed for all time."

"This must be a dangerous mission for you!" Dalnia sounded concerned.

"Not particularly," Renno assured her, "but it is a nuisance, coming so soon after the end of our campaign. I would much rather spend the time here with you instead of absenting myself for another eight days or more."

"I will be here," she said, moving nearer to him. "I will be waiting for you whenever you can come back."

Soon she was sound asleep, but Renno remained

wide awake. He had put his plan into motion. By the time it reached its climax, he would know whether Dalnia was indeed the spy who was guilty of such terrible treason.

The following day, Renno went to his father and outlined his scheme. Ghonkaba listened quietly, and by the time his son finished speaking, he was frowning. "I quite agree that a spy was in our midst giving our military plans to the Choctaw," he said. "I see no doubt of that. I can also understand your desire to determine whether Dalnia was the guilty party. What I do not like about your scheme is the needless risk you are taking with your life."

"I will be taking a very slight risk, at most," Renno promised. "But I must know. I have asked Dalnia to marry me, and my honor requires that I fulfill my pledge and make her my wife if she is innocent. If she is guilty, however, I shall . . ." His voice faded away and he paused momentarily, then spoke again with greater emphasis. ". . . I shall be obligated to revise my plans. I assure you again, my father, the risk will be very slight."

"How so?"

"I shall arrive at the great bend in the mighty river a full day earlier than I told Dalnia that I would. I have no intention of going on to the town of the Choctaw. I shall proceed no farther than the great bend. There I will climb into the branches of a high tree and wait. If Dalnia is guilty, she will have somehow communicated the false news to Solomba and Rattlesnake that they are to be attacked by an assassin. In that case, a company of warriors will appear, ready to do away with me when I come down the river. It will not be difficult to identify Dalnia as the Choctaw spy. Nor will I have long to await the answer to this question that so perplexes us."

"Your mission makes me uneasy, my son," Ghonkaba replied, "but since I can think of no better scheme, I must allow you to proceed with it. Do what you think you must. And may the manitous watch over you."

As Renno slept with Dalnia on the night before his departure from the land of the Cherokee, he could not help wondering whether they were making love for the last time or whether they would marry upon his return. He believed he had allowed ample time for her to transmit the message of his pending arrival to the leaders of the Choctaw. Beyond that, he could do nothing more.

Renno's spirits were low when he left on his self-appointed journey, but his youth and his joy in his surroundings had their customary effect. The majesty of the limitless wilderness inspired him as it always did, and by nightfall he felt much improved. He paused to rest for only moments at any one time, and occasionally he broke into the Seneca trot, which he maintained for several hours before slowing his pace again. By sunrise he was a full day ahead of the schedule that he had told Dalnia he planned to keep. Thereafter, he enjoyed himself thoroughly, shooting small game with his bow whenever he became hungry, then cooking his meal over a little fire. His route was

easy to follow once he came to the river, and his
spirits continued to rise. All the same, the possibility
of Dalnia's perfidy continued to hang over him. He
realized that he never would know real peace or
pleasure until the issue was settled.

He caught a large fish in the river and, wrap-
ping it in some large green leaves, cooked it for his
supper. Finishing his meal with some ripe berries
plucked from a nearby vine, he dropped asleep and
slept soundly beside the riverbank.

The following day, after another couple of hours
on the trail, he came to the great bend in the river.
A large tamarack offered the greatest concealment.
Before climbing it, Renno obliterated all signs on the
ground of his presence. According to his estimate, a
band of Choctaw might be expected to appear at any
time before late evening. He made himself as comfortable as he could in the branches.

The day passed slowly. An insect droned nearby,
a talkative bird chattered overhead, and a pair of
squirrels playing in the lower limbs paused to peer at
Renno and then took flight. The young Seneca dozed,
but kept his bow and a quiver of arrows within easy
reach. Now that the climax was at hand, his calm was
monumental. He felt under no pressure to obtain an
answer to his problem.

After he had idled away several hours in a som-
nolent state, Renno suddenly became wide awake
and alert. His extraordinary hearing enabled him to
pick up the faint but unmistakable sounds of a small
group approaching cautiously. He made certain again
that the branches in which he was hiding would

completely conceal him from the ground below, then peered down expectantly. The next few minutes would give him the answer.

When a party of five warriors—all wearing the Choctaw black and white war paint—came into view, Renno felt a stab of grim satisfaction as he saw a half-breed he knew must be Rattlesnake.

The Choctaw party halted near the base of the tree, and Rattlesnake gave specific orders to his men. He spoke in a low tone of voice, and Renno could not hear his words, but the intent of his instructions was clear. Two warriors were sent off to follow the river's winding course while two more were dispatched to search an area to the south of the river.

No longer could he have a shred of doubt that the Choctaw were hunting for him.

As the braves went off, Rattlesnake sat down, resting against the base of the tamarack. He was only partly visible now from the heights above.

Renno, who had killed Anthony Simpson, knew that the British agent's son was equally dangerous; he could do great harm to the American cause and to the combined interests of the Seneca and Cherokee. It would be a relatively simple matter to put an arrow into Rattlesnake while he sat below, and to end his threat. Renno was sorely tempted.

But his high sense of honor would not permit him to launch a surprise attack on an unsuspecting foe. Before he shot Rattlesnake, he felt obliged to notify his enemy that such an attack was about to be made. Only if the half-breed had an opportunity to defend himself would Renno feel justified in committing such an assault.

Perhaps he could give Rattlesnake fair warning, and then attack. Such a course would be difficult, however, because the Choctaw leader's followers would immediately know that the Seneca was on hand, and they would bend every effort to find him.

For the moment, Renno reasoned, he had a mission far more important than killing Rattlesnake. Because of his own stupidity in talking out of turn, a traitor had been able to penetrate the most confidential secrets and betray his or her countrymen. Recalling only too vividly the bone-chilling dream that had inspired his present search, he knew that his mission took precedence over everything else. His feud with Rattlesnake would necessarily wait until he could devote his full time and attention to it. First he had another vital score to settle.

Renno remained silent and unmoving for another two hours, until at last the Choctaw scouts began to return, all empty-handed. They reported to Rattlesnake, who conferred with each in turn. The entire group rested interminably, eating emergency rations and dipping their bare feet into the river.

After the last member of the party had an opportunity to eat and to rest, Rattlesnake put them all into motion again. Apparently he had decided not to give up the search, for he and his companions pushed on, following the river.

It was a simple matter now for Renno to wait for another hour to pass before he descended. Then, making sure he was leaving no footprints, he plunged into the river and swam to the north bank. There he emerged and struck out on a route that would take him due north. In time, he would turn west again and eventually would reach his destination in the land of the Cherokee.

Until then, however, he reasoned, he would be relatively safe, and Rattlesnake and his Choctaw would not find any sign of him in the forest.

Chapter IX

As Renno sped homeward through the wilderness, he tried in vain to slow his pace. He had no reason to hurry; no crisis made it necessary for him to rush. But the memory of his explosive dream goaded him, and as he remembered the bloodless faces of the warriors who had been killed by the Choctaw, all accusing him of responsibility, he forced himself to the limit. He knew he could not rest until he had avenged their deaths at the expense of the person who was truly responsible. Although he was tired, he found it impossible to pause, and even when his bones ached, he could not sleep.

He had repeatedly spoken out of turn, freely discussing military plans with Dalnia, and never once dreaming that she was somehow passing along secrets to the Choctaw. He could argue, to be sure, that he had lacked any way of knowing that Dalnia was disloyal. He blamed himself. The principle had been drummed into him since boyhood that military plans were to be revealed to no one except authorized personnel. Certainly no woman—including his mother and grandmother—belonged in that category. Although Dalnia's treason was shockingly unprecedented in the long, glorious history of the Seneca, he nevertheless also realized that he should not have been indiscreet in her presence.

As yet he had not formed an idea how he would use the information that he had managed to piece together regarding Dalnia's guilt. His dismay, anger, and shock were still too intense for him to think clearly. But he knew that he must confront her with evidence of her perfidy as soon as possible.

His face gaunt, his expression bleak, Renno arrived home in midmorning. Passersby, including those who assumed that he had been dispatched on a new mission by Ghonkaba and Wegowa, took one look at his face and avoided contact with him. His burning eyes and the thin set of his lips showed that he was in no mood to exchange pleasantries.

Ordinarily, Renno would have gone directly to his father, but he had matters to settle with Dalnia. He went straight to her house, wondering if she would be bold enough to remain after arranging a meeting that she assumed would result in his death.

In spite of the hour, Dalnia was still asleep. Renno paused at the entrance to stare at her.

Never had she looked lovelier, more defenseless, or more appealing, and he had to harden his will as he gazed at her.

Gradually, she became conscious of his scrutiny and stirred. She opened her eyes, and saw him, and smiling to cover her surprise, extended her arms to him. He knew she must be almost overcome by amazement to see him alive. He could not understand why she had delayed her departure from town.

Renno realized that in spite of what he had learned about her, he still wanted her. But he knew that desire could no longer be fulfilled. He extended an arm and pointed a forefinger at her. "Woman," he said somberly, "you have kept the Choctaw informed of our military plans. You have told the enemy all the information you have gleaned from me about our operations."

Dalnia was suddenly jarred wide awake. She was tempted to deny the charge, but one long look at Renno's face convinced her that the truth was preferable. Never had she seen such an expression in his eyes. He was showing no mercy, feeling no compassion. She realized that he demanded the truth at any cost. Unable to meet his gaze, she looked down at her short nightdress of doeskin, which revealed her long legs. She took a deep breath.

"When the Choctaw captured me and took me back to their town with them," she said, "on behalf of Solomba, their military leader, finally it was Rattlesnake who made a hard bargain with me. He threatened to kill me unless I cooperated. He promised a considerable fortune in English money if I provided him with information on the military plans of the Seneca. I—I was reluctant to accept, but I had to protect myself in case the Seneca were defeated by the Choctaw, or if you were killed in battle."

He brushed aside her excuses. "Exactly how did you operate?" he demanded.

"In the wilderness not far from this town there is a hollow tree," she explained reluctantly. "I was instructed to place a pine cone in the hollow whenever I had a message to impart. Then a certain number of days later, I was to return to the tree and there I would find a courier of the Choctaw awaiting. That is the system I used. It was very simple. I gave a message to the courier, and that was all, as far as I was concerned."

"You consider it the end of the matter when scores of our warriors died because of your treachery?"

Stunned by his tone, Dalnia felt a stab of fear for the first time.

"You are a traitor to the Seneca people," Renno said in a low, intense voice.

Terrified, Dalnia fled from the house into the open. Renno followed her, and cutting off her retreat, he began to call out names of warriors killed in the battle. His voice was toneless, his expression unrelenting, impersonal, almost cruel.

A large crowd began to form and grew quickly. Ghonkaba and Toshabe came, accompanied by Ahwen-ga, and they knew at once what Renno was intoning. Dalnia's parents appeared on the scene and feebly tried to push through to the front of the crowd where they would find it possible to intervene, but Ghonkaba waved them back. He realized that Renno must deal with this matter in a way that would satisfy the manitous as well as himself.

Renno again pointed a forefinger. "You alone," he declared, "are responsible for the death of many men. You alone are responsible for having made me a fateful part of your scheming. The time has come when you must pay for your crimes!"

He took a single step toward Dalnia, then another. His tread was measured; one hand was on the hilt of the hunting knife that he carried in his belt.

Dalnia now realized her extreme peril. She began to babble desperately. "I had no choice," she cried. "Solomba and Rattlesnake forced me to act as I did. They swore that Rattlesnake soon will kill you in cold blood, and I believed them. I also believed that my own life was threatened, and that the only way I could save it was by becoming a spy."

Renno continued to advance toward her, the knife firmly in the grasp of one upraised hand.

His intent was plain: when he came within reach, he intended to strike.

Dalnia looked around wildly, but the crowd cut

off every avenue of escape, and the Seneca, having heard Renno's allegations, were in no mood to open a way out.

She took a deep breath and, breaking into a sudden run, she tried to brush past Renno. Instead, she crashed into him, which forced him to lower the hand that held the knife.

Using all her strength, Dalnia made a wild attempt to break away. He was holding the knife in such a way, however, that the point of the blade was aimed directly at her.

As Dalnia blindly threw herself forward, she forcibly impaled herself on the knife blade, which penetrated deep into her body.

She gasped as she staggered and fell to the ground, a look of incredulity and horror on her face as she died.

Renno insisted that he alone, unaided, would attend to the burial of Dalnia. Her parents, shamed by their daughter's acts, silently assented. All other Seneca turned away.

Going a short distance into the wilderness, he dug a grave. Then, refusing Casno the privilege of conducting a ceremony, he picked up the bloody, crumpled body and slowly carried it to the grave. He was followed by scores of fellow Seneca, who observed him in utter silence.

He stood for a long moment, an expression of utter contempt on his face, and then he threw her body into the pit.

It was noon, but as Renno began to shovel dirt

over her, the sky grew dark, and soon the day was as black as night. A single, bright beam of sunlight shone through the darkness and picked up Renno in its rays. He alone was illuminated.

Peal after peal of thunder sounded in the distance, as though the manitous were applauding what Renno had just done. As soon as he finished his grisly task, the sky grew lighter again. Renno dropped his shovel, picked up his bow and quiver of arrows, and started off into the forest.

Ena and Rusog, who had been watching from a distance with the greatest sympathy, started toward him, intending to join him.

But they were stopped by Ghonkaba, who also halted the approach of several warriors who fought under Renno in battle.

Of all those present, Ghonkaba alone appeared capable of understanding that, at a moment like this, his son desperately needed to be alone.

Renno walked far into the wilderness, seemingly paying no attention to where he was going. But he had in the back of his mind a destination. Jejeno had told him of a hot spring of bubbling water that had once existed. Though it had not been active for many years, it was a favorite place for the Cherokee to commune in private with their gods.

When Renno finally reached the place, he lowered himself to the ground in front of the spot where the spring had been and began to pray aloud.

"I beg you, O manitous, cleanse me of guilt. I have erred and I fear that I have displeased you. I have this day dispatched from the land of the living one who was a traitor to the Seneca nation and caused many men to die before their time. I acted as I did so that others who are weak of will do not follow in the footsteps of treason. If I acted as I should and pleased you, O manitous, send some sign to indicate that I followed in the right way."

To Renno's astonishment, he heard a faint but distinct gurgling sound. All at once, the dormant spring before him came to life. A steady stream of water shot up some eighteen inches into the air and then cascaded down again, forming a little stream as it ran off.

He stared at it for some moments, then reached out a tentative hand and let the stream play on his fingers. The water was hot. He saw it as proof that he had won the favor of the manitous by ridding the world of Dalnia.

Renno reached out and let the spring play on the hand that had held the knife responsible for Dalnia's death. The heat of the water pained him, but he gritted his teeth and submitted to it. Eventually, he no longer felt the heat.

When he withdrew his hand, he sighed deeply and looked at his fingers, which had turned almost scarlet.

He could not explain his reaction, even to himself, but suddenly he felt cleansed. Dalnia had fallen onto his knife and had died accidentally, but he had intended to do away with her, and he could not pretend otherwise.

Bending forward over the spring, he drank a large quantity of the water. He felt that his insides were on fire. When he could drink no more, he raised his head and let the stream play on his face and forehead. Now, surprisingly, the sensation seemed very pleasant, and he had the feeling that he had been forgiven for any act that he might unwittingly have committed. The manitous, like the gods they represented, rejoiced because Dalnia was no more, and Renno felt that they had absolved him of permitting himself to be a tool that she was able to use and manipulate in furthering her evil ways. He realized that now, at last, he could put her out of his mind for all time, and he made a solemn pledge to the manitous. Never again would he think of Dalnia, never again would he mention her name to another living human being. His thoughts would be on the Seneca and how he could serve his people.

Taking a last drink from the hot spring, Renno started to walk back to the town. He held his head high, his step was light, and most of his troubles were behind him. He went straight to the house of Ah-wen-ga. She took one look at him, saw that he was erect and clear-eyed, and smiled.

"You are recovered from the illness that has afflicted you for so long," she said.

Renno agreed. "I am healed."

His tone reverential, he told her in detail about the awakening of the dormant spring.

She nodded solemnly. "You are favored by the manitous," she said, "and you live under their guidance and with their blessings."

"Never again will I stray from the paths on which they lead me," Renno said. "I cannot bring back to life those who have died, but I can make certain that they did not lose their lives in vain. I have dedicated myself anew to the Seneca, to their greatness and glory."

Looking at him, Ah-wen-ga recognized his potential. She knew beyond doubt that he had been chosen by the manitous to walk in the footsteps of his ancestor, the great Renno.

"Now that you have cleansed your mind and heart and body," she told him, "you are prepared to begin a new life."

"I feel as though I am already embarked on that life."

"The time has come," his grandmother went on, "for you to think in terms of your own future, as well as the future of our people. Turn your thoughts to the young women whom you know so that you may select one of them, marry her, and raise a family."

To her surprise, Renno no longer was able to meet her level gaze. He lowered his eyes and began to fidget. "I have already thought in such a way," he admitted, "and I have become confused. I have determined to stop trying to push, to stop trying to insist that my own will be done. I am content to leave all such decisions to the manitous."

Ah-wen-ga vividly recalled the time, more than a half century earlier, when she had waited impatiently for Ja-gonh to make his feelings clear and unmistakable. "Do not force someone to wait too long," she advised.

"She has no idea of my interest in her," Renno

said, and then added, "besides, many complications exist."

Ah-wen-ga's unchanging expression gave no clue to her realization that inadvertently he must be revealing the identity of the young woman he had in mind.

"But I cannot let myself dwell on my future and worry about it," he went on. "Having dedicated my life to the Seneca, I rely on the gods and the manitous who represent them to guide me and to lead me in the right direction. If their will is that I marry, so I shall. If it is their desire that I remain single, I will take no wife."

He sounded like a medicine man, Ah-wen-ga thought, but she knew he was too robust, too energetic, too filled with a love of life for such an existence.

His grandmother bowed her head to conceal her broad smile and then murmured, "So be it."

Renno announced his intention of going hunting to celebrate his release from the worries that had been wearing him down. Shortly after that, he went on his way.

Ah-wen-ga waited until he had departed, and then went to see her son and daughter-in-law. She lost no time in coming to the point of her visit. "Now that Renno has cleared his mind and his soul," she said, "he will soon be at loose ends for things to occupy his attention. If you have any urgent dealings with the settlers, I urge you to send Renno there as your courier."

"Why do you have that in mind, my mother?" Ghonkaba asked.

"The settlers, I believe, engage in many pursuits that would be of great interest to Renno," Ahwen-ga told them. "If we lived in the land of the Seneca, he would use such an occasion to begin his preparations for the day when he will become the sachem of our nation. The blood of white ancestors flows through Renno's veins. It is only right that he visit a white community and learn more about the ways of civilization. It is wrong for him to think only of Seneca as his ancestors."

Ghonkaba laughed. "The manitous must be prompting your speech, my mother," he said. "Let me show you a communication that I received this very day. It was delivered by a courier from Lieutenant Colonel Roy Johnson." He went off into an adjoining room and returned with a sheet of parchment, which he handed to his mother.

Ah-wen-ga read an extremely cordial letter that Colonel Johnson had sent to the Seneca leader. He had also written to Loramas and Wegowa of the Cherokee, Colonel Johnson said, and he included anyone else that Ghonkaba cared to designate. The Seneca and Cherokee leaders were invited to join in discussions with the officers of the militia battalion on their common future, as well as to review their victory over the Choctaw and to consider its significance.

"The manitous must have guided your thoughts, my mother," Ghonkaba said. "Wegowa already has asked Rusog and Ena to accompany him on this journey, and in the normal course of events, I would have asked Renno to come with us. Now I shall be certain to include him in our party."

Renno and Rusog were appointed as commanders of the bodyguards for their fathers on the journey through the wilderness. Ena was made head scout, giving her the pleasure of performing a duty that she accomplished so brilliantly. Casno accepted a liaison responsibility. Loramas, though feeling relatively fit for a man of his years, declined to make the long journey.

Toshabe accompanied Ghonkaba. Together, they would be guests at the home of Roy and Nora Johnson. Wegowa, recently a widower, would be housed in the dwelling of the major who was the battalion's second-ranking officer. The journey was uneventful, the weather was warm, and no hostile Indians were encountered. The Choctaw had been thoroughly vanquished, and any of the small tribes steered clear of the party.

Observers in the fort's watchtowers noted the approach of the Indian leaders from a distance of two miles or more, and the palisade gates were opened, with Colonel Johnson and his staff coming out to meet the visitors.

Renno, who shared the cordial greeting of Colonel Johnson, accompanied his parents to the Johnson house. Now that he was about to see Emily Johnson again, he allowed himself to think about her at length for the first time. He was aware of her popularity with the young men of the fort, and he half expected her to be betrothed if not already married.

Nora Johnson was in the doorway of her home, waiting to greet her guests. Her daughter was at her side. Colonel Johnson presented Ghonkaba and Toshabe to his wife and daughter. Renno caught a glimpse of Emily, fresh-faced and smiling, her wheat-blond hair tumbling below her shoulders. From that moment he had eyes for no one else.

At last the time came when they were face to face. To his consternation, his power of speech completely deserted him, and he stood mutely before her, feeling awkward.

Emily salvaged the embarrassing situation by smiling and telling him she was happy to see him again. She held out her hand.

As Renno touched it, he felt as though a bolt of lightning had struck his fingers. His whole arm tingled from the shock; but almost at once, he regained the ability to speak. "How are you, Emily?" he asked, and was annoyed with himself because it sounded so inane.

His mood was not improved when he saw his mother and Mrs. Johnson exchange a significant look. Their meaning escaped him; but he knew they were referring to him, and his sense of discomfort increased.

That night, the officers of the battalion gave a dinner in honor of Ghonkaba and Wegowa in one of the assembly rooms of the fort. The meal was prepared by wives of the officers.

Ghonkaba, whose command of English was

perfect, replied to some brief remarks by Colonel Johnson.

Renno, who had no official duties to perform, was delighted that he had been chosen as Emily's escort for the evening. They found themselves seated at a table with a half dozen militia officers, with all of whom Renno was on friendly terms. Painfully self-conscious at the start of the festivities, he gradually thawed under the combined influences of Emily and his wartime companions. The speeches delivered by Ghonkaba and Colonel Johnson were short, and by the time they were finished, Renno, who had been exchanging toasts in beer with his former colleagues, felt completely relaxed.

Emily could not help contrasting him with his sister and brother-in-law. Ena and Rusog, at a nearby table, were stiff, ever-conscious of their Indian heritage. They behaved like uncomfortable guests rather than joining in the evening's fun. By this time, Renno had so entered the spirit of the occasion that nothing in his behavior made him seem different from the other young men at the table.

The residents of the fort were strictly forbidden to go beyond the palisade after dark. When the festivities ended, the majority of the young people decided instead to climb to the walk atop the parapet that encircled the fort. Here, in the moonlight, with their wives and sweethearts listening appreciatively, the young men began to speak of the future they envisioned and of their own aspirations of taking part in building the future. At last it was Renno's turn.

"Several of you have mentioned great cities you

would like to see built here in the wilderness," he said. "I have no desire to see such cities transforming the land. Nor do I look forward to the day when mines will bring up iron and coal from the earth. Or when the wilderness will be transformed into a modern place where factories take the place of trees. I know and appreciate the meaning of being an American, and I understand the value of the freedoms that we possess." He noted that Emily was listening closely to his words, her expression as unfathomable as that of an Indian.

"I was in my early teens when I first took up arms for the American cause, and I still bear them," he said. "The price of liberty is as high as its taste is sweet, and we who cherish it must be prepared to defend it at all times.

"I have listened to some of you outline the America you want. That is not the America I seek. Let me say only that in a land as vast as ours, both our dreams can come true. I see no conflict between them. We have room for great cities and factories, as well as ample room for the wilderness where one survives on the hunt.

"In my blood flows the heritage of two cultures, that of the whites and that of the Indian. I choose that of the Indian, and I seek to make it secure. I seek the wilderness where those who choose it as their home may live in peace and in plenty with their neighbors, where no man fires an arrow or hurls a tomahawk at a fellow man. A land where all who have elected to live close to nature may enjoy her bounty."

Embarrassed because he thought he had said too much, Renno now fell silent.

"Who among us," Emily called out, "can dispute the vision that Renno has just described? Does anyone here seek a deeper, more enduring peace? Or seek a more satisfying life? I doubt it!"

Renno was astonished by her support. The discussion went on, but he heard none of it and kept returning to her words. Not until the group gradually broke up and he and Emily were left alone sitting on top of the palisade did he have the opportunity to pursue it with her.

"You think I am arrogant," she said, "because I claim the right to pleasures in the forest that you feel only you have the right to enjoy. Is your Indian sense of smell so keen that only you can differentiate and appreciate the wonders of the forest after a heavy rain? Is your Indian sense of hearing so keen that you hear notes that are denied to my hearing when the birds of the forest start to sing? I think not. All you can rightly claim is that you were here first. You were the first to smell the good earth and the trees after the rain. You were the first to hear the chatter of birds and the jabber of small animals. You were the first to taste the berries and the roots that were planted by no man, but does that make them any less easy on my tongue? I think not."

"Your words suggest sincerity when you speak of the wilderness," Renno replied, "but you protest in vain when you say that I would deny you its joys. Have I tried to drive you out of the wilderness? Have my people tried to drive you out? Have the

Seneca sought to prevent you from sharing in these pleasures? If so, they are not true Seneca!"

"The first thing one learns about the wilderness," Emily said with dignity, her tone injured, "is that he who seeks its pleasures for himself is soon denied them and gets nothing. The wilderness must be shared if it is to be loved and appreciated."

The thoughts she had just expressed were so similar to his own views that Renno was left speechless. He groped in vain for a reply.

Thinking that she had won a debate, or at the very least that she had enlarged the scope of Renno's thinking, Emily had a satisfied look on her face as they terminated the discussion in order to return to the Johnson house.

The recuperation of Loramas from the illness that had almost taken his life was slow but steady. In time he felt well again. As his rejuvenation went on, he realized that he felt livelier and younger than in a very long time. Everything around him commanded his active interest.

Somewhat to his surprise, he found his thoughts turning frequently toward Ah-wen-ga. Unable to get her out of his mind, he nonetheless hesitated to call on her.

Early one afternoon when the sun was bright overhead and the air unusually balmy, he could resist the temptation no longer.

At her door, he called loudly, "Hail, Ah-wen-ga!"

If Ah-wen-ga was surprised to see the Grand Sachem of the Cherokee, she did not show it. "Good afternoon, Loramas," she said politely. "Won't you come in?"

They sat down on opposite sides of the stone pit in the center of the room where she did her cooking.

"You are looking well," she commented politely.

"I never have felt better," he said. "And our climate appears to agree with you. You, too, seem in the best of health."

"Indeed," she told him, "I love living here. The atmosphere in the North had become oppressive. You perhaps cannot imagine what it was like there among the Iroquois nations who had chosen the wrong side in the American war of independence. In contrast, I have found that our people here are full of life and high spirits. They actually look forward to each new day and to the future. Now I am finding that, even at my age, I am responding in the same way."

"You are not as old as you make yourself sound," he protested. "If your gods are willing, you have many years left to spend in this world. I, too, have a long life ahead of me here. The Corn Mother spared me, and as a result, the Breath Holder promises many functions for me to perform before I am called to join my ancestors."

"I know what you mean," Ah-wen-ga agreed. "When my late husband was alive, he took care of most business matters. I had little to do with the governing of the Seneca. But here, where I am the most senior of all Seneca, many problems are thrust into my lap for solution. I am required to be wise and farseeing, compassionate but at the same time just. It is quite a responsibility."

"If you find that your duties are too onerous," Loramas said hastily, "you may wish to refer some problems to me, one by one. I spend much time listening to disputes and settling problems of the Cherokee. If it would be of help to you, I would gladly take on whatever burdens you might wish to share."

"Throughout my life," Ah-wen-ga said, "I have grown accustomed to doing my duty at all times and never shirking my responsibilities. You are very kind. But I never could take advantage of your generosity by adding to your burdens. That would be unfair."

"I already bear responsibility for thousands of my own people," Loramas replied. "Certainly it would be no additional weight if I also attend to similar duties involving only some hundreds of Seneca. I would be delighted to do this. But you must not consider yourself indebted to me."

She shook her head.

Loramas smiled indulgently. "The Seneca are a remarkable people," he went on, "and of all the breed, I see you as the most remarkable. Ask yourself this: have you ever failed to live up to the principles that guide your existence and that you regard as so dear?"

Ah-wen-ga considered the question. "Not to my knowledge," she said. Suddenly she grinned at him. "I sound so lofty, so elevated, but between us, I am not. Often I am compelled to struggle when sitting in judgment on my people. I am required to maintain a solemn air. But occasionally I feel like laughing until tears come to my eyes."

"Really?" He was surprised and pleased. "The same thing has happened to me, more often than I can tell you," he confided. "It is very difficult to be the court of last resort. I sometimes wonder how the Corn Mother and the Breath Holder must feel. Might they not sometimes want to relax and enjoy themselves."

Ah-wen-ga's tone became conspiratorial. "I wondered the same thing about the manitous. If you think we have a difficult time, how much more so it must be for those who are immortal. Your late wife and my late husband must look with disapproval when they contemplate our present lives."

"Not if they remember how hard they found it to maintain their own dignity day after day, month after month, year after year."

"I could never discuss such matters with Ja-gonh," Ah-wen-ga said. "I never have told this to anyone else. He often was so austere that I felt a little afraid of him myself. I did not dare joke about his precious dignity."

"Now that you mention it," Loramas said, "I had to be on guard with my late wife, too. Because her family was of the nobility, she was accustomed to much pomp in her relationships. I was an ordinary person at birth, the son of a warrior and squaw. Only through chance I rose to the top. Therefore I possess a sense of humility that some of the aristocracy seem to lack."

"What you say about sensitivity is true, but I must take issue when you claim that you rose to the top by chance," she protested. "No real ruler rises by accident to a place above his fellows, and you know it. You are guilty of false modesty when you fail to take into consideration your own superior qualities."

"What makes you so sure my qualities are superior?" he demanded, challenging her.

"I have eyes in my head, so I can see you," she replied defiantly, "just as I have a mind of my own and can make it up accordingly. You have the drive and the inner strength to lead your people. Above all, you care about them sufficiently that you want them to move harmoniously in the right direction. Believe me, even if I did not know you as the Grand Sachem of the Cherokee nation, I could discern it by your attitude. Unknowingly, you give yourself away— to me, at least."

"Because of your own position," Loramas answered, "you are sensitive to the needs of those in positions of authority. Perhaps you recognize certain qualities because they are similar to your own."

"Perhaps," she agreed. "This discussion is fascinating. Perhaps you would care to stay for dinner, while we continue the talk at our leisure."

"I do not want to impose—"

"Nonsense!" Ah-wen-ga interrupted. "I must eat, too, you know. It is no more trouble for me to prepare a meal for two persons than for one."

Loramas's resistance vanished. "Well, if you insist . . ." he murmured.

"I do insist," Ah-wen-ga told him firmly. "How do you like your venison cooked?"

"I well remember one time when I ate it at the

house of your son and daughter-in-law," Loramas told her. "She had an unusual way of preparing venison that I found absolutely delicious."

Ah-wen-ga giggled. "Of course," she said. "I gave Toshabe that recipe. If you will please gather some firewood, I will prepare the dish the way you want it."

Like any ordinary brave, he went outside, picked up an armload of wood, and bringing it back to the pit, built a fire.

Then Ah-wen-ga went to work putting a venison steak on the fire and basting it with a mixture of oil and herbs.

Neither of them was giving it a thought, but their behavior markedly resembled that of many hundreds of Cherokee and Seneca couples at the same hour.

Because Nora Johnson had to meet with senior officers' wives to plan another fete, she briefly left her visitors behind with apologies. Toshabe found sewing equipment for her use in completing a task for Ena. There Emily came to join her but stood hesitantly in the doorway.

"Come in, child," Toshabe called with a quick smile. "No need to stand on ceremony."

Emily came slowly into the room. "I did not want to intrude on you."

"You are hardly intruding," Toshabe assured her. "I am just finishing this skirt for Ena. As a scout, she is the equal of any brave of the Seneca or the

Cherokee, but she is none too clever with a needle, and without help she cannot finish this skirt."

Emily seated herself and took knitting from a bag she was carrying.

"What are you making?" Toshabe inquired.

Emily held up the garment. "A vest."

"It is very attractive," Toshabe commented, and asked idly, "For whom is it intended?"

"I am telling people that I am making it for my father, but that is not strictly true," Emily said, and then paused for a long moment.

"Do you suppose Renno would wear it if I gave it to him?" she asked in a small voice.

"He certainly would," his mother replied. "He would be overwhelmed." She looked long and hard at the younger woman. "But I cannot be so sure that you would wish to give it to him if you understood the customs of our people."

"Oh, dear," Emily murmured, looking distressed.

"It has long been a rule of the Seneca," Toshabe explained, "for items of wearing apparel to be exchanged only by husbands and wives—or by those who are betrothed to be married. By presenting such a gift to Renno, you would be signifying to the people of our nation that you have reached a private understanding with him and have consented to become his wife. And by accepting such a gift, he would be signifying to the Seneca that he is intending to take you as his wife."

Emily turned beet red. "I am so glad you told me," she muttered. Her hands, holding her knitting needles, suddenly became very still. "I—I could not do so, now that you have told me."

"On the other hand," Toshabe went on with a smile, "you have no reason to be familiar with the customs of our people. So you surely are free to do as you please."

"If I had remained in ignorance, I would have been free," Emily rejoined. "But I simply cannot ignore Seneca tradition. Renno would never forgive me for tricking him if he discovered the truth."

Toshabe spoke deliberately. "If my son realized that you made him a vest in spite of being aware of the traditions of our people, he would be very pleased to accept the gift."

Her observation was so unexpected that Emily blinked in surprise. Toshabe laughed softly.

"Do I make my feelings for Renno so obvious, then?" Emily asked.

"Only to your mother and me," Toshabe said, "and I question whether anyone else could have the slightest idea. Certainly, I have no intention of telling. As for Renno himself, he is like all the men of our family. He has no idea."

"I—I hardly know what to say," Emily murmured. "I believe I am safe in saying that my father has no idea, either."

Toshabe started to respond that she thought Roy and Nora Johnson were also aware of their daughter's feelings. But she stopped, and said nothing, deciding that was between Emily and her parents, and she had no right to interfere.

Emily steeled herself. "What do *you* think?" she asked quietly.

Toshabe replied hesitantly. "If you are destined to become the wife of Renno," she said, "I will thank the gods. My trust in the judgment of the manitous will be confirmed. If it were your destiny to marry another, however, I would abandon my faith in the manitous and never again bow my head to them."

Emily, realizing that she was in earnest, was deeply impressed.

"If your wish is to become the wife of Renno," his mother said, "and I assume it is, then listen to the advice that I give you and heed it well. Above all, be patient in your dealings with him. He must come to terms with himself and must acknowledge that he is in love with you. Only then will he be prepared to act on that knowledge."

Emily felt as though she had received a blow in the stomach. The revelation that Renno did not know the state of his own feelings toward her came as an overwhelming shock.

"I wonder if you have heard of his infatuation with Dalnia," Toshabe asked, "and of what became of her?"

Emily shook her head. "I never have heard that name."

Toshabe started to relate the tale, beginning with Renno's early infatuation with Dalnia.

"I don't think I should listen," Emily murmured.

"You must. Every word that I speak is common knowledge among our people."

She revealed how Dalnia had abused Renno's

trust in her and had inveigled him into inadvertently revealing military plans. But Renno had learned the truth, and after proving to his own satisfaction that Dalnia was a traitor, he had been responsible for an act that killed her.

"The gods approved and so did our people," Toshabe concluded. "In some way that I do not know and would not ask him, Renno has found release from the turmoil of his guilt. Now, at last, he is free to resume his life as the gods intended him to live. And the most certain sign that he has recovered is his interest in you."

Too bewildered to reply, Emily sat very still, pressing a scented handkerchief to her nose as she tried in vain to reassemble her reeling senses. She politely thanked Toshabe for revealing the story, then asked to be excused and went off to her own room. She closed the door behind her, kicked off her slippers, and collapsed onto the bed.

What disturbed her most was the revelation that Renno was capable of being a murderer, that he would deliberately kill another human being as punishment for wrongs committed against him and against the Seneca people.

As she reconstructed the situation, Renno had seen it as enough that he had satisfied himself that Dalnia was guilty. Accordingly, he had felt no need to present the evidence to others; having established her guilt to his own satisfaction, he had appointed himself as her executioner and had carried out a death sentence, with no appeal, no plea for extenuating circumstances, no excuse of any kind. To Emily, his vengeance appeared as swift, terrible, and all-consuming.

The thought occurred to her that she had developed a deep interest in a man who, in spite of his adoption of a surface veneer of civilization, was at heart a barbaric savage. She could think of no white man who would take the law into his own hands with such impunity, decide a matter of life and death, and then carry out the sentence.

Would he be judge, jury, and executioner in all things? His mother had shown no distress when she related the story, and it seemed that she did not blame him for what he had done. As a matter of fact, she appeared proud of his conduct.

Emily warned herself to draw back. Was she willing to compromise her own principles and standards for the rest of her life? This she very much doubted. She had to think it all out thoroughly, determine where her relationship with Renno might be leading her, and thereafter act accordingly.

Emily emerged from her long hours of thoughtful isolation with the determination to defer any decision. In spite of his mother's confidences to her, Renno had not yet expressed an intimate interest in her. She decided to wait until he did so before she even tried to determine whether she really would want to make her life with the Seneca in the wilds.

Ghonkaba, Wegowa, and their respective parties dined privately with their hosts in a gazebo behind the home of the Johnsons. The main course was roast lamb. It was a dish little known to the

Indians, who pronounced it delicious. After the meal, the older people settled down to an evening of serious discussions, dismissing the younger generation, including the aides-de-camp.

Delighted to have time to themselves, Ena and Rusog immediately departed for the house in which they were staying, while Emily and Renno were left to their own devices. Renno appeared to be in high spirits, and Emily found it exceptionally difficult to realize that this ebullient young Seneca was actually a potential killer.

They made their way to a stone bench that Roy Johnson had fashioned from a boulder; it was at the far end of the garden. When they reached it, Renno spread a handkerchief so that Emily would not soil her gown. She lowered herself to the seat and looked up at him expectantly.

Having thought about her to the exclusion of almost everything else, Renno had finally concluded, in typical Seneca fashion, that he should leave in the hands of the gods the question of what to do about her. Because, in his own view, his stature and his natural dignity would not permit him to risk rejection in the event that he proposed, he had decided the time was not yet ripe for a proposal. First, he must demonstrate to her that she was increasingly in his thoughts and in his heart. After devoting hours to the problem, he at last had solved it according to his own lights. Permitting the future to take care of itself, he would concentrate only on day-to-day developments. His trust would be in the manitous to guide him toward the solution he wanted, always provided that they deemed it best for him.

Renno had prepared and rehearsed a little speech, but now it sounded stiff and false as he ran it over in his mind. He hastily discarded it.

"You love the wilderness," he reminded her, "and think of it as your home. But, as you know, the forest can be dangerous for anyone who fails to take the needful precautions. I have made a small keepsake that will, I hope, protect you from harm there."

He reached into a pocket and produced a knife with a razor-sharp blade about four inches long. The blade bore a stamp showing that it had been fashioned in Sheffield, England. The handle was made of shells woven together to form the symbolic bear of the Seneca. This motif was repeated in the rawhide scabbard that covered the blade.

Renno had captured the knife in a battle with the redcoats, but he had remade the handle and the sheath himself.

Emily was as surprised as she was pleased. "Thank you!" she exclaimed. "This will be very useful." She turned the knife over and over in her hand, examining it. "I know something of the quality of knives, as you may not be aware. And the handwork on it is striking."

Suddenly shy, Renno could only stammer. His mother had taught him to draw, and he had learned the art of needlework from his grandmother, but these were accomplishments of which he never boasted. Only the members of his immediate family knew of his talents, and the thought suddenly struck him that he was exposing himself to ridicule.

But Emily had no intention of ridiculing him. "You are so very clever," she told him. "I wish I could use my fingers as well." Beyond his mechanical skills, however, she realized that she was greatly impressed by his tenderness and awareness of her. The conflict with what she feared him to be—a killer without mercy—was confusing at the same time that it was somewhat reassuring.

He had always taken his skills for granted and was embarrassed by her praise for his work.

Seeing that he was ill at ease, Emily reached into her reticule and drew out a Rhode Island silver dollar that featured an engraving of an Indian warrior on its face. Through a small hole drilled in it, a chain had been inserted. Actually, like the currency being issued by a number of the individual states, the coin was worth many times its face value. The silver was part of a sunken treasure recovered from a Spanish galleon by Rhode Island authorities.

"The brave reminds me of you," Emily remarked quietly, studying the figure on the coin. She handed it to him.

Renno looked closely now at the figure of the Indian and felt blood rushing to his face. The likeness was an idealized version of a brave. No warrior ever had been that handsome or superbly muscled.

Emily took back the coin and draped the chain around his neck. The coin hung down over his chest. "There!" she said. "That's the way it should be worn."

"I shall wear it for all time," Renno told her. "It

shall rest upon my chest and serve as a reminder to the manitous to protect me from harm, thanks to you."

He could have had no idea that his gracious words spoken as a prophecy would be put to the test, and far sooner than he might have anticipated.

The following morning, games of prowess and skill were held on the green for the guests' entertainment. The young Seneca and Cherokee were invited to participate, as were the fort's inhabitants. Members of all three groups volunteered.

Among the events on the schedule was a knife-throwing contest. Although Renno was an expert in the art, he had no desire to participate. When his intentions became clear to Emily, she surprised the assemblage by stepping forward and announcing that she intended to be a contestant.

Her revelation created an uproar, but nothing in the rules prevented a woman from competing.

Renno hurried to her side as others also entered the fray, one by one. Emily greeted him cheerfully. "When I was small," she said, "my father taught me knife-throwing as a means of self-protection. I want to try my luck with your gift knife."

"I gathered that you might use it," Renno told her. "Let me show you one or two of its peculiarities."

She handed him the knife.

"The blade and the hilt are perfectly balanced," he explained. "The trick in throwing it is to maintain that balance."

Grasping the blade lightly, he went through the

pantomime of throwing it. "Keep your motion fluid and easy, without jerkiness," he advised, "and when you release it, do not give it an extra thrust. Just open your hand when your arm reaches the top of its sweep. Here, take the knife, and I will show you."

Emily grasped the blade and simulated the throwing of the knife while Renno guided her arm.

So engrossed in what they were doing and with each other, they failed to realize for several moments that a man standing nearby was glaring at them. It was the rawboned Captain Ben Whipple, whose disapproval of Emily's entrance into the contest was evident. His annoyance with the lesson Renno was trying to give her was also very clear, but Renno was not conscious of the animosity that he exuded. "Good morning, Captain," he called. "Miss Johnson is aiming to make the knife-throwing contest more interesting for everybody concerned." He turned back to Emily and the lesson.

Glowering steadily, Whipple made no reply.

An expression of exasperation crossed Emily's face, but she managed to control her feelings as she continued to concentrate on Renno's instructions. Once again, she was pleased by his concern for her, obviously very sincerely felt. None of her many other suitors, actual or prospective, possessed the personal qualities that this young man had.

Turning her back to Whipple, she tried to hide her concern. Whipple, she knew, invariably was jealous of any man to whom she paid any attention. Furthermore, he hated every Indian. She had managed to keep his volatile temper under control in her presence, but she had always assumed it would only be a matter of time until he exploded. She prayed this would not be the day he gave in to a temper tantrum. Renno, she suspected, never would tolerate such behavior. Even if she managed to curb his likely reaction, her father might intervene, also with predictably disastrous results.

Gradually becoming aware of Emily's increasing nervousness and of Whipple's icy stare, Renno deliberately placed himself between the two of them as he continued to instruct her. Eventually, the tension seemed to ease, and the near-incident passed without harm to anyone.

Then the contest began. Emily encountered no difficulty in qualifying, and with the young women cheering her every move, she racked up a reasonably decent score, striking three targets out of five.

In the second round, her skill and her score slipped somewhat, and she came close to being eliminated. But she managed to rally. As she passed on to the finals, she compounded the surprise of the men who were opposed even to her participation.

Renno stayed beside her throughout, coaching, soothing, helping in every way he could. His assistance was at least partly responsible for keeping her in the running as others were eliminated. Finally, only Emily and four men remained, one of whom was Ben Whipple. The judges called for a respite of a few minutes, and Renno moved close to Emily, advising her in low tones.

"The only opponent you need to worry about is Whipple," he told her. "The others are erratic. Now, you cannot influence the target strikes that Whipple achieves, but you do have a very great influence on the final score he obtains. Under the rules, you are allowed to knock his knife from the target in order to cut down on his points. That is what you may have to do."

"I never have dislodged anyone else's target," Emily objected with doubt in her voice.

"It is quite simple," Renno assured her. "Aim for a place in the target a tiny fraction above the spot where his shot lodges. The momentum that your knife attains will not only knock his knife to the ground, but will assure you of a lodging place in the target. Never forget that you have a double objective: first, to dislodge your opponent; second, to achieve a score yourself. You have drawn fifth. That is all to the good, because you will throw after him. I am not saying it will prove necessary to knock anyone's knife from the target, but if they should score too well, do not hesitate to get rid of them. It is legal, and good sportsmanship as well."

Ribbons of different colors were fastened to the shaft of each knife. Emily, handed a ribbon of white silk, attached it before announcing that she was ready.

The target was a narrow white birch tree, difficult to see in the dazzling sunlight of midday. No more than eight inches in diameter, it would have been easy to miss under the best of circumstances.

The first contestant, giving in to his nerves, wildly overshot the target and missed the tree completely. The second and third did better, but they used too strong a throw, and their knives soared high and landed just below a divide in the trunk, about eleven feet above the ground. They were not disqualified, but their shots would provide no real competition for those who kept their head and maintained their aim.

Now it was Whipple's turn. Demonstrating surprising calm, he took aim, measured the distance, then let fly. His shot appeared gentle, but his blade nevertheless embedded itself in the trunk of the tree, directly below shoulder height.

He had achieved the most difficult of shots. The judges were certain to award him the highest possible score.

Whipple was not popular with his colleagues, but his skill, nevertheless, elicited a smattering of applause. He acknowledged it by grinning and bobbing his head.

Beating him would be exceptionally difficult. He glanced at Emily and smiled triumphantly. His expression was arch. His lips parted in an unpleasant sneer as his gaze flicked past Renno. His attitude was plain: he had come as close to a perfect strike as it was possible to achieve, and he was defying his opponent to try to equal his skill.

Renno lowered his voice to a near-whisper as he spoke to Emily. "You have only one way you can beat him now. You must knock his knife to the ground and make certain that your knife sticks."

"I don't think I can do it," she responded dejectedly.

"Of course you can! Look here." He took the knife and illustrated. "You want the blade to glance against the shaft of Whipple's, hitting it just hard enough to dislodge it. Because the handle is much heavier than the shaft, his knife will then fall."

Concentrating her whole being on the task that confronted her, Emily pushed back a lock of her blond hair, then took the knife. Though already completely familiar with it, she weighed it again in her palm.

Renno stepped back out of her way.

Emily was an apt pupil, her hand was steady, and her eye was exceptionally good. Her blade glanced against Whipple's knife, knocking it to the ground. And then hers embedded itself in the tree trunk. She was the sole, undisputed winner of the contest.

Ben Whipple failed to appreciate Emily's skills. His face livid, his eyes burning, he pointed an accusing forefinger at her. "You cheated!" he roared.

She tried to brush past him, but he refused to give ground.

"You played an unfair trick on me," he shouted. "If you had not struck my knife, I would have beaten you!"

Incensed and scarcely knowing what he was doing, he gave her a quick shove, knocking her somewhat off balance.

Emily staggered and would have fallen, but Renno held her until she regained her balance. Then he released her and, turning to Whipple, grasped him by one shoulder and swung him face to face.

Whipple was so astonished that he failed to react and could only blink.

"If you know what is good for you," Renno said,

speaking slowly and distinctly, "you will keep your distance from Miss Johnson—now and in the future! I will teach you a lesson that will help you remember."

Deliberately electing to fight in an American style rather than one favored by Indians, Renno cocked his right fist. He delivered a short, sharp punch that traveled no more than twelve inches. Such force was behind the blow, however, that it landed with explosive impact against Whipple's cheekbone. The officer instantly collapsed to the ground, hands involuntarily flung above his head, his legs akimbo, his jaw slack.

Renno took a backward step and waited for his opponent to rise. He had no idea whether the fight was ended or was just beginning. He prepared for either eventuality. Balancing his weight on the balls of his feet, he was ready to strike again if necessary.

Whipple hauled himself to his feet, a bruise mark marring his cheekbone, which he nursed with one hand. "Damn your filthy hide, Indian!" he shouted. "You not only helped Emily cheat, but you caught me unaware just now. We will soon see if you have any real courage! I challenge you to a rifle-shooting contest. Right here, within the next twenty-four hours!"

"I accept," Renno answered quietly, "and as is my right, I challenge you in return to a similar contest with bows."

Whipple immediately interpreted Renno's words to mean that he was weak with a rifle and preferred to fire the traditional Indian weapon. Laughing boastfully, he replied, "Agreed! Provided that you will add a contest in pistol-shooting to our competition."

"Very well." Renno remained unruffled. "Can I interest you in a contest with tomahawks, as well?"

"Why not?" Whipple was openly contemptuous. "And you should have no objection to a knife-throwing contest after the unfair advice you gave Emily."

"You wish to throw knives, as well?" Renno asked quietly. "I see no reason to refuse."

Colonel Johnson, intervening, called a halt before the two young men went beyond reasonable bounds. Fearing they would become involved in actual bloodletting unless someone stopped them, he stepped between them and announced that their contest would be at the same hour on the following day. Disappointed by the postponement of the rare sport they were going to witness, the onlookers finally accepted the delay in good spirits.

Emily went directly to Renno. "Please call off this competition with Ben," she urged. "I distrust the possible result of such a conflict."

The very thought of canceling the contest was abhorrent to Renno. He was astonished that Emily would offer such a suggestion. "I cannot call it off," he said. "My honor is involved, and so is yours."

"You do not understand," she told him earnestly. She was surprised to realize anew how much she cared for him, despite the doubts she had felt. "Ben has been interested in me for a long time. He is wildly jealous. All I have to do is show a slight interest in a man for him to become combative and unreasonable and—well, almost demented. When you knocked him down, you insulted his manhood. He feels compelled to even the score. I feel dreadful about all this, because I failed to warn you of his insane jealousy."

"I would not permit his jealousy to stop me from doing what I did," Renno answered flatly.

"I am grateful to you for it," Emily acknowledged, and meant it deeply. "At the same time, I am somewhat shocked. He has intimidated every single man for a long time now, and I had become unaccustomed to having someone act on my behalf." As she said it, she knew that here was a man truly capable of winning her heart completely, no matter what else he might ever do.

"Then I see it as high time," Renno replied, "that Ben Whipple really be taught a lesson that he will not forget—as I have already promised him. He may learn hard—but learn he will!"

On the surface, Ah-wen-ga and Loramas maintained a primly correct, formal relationship. As befitted two heads of state, they never broke down the barriers of reserve, propriety, and protocol.

In private, however, their conduct was far different. Ah-wen-ga stayed at home two evenings a week, instead of going next door to her son's house for supper or attending one of the feasts that her position ordinarily made advisable. On these occasions, Ghonkaba, Toshabe, and their children did not think of disturbing her by calling on her. And frequently they were absent from the town. The Seneca in the community followed her family's example in keeping their distance.

It was easy, therefore, for her to entertain Loramas in strict privacy at supper twice each week.

They made no attempt to keep their relationship a secret. On the other hand, they mentioned one another to no one, including their children and grandchildren. Consequently, no one knew the extent of the growing romance, and it was not a subject of speculation. Occasionally, a Seneca or a Cherokee returning home late in the evening might happen to glimpse Loramas leaving Ah-wen-ga's house, but it was invariably assumed that he was there on a matter of state.

As a result of these unusual circumstances, the elderly couple was free to explore each other's personalities at their leisure. They felt no pressures while determining where—if any place—they wanted the relationship to lead.

One night, after several gourds of a particularly delicious buffalo meat and vegetable stew that Ah-wen-ga had prepared, Loramas groaned when she offered dessert.

"Really," he said, "I can eat no more."

"I already have poured syrup on the blueberries. They will not keep," Ah-wen-ga told him. "You must eat some. Besides, you yourself brought these berries tonight. Would you have me be a poor hostess and refrain from serving them? I hope I have better manners than that!"

He accepted the dessert without further objection and began to eat with a long wooden spoon.

"They are good for you," Ah-wen-ga reminded him. "Besides, you need more fresh fruit. Increase the amount, and you will not fall sick again."

Although Loramas allowed no one else to lecture him, not only did he lack the authority to silence Ah-wen-ga, he was reluctant to try, for fear of hurting her feelings. And he recognized the validity of what she was saying. If he sought to deal firmly with her, he could expect her to point out, as she had on several occasions, that she had only his own welfare at heart. Her rebuttal left him defenseless, as they both knew, and Loramas could do nothing about it. He tolerated her remarks in good-humored silence.

At last Ah-wen-ga ran out of breath. She smiled at Loramas virtuously, picked up her own gourd, and began to eat. Her berries were not covered with syrup, because she was careful not to eat foods that would add to her matronly figure.

After a lifetime of dealing with women, Loramas had learned that he usually could forestall criticism by changing the subject with a compliment. More to the point, his compliment ordinarily was sincere. "You did beautifully," he now told her, "this afternoon, when you settled the dispute between the two brothers who fought with knives over possession of the bow and arrows that both claimed."

"That was a rather interesting matter," she admitted.

"Rather interesting? I found it fascinating! I could not determine which was the wronged party, but you ferreted out the truth when you threatened to confiscate the bow and arrows permanently if they disturbed the peace again. One brother did not care what became of them while the other became very distressed. Your wisdom sorted them out with great speed and efficiency."

"I did nothing original," Ah-wen-ga said. "I simply remembered a matter that came before my father-in-law—the great Renno—many years ago. He used the same strategy under circumstances that seemed fitting. I merely adopted his approach. And you are trying to spoil me!"

"If I am, it is only because you deserve to be spoiled!" he retorted.

They looked at each other, and their gaze held for a time. Then Ah-wen-ga broke the spell by looking down at her folded hands in her lap. Flustered, she muttered, "We're too old for such nonsense."

"What nonsense is that?" he demanded.

"Behaving like a pair of young romantics the ages of our grandchildren."

Loramas worded his response with utmost care. "When I was the age of my grandson," he said, "I lacked the depth and understanding to appreciate a woman with your qualities. I have needed a lifetime to evaluate them, much less enjoy them."

"You flatter me," Ah-wen-ga said, "but you disregard your responsibilities, as you apparently would have me disregard mine."

"I am acutely aware of your responsibilities and of my own," Loramas assured her. "If it were not for our consciences, and for the high positions that we enjoy, I would have asked you weeks ago to marry me. I ask it now in the full consciousness of our responsibilities. As my wife, your position would in no way hamper your responsibilities as the first-ranking member of the Seneca. Nor would I be restricted in carrying out my responsibilities to the Cherokee."

Ah-wen-ga placed a hand on his arm to silence him. "I am not questioning your motives in any way, Loramas," she said, "just as I am not questioning my own. I believe that both of us are sincere and honorable in our intentions. If we had no obligations to our respective people, I would not hesitate to accept you. You do me a very great honor in asking me to become your wife. For the rest of my days, I shall be grateful to you for it."

"Does that mean that you reject my proposal?"

She shook her head. "No, it does not. If the truth be known, I am procrastinating. I have no desire to look foolish in the eyes of the Seneca, nor to have you appear foolish to the Cherokee. Our dignity must be preserved, as must the high public regard for our positions."

"I have searched my heart," Loramas said, "and I cannot see how it is possible for our marriage to compromise our stature with our people."

"I am glad for you that you have arrived at that state," Ah-wen-ga told him. "As for me, I am not there yet. Perhaps that reflects one of the principal differences between a man and a woman. I need more time to weigh the idea from every possible angle. Then I would discuss it with my son and daughter-in-law—not that I seek their approval. Whatever we do, we shall do regardless of what they may think. But I would wish to notify them of my decision to marry you. I say that because, all things being equal, I will marry you, Loramas. I keep searching for some reason why I should not. Only if I find one will I refuse you. I know that time is precious to both of us. Neither of us has much longer to enjoy what pleasures there may remain in this life. Nevertheless, I must beg you to please be patient until I can come to you with a clear heart and a clear mind."

Chapter X

"Captain Whipple is a competent officer who carries out his assignments well," Colonel Johnson told Ghonkaba. "He is efficient, and though the troops have no personal liking for him, the men nevertheless respect him because of his ability. One result is that I have been reluctant to punish him. What is more, though he is jealous of my daughter, he is

generally clever enough to keep his feelings in bounds.
For example, he undoubtedly knew that if he had
challenged your son to a duel, I would have intervened at once and forbidden a fight. But by challenging him to a contest of skills, he gave me no legitimate
reason to intervene. As a matter of fact, he may have
actually managed to increase his stature by appealing
to a certain element among us."

Ghonkaba nodded, and his voice was dry as he
replied, "Yes, I recognized the appeal to anti-Indian
attitudes. I am sure some people here, as in every
frontier town, have no use for Indians, even for those
of us who fought for American independence and
whose loyalty to the United States is assured. That
entire group will be supporting Whipple, cheering
for him, and hoping for his victory."

"The people who hold such views," Colonel Johnson said, "make up a very small proportion of our
population. All the same, Emily's views cause me to
wonder whether I should call a halt to the contest."

"I hope you would not be calling it off for Renno's
sake," Ghonkaba protested.

"Partly for him, and partly for my daughter,"
Colonel Johnson replied. "I have no clear idea how
serious their mutual interest may be, but I would
much prefer to see their relationship develop outside
the public gaze. They would be under far fewer
pressures that way. And their judgments could be
more seriously reached and more valid."

"I cannot predict what is to happen, either,"
Ghonkaba agreed. "But let us suppose that they do

develop a relationship in earnest. Would you and your wife have any objections to Renno?"

"Because he is part Indian?" The colonel roared with laughter. "I can tell you that Nora and I would be damned proud to have as a son-in-law the inheritor of the name and the mantle of the most renowned warrior in the history of this country." His smile faded, and he peered hard at the Seneca leader. "Do you and your wife object to Emily?" A hint of belligerence entered his tone.

It was Ghonkaba's turn to smile. "If the manitous gave me the right to select a wife for Renno," he said, "I would choose Emily ahead of every other woman on the continent. I happen to know that Toshabe feels exactly as I do."

They looked at each other, smiled broadly, then shook hands.

While they inched their way toward a meeting of the minds, their wives were far more blunt.

"Ordinarily," Nora Johnson said as she threaded a flat needle that she used for sewing leather, "Emily is very frank with me. She tells me in great confidence about her feelings and holds nothing back. But it is different these past few days. She has not mentioned Renno ever since he arrived, any more than she confided about him in the past. For whatever my opinion is worth, I am convinced that she is seriously in love, but that she cannot yet recognize her own emotions."

"Renno adheres to a long tradition among men in our family," Toshabe said. "When a male is a boy, he tells his mother everything. But once he becomes a warrior, the flow of information stops abruptly. Then he confides in no one. His mother tells me how frustrated she was when Ghonkaba grew up—seemingly overnight. I know exactly how she must have felt. All the same, I have eyes, and I have watched as he becomes increasingly adult. I watched in silence as he went through a painful physical infatuation with a worthless creature. I have watched him come back to life as he outgrew that infatuation. Now I am sure he is in love with Emily. The one thing I do not know is whether he realizes it. Very much like his father, he keeps his own counsel until he feels it necessary to speak. But his actions alone persuade me that he loves Emily. That is why he is involved in this contest of martial skills."

Nora smiled and shook her head. "How interesting that you should feel as I do about it."

"In my opinion, it will be a sheer waste of time," Toshabe said, "proving nothing and solving nothing."

"Exactly," Nora said, "but Emily regards it with the utmost seriousness. So does her father."

"I never have known my husband to regard any contest as an event of less than national importance," Toshabe told her, "and this one is no exception. We can be grateful that they are not to be fighting a duel of some kind and endangering each other's life."

"I will be satisfied," Nora said, "if some good can possibly come out of this whole experience. If Emily and Renno are wise enough to recognize their love and plan their future accordingly, I will consider it a step forward."

"When my daughter was married," Toshabe confided, "I did not feel as I do now. So much more is at stake now."

"Everything is at stake," Nora said soberly. "A marriage between my daughter and your son probably would assure us of peace on the frontier. Perhaps for at least a full generation to come."

"Aside from the personal joy I would feel at welcoming Emily into our family," Toshabe agreed, "I can think of no event of greater benefit to the Americans, the Cherokee, and the Seneca than their marriage would accomplish. But I know better than to push—or to interfere in any way. If Renno and Emily are to settle on each other as the mates they choose for the rest of their days, they must act completely on their own initiative. They must know that they alone found each other, and they alone realized they could find lifelong happiness together."

The day of the contest dawned clear and warm. Shortly after sunrise, people began to arrive at the parklike green to watch the forthcoming events. The ordnance department of the militia battalion provided two long rifles of late manufacture. Tested by battalion sharpshooters and by Seneca warriors familiar with the use of firearms, these were found eminently satisfactory.

The second in command of the battalion came with hair-triggered dueling pistols, handcrafted in

England shortly before the Revolution. The weapons were finely tuned, responding to a light touch on their triggers. Both were approved.

Wegowa's bodyguard supplied bows and arrows, and those who tried them described them as of equal strength and resilience, leaving little to the imagination.

Ghonkaba's Seneca supplied the tomahawks, well-balanced, with razor-sharp blades.

The throwing knives, of the finest Toledo steel, were crafted in Spain before being brought to Spanish Florida. They had been captured several years earlier when an expedition conducted by ever-belligerent Seminole Indians from the Floridas led a party of Spanish marauders north to attack the Cherokee.

Many spectators already were on hand when, a half hour before the contest was to begin, Emily arrived, escorted by her father. She was dressed for the occasion in a peach-colored gown of glazed cotton with a square neckline and a full, ankle-length skirt. She acknowledged the cheers of the crowd with a slight, dignified nod that caused her blond curls to dance up and down. Thereafter, she stared straight ahead and appeared to take no interest in the drama that was imminent.

Soon after, Ben Whipple arrived, his manner so somber as to be almost lugubrious. He acknowledged the wild greeting of friends in the throng by raising his arms and waving, and then he began various limbering exercises after removing his swallowtailed coat and rolling up his shirtsleeves. Emily purposely showed no sign of recognition and turned her back.

The Indian contingent arrived, led by Ghonkaba and Wegowa. Stationing himself near them was Rusog, whose wife, Ena, found it difficult to curb his loud exuberance.

Renno suddenly materialized in the midst of his comrades. One moment he was absent, the next he was there beside them. How he could have approached through the park without being observed was a source of considerable mystification to the throng and led to yet another legend about him.

The two principals resolutely ignored each other. Whipple was flexing his muscles and waving his arms. Naked to the waist, and with the Rhode Island silver coin dangling on his chest, Renno stood immobile. He seemed unaware of the stir he created in his war paint. The approval of the other Indians and of a large number of his military colleagues in the battalion was evident. Folding his arms across his chest, he stood unmoving as he stared into space. Physically he was present, but mentally he might as well have been far removed from the scene. The coming trial, in which he would be pitted against Whipple, seemed far from his mind. He appeared tranquil, completely at peace within himself, and paying no attention to the mounting hubbub.

Emily stared hard at him. She was reluctant to interrupt his reverie but, at the same time, wanted to wish him well. He gave no sign that he even recognized her presence.

Ghonkaba approved of his son's seeming remoteness. Only he and Toshabe knew that Renno was far from feeling indifferent about the coming struggle. On the contrary, they realized that he was communing with the manitous, imploring them for help and guidance.

Acting in his capacity as the referee, Colonel Johnson called the two contestants to him.

Whipple swaggered forward, his self-confidence and his contempt for his opponent obvious to everyone. Renno dropped his arms to his sides and glided several steps toward the colonel. He twice bowed his head slightly, first greeting Roy Johnson, and then acknowledging Whipple's presence. He did not speak, but waited patiently for the instructions that were to precede the contest.

Colonel Johnson pointed to two identical tree stumps, which stood side by side. Both were large and substantial, at least two feet in diameter and the better part of six feet high. All branches had been stripped from them, as had their bark. At Colonel Johnson's signal, several militiamen came forward and with difficulty moved the stumps until they stood about a half dozen paces apart. Then the colonel took two large, ripe melons, about the size of human heads, and placed one on top of each stump.

"These are your targets, gentlemen," he said. "If either target is destroyed, it will be replaced with another melon for the next round of the engagement. You may select either melon as your target. You are now free to begin the contest with rifles whenever you are ready." He handed each of them a long rifle, a powder horn, and a bar of lead, along with a bullet press.

Then he walked them to a point somewhat farther than fifty paces from the two targets. Someone handed him a long stick, and he drew a straight line with it in the dirt. "You may station yourselves wherever you please," he told them, "provided you stay behind this line. If you completely miss the target—that is, the melon and the pedestal on which it stands—you will be allowed a second shot. In the event that you hit the target, however, that strike will count toward your final score, and you may not fire again. Do I make myself clear?"

The contestants nodded.

"Fire when ready," Colonel Johnson called. He backed away to the far end of the line he had drawn.

Whipple did not waste a moment, and it was apparent that he was determined to fire the first shot. He hastily loaded his rifle, then raised it to his shoulder and, squinting down the barrel, he fired.

Watching Whipple's display, his face registering no expression, Renno saw that the bullet missed one of the melons by inches.

The rustling sound revealed to the entire audience that the shot had ripped through the foliage of the trees that formed a dark green background behind the targets.

Undeterred and undismayed, Whipple expertly reloaded and again took aim and fired.

This time, his aim was better. His shot nicked the edge of the top of the tree stump on which the melon rested. A small chip of wood flew into the air, as if certifying that he had made contact.

"If that shot had been aimed at a human target," Colonel Johnson announced, "it would have wounded the man in the shoulder."

A number of onlookers applauded.

Whipple turned to his opponent, and although he did not speak, his expression was daring his foe to equal his mark.

Renno reacted in his own way. Taking his time, he first raised his weapon to his shoulder, then squinted down the barrel at the target. When the weapon felt comfortable in his hands, he lowered it, made a bullet, dropped it into place, and tapped powder into the pan. His movements were leisurely.

When he raised his rifle to his shoulder, he once more looked down the barrel at one of the melons. Holding the weapon steady, he gently squeezed the trigger.

The onlookers shouted when they saw pulp shoot up into the air. It was clear to everyone present that Renno had hit the target in as accurate a shot as it would be possible to achieve.

Ben Whipple, failing to acknowledge his opponent's superiority with a rifle, turned his back to Renno.

Colonel Johnson came forward and, taking possession of the rifles, handed each contestant a bow and two arrows. His instructions were the same. They waited while the melon that Renno had destroyed was replaced with another.

Again, Whipple demonstrated his lack of patience. No sooner was he given the weapons than he strung an arrow into the bow and stood with the shaft pointed downward at the ground until the new target was in place. Then, scarcely waiting until the militia-man had retreated, he took rapid aim and let loose.

That he knew very little about bows became very evident to all the spectators. He missed the target completely, his shot going wild by four yards.

A number of people laughed aloud, and one young woman's high-pitched giggle was particularly penetrating.

Mortified and angry, Whipple flushed and then compounded his error. Instead of taking his time, he became even more frenzied. Seizing his arrow, he fitted it into the slot and let loose.

His aim was even worse, and his shot soared high in the air and went wide by a great margin. The arrow disappeared into the trees. Whipple had left both targets untouched.

Acting as though he were alone in the forest, Renno tested the bow, found it less taut than he liked, and adjusted it until the tension suited him. Then he practiced firing twice to get the feel of the bow in action. Only when he was fully satisfied did he fit an arrow into the slot and take aim. He stood in the classic pose, his left foot pointing toward the target, his weight balanced on his right foot, behind it. His left arm, holding the bow steady, was extended. His right arm grasped the all-important arrow. The muscles in his arms and back rippled as he pulled the bow taut.

Ghonkaba was pleased to see his son remaining cool, remembering the proper technique with each weapon, and the Seneca leader was in no doubt about the outcome.

As Renno let fly, the crowd was so silent that the sound of the arrow humming like an angry bee could be heard.

The arrow broke through the outer shell of a melon, and the point buried itself in the soft interior flesh. A collective sound like a sigh went up from the spectators.

For the second time, Renno had, without question, won the round.

Emily Johnson was almost overcome with relief. She felt a great stirring of pride in Renno's accomplishments. She wondered how she could have doubted his abilities. He was the most accomplished warrior she had ever seen; without doubt he would put Ben Whipple to shame, no matter what weapons they used.

Interest in the duel faded, and most of the spectators wrote off Ben Whipple as a worthy opponent. Attention was centered exclusively on Renno and his ability with each type of weapon. Those who had served with him in battle were well aware of his expertise; others, seeing him in action for the first time, began to recognize him as an extraordinary fighting man, one well versed in handling any weapon.

Again the damaged melon was replaced, and Colonel Johnson made a mild joke to the effect that he hoped the supply of melons on hand would be adequate as targets. Renno smiled, and the audience laughed appreciatively, but Ben Whipple was hardly amused. He glared, first at his commanding officer and then at Renno, whom he held responsible for his own miserable showing. No longer rational, he was convinced that Renno was directly responsible for subjecting him to ridicule. His hatred for the young Seneca threatened to overwhelm him. He managed to curb all outward displays of emotion, however, so neither Colonel Johnson nor anyone else realized how close he was coming to the loss of all self-control.

The next contest was a demonstration of skills with a tomahawk. Colonel Johnson moved to a point about fifty feet away from the targets. The same rules applied; each contestant was given two tomahawks and was instructed to use the second only if he completely missed his target with the first.

It should have been Renno's turn to go first, but Whipple was in no mood to behave with politeness. Rudely shouldering Renno out of his path, he threw a tomahawk with great force. It landed with a jarring impact against the tree trunk that served as the base of his target, the flat of the blade hitting the wood hard. The impact was so great that the melon resting on the top was jarred, rolled off the flat surface, and fell to the ground.

Some onlookers tittered nervously, but all were impressed by the sheer force of Whipple's blow. One of Colonel Johnson's aides replaced the fallen melon atop the stump.

Renno deliberately stepped in front of Whipple.

He had no intention of allowing his opponent to take advantage of him by having two shots to his one. In fact, nettled by the other's conduct, he was determined to even the score in his own way. Shouldering Whipple out of his path, he stepped up to the starting line in the dirt. He carried a tomahawk in each hand and was twirling both as he studied first one target, then the other.

A deathly quiet came over the audience as his intentions dawned on them. Emily gasped, unconsciously raising the back of a hand to her mouth. She gnawed nervously at a knuckle.

Toshabe sighed and shook her head sadly. She recognized that her son, goaded beyond endurance, was overreacting. He was taking on a task too great for any man to perform.

The audience watched in almost stupefied silence. What the young Seneca was preparing to do was so extraordinary that no one could believe the evidence being presented before their eyes.

Only Ghonkaba remained calm, his faith in his son's abilities undiminished. He knew that what Renno intended to do was without precedent, yet he realized, too, that if anyone could accomplish the seemingly impossible feat, his son was the man to do it.

Twirling both tomahawks, Renno studied his targets for an extended time, oblivious to the mounting tension in the throng.

Whipple sneered openly, contemptuously certain that his opponent would fail miserably.

Colonel Johnson sympathized with Renno but

nevertheless could not believe that he could succeed in any feat that required a perfect eye, perfect reflexes, and a perfect release of both weapons.

Conscious only of the superhuman task he had set for himself, Renno concentrated his whole being on it. He spun the two tomahawks more and more rapidly, then released them simultaneously and watched as they sped toward their targets.

Those who witnessed the extraordinary act never would be able to forget the climax.

At almost the identical instant, the tomahawks sliced into the melons perched on top of the targets. Each lopped off a chunk. If the targets had been human beings, they would have been killed simultaneously.

The spectators reacted as though deprived of their reason. Shouting, gesticulating, and cavorting, Indians and settlers alike crowded around to slap Renno on the back and shake his hand.

Through all the excitement, Renno remained remarkably calm. Looking past those who surrounded him, he caught sight of Emily standing alone, some distance away. They had no need for words. With their eyes, they achieved an almost perfect understanding. Emily was telling him that she was proud of his exceptional exploit. That much was clear. In return, he was informing her that he had sought victory for her sake and believed that now she had been vindicated. But Renno also realized that more was in Emily's expression than he had first thought. She was telling him something further. He concen-

trated harder, finally concluding that she was trying
to warn him. But her message remained blurred and
indistinct, impossible for him to decipher. He assumed he would have to wait until they were alone.
For that, he would need patience, as the contest had
not yet ended.

Throughout the excitement, Ben Whipple was
virtually forgotten. He had become very pale, and
the pupils of his eyes were reduced to pinpoints of
light. He was silent, withdrawn, and appeared to be
sleepwalking.

At last the clamor subsided. Only Colonel Johnson seemed to remember that the contest was not
completed. At his request, two aides made their way
through the crowd, asking people to resume their
places and to remain suitably quiet until the match
was finished.

By the time order was restored, the demolished
melons had been replaced, and the colonel opened
the case that contained the dueling pistols. "In this
next contest," he said, "you will use weapons of such
delicacy and sensitivity that you will be permitted to
take only one shot instead of two. These pistols are
loaded. You will each take one. When I give the
signal, you are free to fire at will."

Instead of allowing his opponent to make the
first selection of weapons, Whipple immediately
reached into the case, withdrew a pistol, and pulled
back the hammer.

The next development was so unexpected, so
sudden, that Renno was taken completely by surprise,
as was Colonel Johnson.

Pointing the pistol at Renno from a distance of only a few feet, Whipple pulled the trigger.

As the sound of the explosion filled the air and the principals were enveloped in a cloud of smoke, Emily's high-pitched scream of terror added to the confusion. At that moment, she comprehended fully the depth of her love for this courageous though unassuming man who wished to protect her with his own life if necessary.

Renno stood in a daze, his feet planted apart to prevent his collapse. A trickle of blood glistened in the sunlight as it slowly descended his chest.

In the excitement, Whipple tried to leave the scene, moving closer and closer to the path that could take him directly to the palisade that surrounded the fort. In his right hand, he still held the smoking pistol.

One who did not give in to panic or forget what was expected of him was Ghonkaba. He stepped forward into Whipple's path, intending to stop his departure.

Whipple saw him and reacted instantly. First he threw the pistol at the Indian leader's head, and when Ghonkaba ducked, he gained a precious moment in which to prevent his capture. He drew a sharp, double-bladed knife from his belt and plunged it into Ghonkaba. Leaping over the Seneca's body, he made good his wild dash toward freedom. Before anyone could realize that he was escaping, he was gone.

Ghonkaba was dead by the time he slumped to

the ground, an expression of incredulous astonishment etched on his face.

Few people were aware of his fate because attention was still focused on Renno. To the amazement of everyone, he continued to stand. Gradually, the miraculous truth dawned.

The bullet had hit the coin suspended around his neck. Its force caused it to make a deep indentation in his skin. The coin was badly bent out of shape, even partially pierced.

The young Seneca suffered nothing worse than a flesh wound, where the metal, driven into his chest, had burned his skin.

As soon as he began to recover from the initial shock, Renno realized that the manitous had been protecting him even more thoroughly than he had imagined possible. They had preserved him from harm in an extraordinary demonstration of their power.

But he quickly became aware of his father stretched on the ground nearby, his buckskin shirt soaked with blood.

Dropping to his knees, he assured himself that his father was beyond help. Then he fully raised his head and, staring out into space, emitted a high-pitched baying sound that sent shivers up the spines of all who heard him. Some swore that a demon took possession of him at that moment and that the creature cried out in pain, demanding revenge. Emily had to admit that the cry was unlike any human sound she had ever heard.

By the time that Colonel Johnson and Casno

formed a posse and sent it out into the forest to search for the killer, Whipple had disappeared. Taking advantage of the confusion, he used his knowledge of the forest in the vicinity to drop from sight. His knowledge of wilderness lore was sufficiently good that he left no visible tracks, and although search parties remained in the field for many hours, they looked in vain.

Chapter XI

The murder of Ghonkaba abruptly changed the holiday atmosphere, and the community was plunged into mourning. The Johnson home became the center of activity. Ena came at once to be with her mother, accompanied by Rusog. They remained close beside the stunned Toshabe, giving her no occasion to be alone.

Renno lacked the experience and inclination to immediately take over from his father. Casno stepped into the breach, making it plain, however, that he was only acting as a regent until Renno could become the leader of the Seneca.

Renno, in fact, disappeared and was nowhere to be found. Emily, who had not spoken to him, became so concerned that she sought the advice of Rusog.

"Do you know what has become of Renno?" she asked.

The Cherokee giant considered the question. "He does that which he finds necessary," he replied woodenly.

She was afraid he meant that Renno had gone off to hunt down Ben Whipple in the forest. "Whipple is too dangerous for Renno—or for any man—to hunt him alone. He has lost his wits and is going to be like an animal at bay."

"You do not understand," Rusog told her. "He has not yet gone to seek the blood of the man who killed his father. First, it is only fitting that he bid farewell to Ghonkaba in a manner suitable for the son of Ja-gonh and grandson of the great Renno. He has gone in the direction of the lands that lie where the sun never appears."

Emily knew that he meant that Renno had gone north, into the forest.

"He has gone only a short distance into the wilderness," Rusog added, "but you must not disturb him until his task is finished."

"What is he doing?" she inquired curiously, certain that the Cherokee was purposely being evasive.

"He does what he is obliged to do according to the customs of his people," Rusog said without explanation as he took his leave.

In Emily's opinion, she needed to follow Renno, offer him her condolences, and do whatever she could to comfort him. Saying nothing to anyone, she left the fort, heading north into the forest. After only a short distance, she heard the sounds of wood being chopped. Slowing her pace, she peered ahead.

Through the foliage she saw Renno. Clad only in a breechclout, he was wielding his tomahawk like an axe and was cutting down dead trees and branches. He had already accumulated a considerable pile. It was evident that the wood had been stacked with almost fanatical care, in a highly regular pattern. Renno, sweating so profusely that his war paint was smudged, was laboring hard, adding many more logs to the pile.

He worked with such a concentrated fury that everything else appeared excluded from his consciousness. Emily was surprised when, without pausing in his labor, he called impatiently, "Don't just stand there, gaping at me! Come out in the open where I can see you, and explain your business."

Emily moved slowly into the clearing.

Renno had stopped working, and he wiped a film of perspiration from his forehead with the back of a forearm. He stared at her, surprised that it was she who had sought him out.

"I—I had to see you and tell you how sorry I am

about your father's tragedy," she said hesitantly. "I did not know him well, but from the little that I saw of him, I know he was kind and considerate."

"He was a great leader and his work was not yet done," Renno replied. "The manitous were protecting me from evil, and they were so occupied that they failed to realize that he was being subjected to harm. They inadvertently permitted a madman to kill him, and I have no doubt that their regret is as deep and as lasting as mine. But what is done cannot be undone. Even the manitous cannot bring Ghonkaba back to life. We who still live must go on and live our lives to the best of our abilities."

Emily was confused. His calm, which tended to give the impression that he was resigned to the untimely death of his father, differed sharply from his ferocious concentration while chopping up trees.

Renno seemed to read her mind. "You wonder," he said, "how I can be so quiet and yet be so angry at the same time. I cannot answer the questions that form in your mind. I know only that braves are taught not to question the reasons for their feelings, but to act on their feelings and to satisfy their desires. Today I lost a father, and our people lost a leader they need to guide and protect them. At the same time, thanks to the gift you gave me, my own life was saved."

Emily looked at the mark left on his chest by the coin, then at the coin, bent almost double by the force of the bullet.

Renno noticed the direction of her gaze and

smiled. "When I have the opportunity," he said, "I shall use the flat end of my tomahawk to straighten out this coin as best I can. But I shall wear it for all time as a memorial of the protection that the manitous offered me in a time of need, and also because it was a gift from you."

She heard the warmth behind his words and reddened.

He studied her, his attitude critical but admiring. "At certain times it is right to speak one's mind," he said, "and at other times it is right to keep silent." He paused for a long moment, disinclined to enlarge on his point. "If you wait until I conclude what I must do," he said, "I shall be honored to escort you back to the fort."

"You have no need to bother," she protested.

"I see every need," he replied firmly, "and I do not regard as a bother what I offer you. The madman who murdered my father and tried to kill me is still at large. You have told me he is motivated by his jealousy of you."

"That is true, but—"

"You cannot know where he may be lurking," Renno went on. "It is all too possible that he might try to attack you. I will be much obliged if you will sit here, out in the open where I can see you, until I am ready to go back."

She had no logical reply other than to thank him for his concern. She walked to a stump, sat, and waited meekly while he went back to his labors.

Renno returned to his task of chopping down deadwood and adding it to the growing pile. He worked hard, in silence, for a long time, before he escorted Emily to the fort. After depositing her with the sentries, he left and soon thereafter jumped into the nearby river, where he swam long and hard to cleanse himself of sweat, grime, and dried blood. When he emerged from the water, he rejoined Emily, who had waited for him, and they proceeded to the Johnson house. Neither was in the mood for conversation. It was enough for both that they were together.

The following morning, the entire community had an opportunity to see Renno's melancholy handiwork. Not knowing what to expect, the men, women, and children of the fort were invited to join their Indian guests at the clearing in the wilderness.

Soon after the settlers appeared, a line of drummers arrived, including members of the Seneca and Cherokee guards. They stroked their drums in unison with rapid abandon, the tempo ever-increasing. Casno began to move in a primitive, yet fairly complex dance.

Watching them, Emily saw nothing strange or alien in their movements. She understood somehow that they were extolling Ghonkaba's virtues and asking the manitous to intervene with the gods on his behalf and speed his admission to the land of his ancestors on the far side of the Great River.

Whirling faster and faster, the dancers reached a climax, and as they did, Toshabe arrived, flanked by Renno and Rusog and followed by Ena. The faces and bare arms of all four were smeared with black paint, and they moved slowly, with great dignity.

The two warriors, unarmed, were imperturbable.
Their only concern seemed to be for Toshabe. Both
her son and her son-in-law kept watch on her to
make sure that she did not stumble, faint, or lose her
balance.

Toshabe and Ena were red-eyed and gaunt; it
was evident that both had been weeping. But they
were in firm control of their emotions now. Though
tradition would have permitted the women a display
of grief on this occasion, they remained expressionless,
their faces showing no feelings, their eyes blank as
they stared straight ahead. When they reached the
large woodpile that Renno had built, Ena and Rusog
sat facing it. With Renno close beside her, Toshabe
continued to stand facing the woodpile, upon which
rested the body of Ghonkaba.

As the drums throbbed in the background, Renno
reached for a pile of wood shavings and kindling that
he had prepared. Then he expertly rubbed two sticks
together and created enough friction to start a small
fire. Picking up a large torch that he had also prepared,
he lighted it and nursed it until a flame of considerable size and intensity was burning. Then he handed
the torch to his mother and sat down cross-legged
beside Ena.

With courage and dignity, Toshabe did what
was required of her. Standing erect, her face betraying
no emotion, she plunged the torch repeatedly into
the woodpile until a roaring fire was built. At that
point, she threw the torch high onto the top of the
pyre. The flames rose higher, and the remains of

Ghonkaba, hidden by smoke and flames, were consumed.

As the flames began to die away and the fire was in its final stages, Toshabe finally moved. She crossed her arms over her breasts, bowed her head, and prayed silently to the gods and to the manitous. She did not raise her head again until the pyre was reduced to glowing coals.

Then, straightening her back and raising her head, she turned and walked slowly toward the fort. Not once did she turn to look at the site that had contained the last remains of her husband.

Renno, watching his mother intently throughout the ceremony, had to conceal a severe sense of disappointment. He had hoped that, like Ah-wen-ga, she would see a vision of her late husband in the smoke that rose from his funeral pyre. Clearly, this had not happened. He was certain that any such revelation would have been evident in her demeanor.

Renno was thoroughly perplexed by his mother's failure. His parents had been devout believers in the gods and in the manitous all their lives. In Ghonkaba's long, honorable life, he had frequently won the favors and approval of the manitous. Why Toshabe had been denied the privilege of receiving an important, final message was not easily understandable to their son. It was not his place, however, to question the will of the omnipotent gods. They had their own reasons for doing whatever they did. In no way and at no time were they to be answerable to mere humans.

When the pyre was reduced to ashes, Renno

rose to his feet, inclined his head to his sister and her husband, and then went in search of Emily.

Word of Ghonkaba's death was carried to the land of the Cherokee by the speediest courier. There, the people—both Cherokee and Seneca—were stunned.

Ah-wen-ga lived up to the highest tradition of the Seneca when she accepted the news of her son's passing with an expressionless face. Saying nothing, she merely bowed her head when the messenger related the sad news.

Subsequently, she consoled her grandson, El-i-chi, and then retired to her house, where she sat in silence, facing the window that looked out across the hills.

Motionless for a very long time, she gave no sign of awareness when Loramas came and seated himself opposite her. He respected her silence for a time but finally spoke. "I offer you my condolences," he said. "It is indeed sad when one's parents go to the land of one's ancestors. When one's child departs from this life before we ourselves go, the pain of departing is almost unbearable."

"I bow to the will of the manitous," Ah-wen-ga said in a toneless voice, "and to the gods who rule this earth as they rule the land of our ancestors in the hereafter. They have chosen to take Ghonkaba, my son, from this life and to transport him into the next world. So be it. I have no voice in their decision, and I must bow my head to the inevitable. Many of my thoughts are with Toshabe, and with Ena. But especially with Renno, who now must prepare himself for a mantle of duty before he may be ready for it."

Her courage was as great as Loramas had known it would be. He waited for a time, then said gently, "I felt the need to come to you at once. Before I leave, I wish to assure you that I am prepared to postpone any consideration of our marriage."

Ah-wen-ga raised her head, looked at him, and smiled sadly. "You are kind and thoughtful," she whispered.

"No," he replied. "I am only being practical. During the time of your mourning, we will suspend all thought of a marriage between us. When your mourning comes to an end, we may resume our plans, if you wish. If you do not wish, we will of course put them farther aside."

She rose, went to him, and put a hand on his shoulder. "As long as I draw breath," she said tenderly, "I shall never forget your thoughtfulness on this, the worst day of my life."

Renno found Emily with her parents, making their way home from the funeral site. His opening words were sad and brief. "It is ended."

In spite of his unbending facade, Emily seemed ready to take him into her arms to comfort him. Through his air of self-contained sufficiency, it was possible to recognize his vulnerability beneath the surface. But he gave her no opportunity to move closer. Proudly self-reliant, he kept her at arm's length, as he did everyone, appearing determined to fight his inner battles alone.

When they reached the Johnson dwelling, however, he found his mother and Casno waiting. He was beginning to realize how much his life would be changed.

He came upon them in the garden, where they beckoned to him.

"We are discussing your future, my son," Toshabe said, making room beside her on a stone bench. "Sit down and listen."

"From the moment of your birth," said Casno, "you were destined to inherit the feathered headdress and the buffalo robe of the sachems. Your place as the leader of our people in your maturity never has been in doubt. Now it is the will of the manitous that the mantle of succession should pass prematurely."

"You have made great progress," Toshabe added, "but I fear that you may need additional time to demonstrate the wisdom and judgment that come with maturity. Those are necessary ingredients to attain success as the leader of the Seneca."

"I am assuming that our councillors would act swiftly," Casno said, "and designate me as a temporary leader of the Seneca in order to prevent fighting among any whose ambitions are so great that they might destroy themselves and perhaps destroy our people, as well. But while accepting the responsibility, I will not wear the headdress of the sachem or don his ceremonial buffalo robe. I agree to act as regent in your stead for a limited period of time. By then, you must be ready to take the place marked for you at birth. At that time, I will happily relinquish the duties that I am sadly assuming. I will make it clear to all our people that, until then, I proclaim my ultimate fealty to you."

The moment was so solemn that Renno instinctively rose to his feet. "Until the day we decide I am ready to accept the responsibilities for which I am destined," he said, "I will swear my total fealty to you in all things. I once erred when I questioned your loyalty to the Seneca. I am grateful that you can forgive that error. I shall not make such a mistake again. You have my unqualified support."

He and the older man clasped each other by the left wrist in a token of their mutual trust and affection.

Toshabe again gestured for her son to sit beside her. Her manner revealed that she had something to say that she regarded as important.

Renno again dutifully lowered himself to the bench.

"Although your heritage has caused you to stand apart from your fellows," she said, "you lack special training for the post that you will hold. That actually is in the true tradition of the Seneca. You are trained, as are so many others, to be a warrior. Thus, you have grown to manhood enjoying a far greater freedom than would have been your lot if you had been schooled exclusively for leadership. You have lived as you have pleased. And you have risen in the hierarchy exclusively through your own efforts. You have earned your advancements."

When Toshabe hesitated, Casno picked up the thought from her. "In the normal course of events, you would have remained free to develop naturally in any ways that you saw fit. But the natural course of events has been terminated by the cruel death of Ghonkaba. While he lived, no one would discuss, or even mention, that some day you would succeed him. That was taken for granted, but you were able to live your own life as you alone chose to live it."

"In this time," Toshabe put in, "you have distinguished yourself. You have made mistakes, to be sure, but you have paid the price that the manitous have exacted from you. Now, however, all that is changed."

"That is right," Casno added. "You are free no longer. It is now general knowledge that the day is not too far distant when you will wear the mantle of Ghonka. Every move you make, every word you speak, will be heard, remembered, weighed, and analyzed by the Seneca. You are free to live your own life no longer."

Renno felt as though a great weight had descended onto his shoulders.

"We are required by Seneca custom, together with Ah-wen-ga," Toshabe said, "to act as your advisors in all matters of importance. You must obey the manitous by coming to us before you make any major step and gain our approval for it."

"We regret the need to bind your ankles after you have walked freely," Casno said, "but, like you, we have no choice."

For a long, tense moment, Renno was silent as he struggled to acclimate himself to the need for a complete change in his way of life. "I acknowledge you as my advisors," he said at last, bowing his head, "and I ask the manitous to help me to heed your words in all matters."

His mother and the chief medicine man of the Seneca showed their pleasure at his words.

"One matter cannot wait," Renno went on, taking a deep breath. "I must ask: will you object if I seek the hand of Emily Johnson in marriage?"

Toshabe smiled for the first time since her husband's death. "Why should we object?" she asked gently.

Renno's reply was blunt. "We are Indians," he said. "The eldest of my sons can be expected to succeed me as the leader of the Seneca. Emily Johnson is not part of our tradition."

His mother laughed aloud, while Casno grinned and shook his head. "The great Renno, whose name you bear," Toshabe said, controlling an urge to laugh again, "was the offspring of American settlers whose blood flowed through his veins. Betsy, his wife, also was white, which means that Ja-gonh, their son, had no Indian blood. Ghonkaba was half white, and you, too, are partly white."

"You waste your time and your substance if you worry about us," Casno added briskly. "You should be concerned about the reactions of Emily and her family. She is the one who will have to make a major adjustment."

"Indeed she will," Toshabe added forcefully. "At the very beginning, she will need to learn our language. The dwelling in which she lives will be different, as will the food she eats and the clothing she wears. Nothing in her life will be as it was. Have you thought of all this?"

"I have thought of little else for many days," Renno replied.

"Yet you are prepared to ask her to give up her own civilization for your way of life?"

Renno flushed and looked uncomfortable. "I hope to offer her compensations," he answered.

"I cannot speak for Emily or for her parents," Toshabe said. "You must go directly to them and with your own ears hear the words they speak."

Renno was pleased that his mother and Casno were putting no obstacles in his path.

He knew, however, that Colonel Johnson could constitute a potential block to his plans. He awaited a meeting with him in nervous apprehension. The opportunity came that evening when he and the militia leader were alone before supper.

Renno's hesitancy caused the colonel to digress onto another matter in an effort to fill in the awkward gap in their halting conversation.

"I wonder if you may have heard," he said, to Renno's surprise, "anything of the news that has only just reached me from one of our couriers. An old 'friend' of yours"—here he smiled—"the notorious Rattlesnake, has fled from the continent."

In response to the young Seneca's inquiring glance, he explained. "He deserted the Choctaw cause in favor of saving his own hide. The word we get is that he successfully made his way to Canada, where the redcoats still have bases, of course, and has sailed for London. I am sure he will find a way to fit in there," he added sarcastically. "But I am equally sure he could one day find his way back here to cause more trouble wherever the seeds of evil will take root."

Renno recalled having heard of the half-breed's fondness for that city's attractions, but when the realization struck him that the information had been reported by Dalnia, the recollection turned sour immediately.

"But we can hope that we have seen the last of him," he responded shortly. "If so, good riddance." He fell silent again, reflecting that he would be well advised, in any case, to remain vigilant against the possibility of the half-breed's return.

The colonel now waited for the question that he knew was yet to come.

Finally, Renno blurted out, "May I speak to you, sir, on a matter closer to my heart than anything else?"

Roy Johnson showed no emotion to suggest that he knew, or even suspected, what the young Seneca had in mind. "Certainly," he replied.

"If the gods who oversee the destinies of the Seneca had allowed the forces of nature to take their normal course," he said, "my father would have remained alive and would have served for another twenty to thirty years as the leader of our people. I would have had ample time to prepare for the day when I would succeed him. Until then, I would have been free to live my life as I wished. Now, however, I am limited and my movements are circumscribed. I must prepare to take up the challenge of acting as

the sachem of the Seneca in the land of the Cherokee.
Therefore, instead of allowing human relationships to
develop at their own pace, I am obliged to hasten
that process." He paused before continuing. "I hope
that I am not speaking or acting prematurely. Colonel,
I have the honor to have fallen in love with your
daughter. I cannot say that I know the state of her
feelings toward me, but if I interpret her correctly, I
have some reason to hope. I request your permission
to pay court to her."

Johnson looked as he did in his courtroom when
he was handing down a difficult decision.

"I cannot say I am surprised by your state of
mind," he said. "I have been observing you ever
since you returned here, and your attitude toward
Emily is plain. My wife and I have discussed the
situation at some length. We have come to the conclusion that we do not object in any way to the fact
that you are part Indian. We have long believed that
integration of Indians and whites is an important
answer to whatever problems they may have in forming a compatible union. It appears that we now have
the opportunity to show we have the courage of our
convictions. Few young men anywhere are endowed
with your qualifications. Mrs. Johnson and I would
be very pleased to welcome you into our family as
our son-in-law."

Renno felt positively giddy. "Thank you, sir!" he
responded.

"Do not rejoice prematurely," Colonel Johnson
said. "My wife and I have observed Emily rather
closely of late, although we have refrained from speak-

ing to her on the subject. We are of the opinion that, at the very least, she is infatuated—to a degree— with you. Whether she has determined that she loves you enough to marry you and give up her home and the life she has led is a matter for her to decide. It is not up to us. She is levelheaded and eminently sensible, so we are prepared to abide by whatever decision she may make."

"That is very fair of you, sir."

"If Emily decides to marry you, she will live in a Cherokee village," her father said. "We will not. She will bring up her children to be Seneca, while we observe only from a distance. I can only add that if my grandchildren grow up to have your qualities, I shall be satisfied."

He and Renno shook hands warmly, but both were aware of the solemn significance of the occasion. They tended toward formality for that reason.

"I think you will agree," the colonel said, "that it is only fair I notify Emily what to expect. If you will pardon me for a few moments, I am sure she is primping before supper."

Renno had little chance to feel apprehensive about the colonel's talk with Emily. No sooner did he leave the room than Toshabe came in with Nora Johnson, chatting quietly.

Renno was drawn into their conversation, though later he was unable to recall a single word of what was said.

After a time, Colonel Johnson returned, escorting his daughter.

Emily curtsied gracefully before her mother and

Toshabe, and somehow managed to include Renno in her general greeting.

Renno stared hard at her, certain that her father had told her of his intention to pay court to her, and hoping to discern from her attitude whether she approved or disapproved.

But Emily demonstrated a rare ability to keep her opinion to herself. Never directly addressing Renno, never looking at him for more than a glance in passing, she spoke of inconsequentials with her parents and his mother. It was ironic, Renno reflected, that Emily was expert at concealing her feelings. He told himself that if they married, she would need no training in the art of becoming a good Seneca wife.

He tried repeatedly to persuade, inveigle, or even trick her into looking at him and addressing some of her remarks directly to him. But Emily proved that she was more agile and clever than he had anticipated. If she was playing a game, she was acting in the full knowledge of what she was doing. Renno got nowhere with his efforts.

Little by little, as they ate, his buoyancy vanished. Perhaps, he reflected, Emily was choosing this subtle means to tell him that she had no interest in becoming his wife. If their parents were aware of the undercurrent, they dealt with it enigmatically and did not reveal a knowledge of her attitude.

By the time they finished the meal, Renno was in despair. As they rose from the table, however, Colonel Johnson looked at him for a moment and lowered his left eyelid.

What is the meaning of the signal? Is it en-

couraging, or is he trying to shield me from a hard blow? Renno did not know the answers.

The colonel spoke in an undertone to his wife and Toshabe, and all three made their excuses, then left the young couple alone. Emily began to fuss. She brought a tray of coffee, cream, and sugar, and inquiring as to Renno's preferences, she poured full cups. Then, going through the same procedure again, she served him with a small glass of mellow brandy-wine.

He tolerated her behavior as long as he could. Finally, he called a halt. "Sit down, please," he urged sharply.

She looked at him in surprise and opened her mouth, intending to protest. A single glance at his expression warned her not to go too far. She seated herself opposite his chair, smoothing her skirts.

"As you undoubtedly know by this time," Renno said in a tense voice, "I spoke to your father earlier this evening. I obtained permission from him to pay court to you."

She was neither surprised nor flustered. "Yes," she agreed, "so he told me."

"How do you react to the idea?" he demanded.

Her poise crumbled, and she revealed her insecurities. "I—I don't really know. I am rather confused at the moment."

Renno leaned forward. "Let me explain my position to you," he said forcefully. "First off, I had a disastrous romance, one that nevertheless taught me many things, including a better ability to distinguish the good from the bad, the real from the unreal.

Most important of all, I have fallen in love with you over a period of months. I failed to completely recognize my own state of mind until I came here on this journey. As I believe you know, I am part Indian and part white. However, I live as an Indian and will continue to do so. So will my children who will come after me, although they will be taught certain aspects of your civilization, as I was. I hesitated to tell you the way I felt because I was unsure that I had the right to ask you to give up your own ways of life. I am still not certain I am doing the right thing. If the idea of moving to a Cherokee community and spending the rest of your life as a Seneca overwhelms you, please say so at once. I shall thereafter never mention the subject again."

Emily folded her hands in her lap and looked at him, her eyes direct and her manner revealing. "Thank you for your candor," she said. "I shall try to be equally honest. I have realized the direction in which we were moving, and I have struggled with the problem within myself for several months. At first, the very prospect of spending my life as an Indian filled me with horror. As I have come to know you, however—and, in recent days, as I have come to know your mother—my outlook has changed. I see many differences between our civilizations, but the similarities are far stronger. You wonder if I could tolerate living an Indian life. I can only say that I have learned a great deal about your own background, and I realize that the wife of the first Renno managed such a feat with distinction. She was a Virginian, as I understand it, and yet she took to Seneca ways and lived happily for many years. Her story convinced me that anything is possible when two people love each other. For some time, I have recognized that you love me. I may have been aware of it before you became conscious of it." She lowered her eyes and looked down at her hands. "I have examined my own feelings with great care, and I believe sincerely that I love you, too."

Her revelation was so great that Renno was stunned. His heart hammered against his rib cage, and he felt so ecstatic that a wave of dizziness almost felled him. Then, gradually, he began to recover.

Nothing in his training in the ways and customs of civilization had prepared him for this moment. He had learned only the ways of the Seneca, and under their system, no physical contact occurred when a couple became betrothed. Their agreement to marry was binding, but they were forbidden all intimacies until they actually became man and wife. He had broken the laws of his people in his affair with Dalnia, and he had paid dearly for that mistake. He had no desire to repeat his error now.

Emily confidently expected Renno to make some gesture after she confessed her love. When none was forthcoming, she was perplexed and slightly annoyed. "Well, really!" she muttered, and spiritedly lifted her chin.

He knew she was irritated because he had failed in some way to live up to her expectations, but he had no idea what he had done wrong or had failed to do. Reluctant to inquire because he wanted their new relationship to begin auspiciously, he said nothing, hoping her mood would change or that she would tell him of his failure.

Seeing his puzzled expression, Emily realized at last that he did not know what was expected of him. Her anger melted away, and in its place she felt a surge of warmth and tenderness. She was facing a test of her ability to handle a Seneca's lack of knowledge of civilized ways, the first of many she would meet in the years ahead. The easiest, most direct response would be to tell him of his failure and give him the opportunity to compensate for it. But she could not bring herself to be so bold. Such an approach would be contrary to her lifelong training as a lady. Furthermore, she well might give Renno the wrong impression and lead him to consider her forward and aggressive, when the contrary was true. No, she needed to devise some more subtle means of putting him on the right track.

"This is an occasion," she said, "that calls for a celebration." She pretended to be lost in thought for a time. "I know!" she said at last. "We will drink some of the wine that Papa keeps for special occasions."

Rising to her feet, she dragged a straight chair across the room to a high cabinet, then pointed to the wine stored at its top.

"I will bring it down for you," Renno offered.

"That's all right, thank you," she replied. "I am afraid you would be too heavy for this chair and might break it." She moved the chair into position in front of the cabinet, then stepped onto it. By shifting her weight experimentally from side to side, she caused the chair to teeter.

"The least I can do is to hold the chair for you, so you will not fall," Renno told her, worried because her balance was so precarious.

"Thank you!" she murmured.

Renno grasped the back of the chair and held it firmly.

Emily, however, swayed even more perilously as she reached above her head to the top shelf. She would have tumbled to the floor if Renno had not caught her.

As she fell, Emily reached out and took hold of him. Her arms clasped around his neck, and she clung to him.

Renno grasped her by the waist, breaking her fall.

She had planned nothing further. Now, their faces were only inches apart. Their love could no longer be denied. Their lips met, their hunger for each other was explosive, and everything else faded from their minds.

Renno's grip tightened, and Emily increased her hold on his head. Her lips parted to receive his tongue, and as their passion mounted, their bodies pressed close together.

Both retained just enough common sense, however, to realize they were playing with fire. They reluctantly pulled apart. Emily gasped for breath, and Renno was unable to tell whether she was laughing or crying.

"To think that I was disappointed," she gasped,

"because you didn't react physically when I told you that I loved you. I see I have a great deal to learn about you, Seneca."

He knew he had much to learn about her, too, but he preferred not to belabor the obvious.

"Shall I fetch the bottle of wine?" he asked.

She looked blank for a moment. "Oh, the wine. I forgot all about it. I don't really want it, do you?"

He shook his head.

"Where are our parents?" Emily asked. "We must tell them our good news."

"After the way they disappeared and left us, I would hardly be surprised if they already know," he said, "or at the very least they have a good idea."

The young couple wandered through the property and finally discovered the Johnsons sitting on the garden bench, conversing with Toshabe.

Emily and Renno were holding hands as they approached their parents. When she tried to disengage herself, the young Seneca clung firmly to her hand and refused to drop it. She flushed and glared at him for a moment. He relinquished his hold instantly.

Nora and Toshabe noticed the interchange, and neither registered surprise when Renno informed them that he and Emily intended to be married.

Their mothers kissed both of them, then Roy Johnson enveloped his daughter in a bear hug and pumped Renno's hand. "I can't say I am surprised," he said. "I regard this as wonderful news."

Tears stood in Toshabe's eyes, and she wished that Ghonkaba could join in the festivities, but she had no wish to dampen the spirits of the happy occasion, so she made no mention of her thoughts.

Sensing what she was thinking, however, Emily silently comforted her with a look and a squeeze of the hand.

Toshabe looked first at Renno, next at Emily, and then spoke to her. "It seems to me," she said, "that you would be wise, Emily, if you were to place yourself in my care for a few weeks before you are married. Let yourself be guided by me and by Ah-wen-ga, the mother of my late husband and the grandmother of Renno. Between us, we can teach you much that it is desirable for you to know about the customs of the Seneca and the ways of all Indians. In this manner, you will be better prepared for the day when you return to the town of the Cherokee and become the wife of Renno."

The Johnsons considered the idea sound and enthusiastically seconded it. Emily was grateful for the opportunity and accepted at once.

It was arranged, therefore, that she would accompany the party led by Casno when they went back to the land of the Cherokee. She would remain for a month and then would come back home to prepare for her wedding.

Particularly pleased by the prospect, Renno was secretly elated that his mother and Emily's parents accepted the idea that they were to be married and placed no obstacles in their path.

But something niggled at a far corner of his mind and gave him no peace. He had no idea what

might be bothering him, but the feeling persisted
and put a definite damper on his joy.

That night, sleep would not come to Renno. He
thought that perhaps the unaccustomed mattress was
responsible and wished he were on his usual bed of
pine boughs.

Eventually, he became drowsy, and at last he
drifted off. Even then, he realized that his sleep was
anything but deep, and he stirred restlessly. Sleep,
it appeared, was merely a prelude for something far
more important.

Then he caught sight of a small clearing in a
forest, a glade that looked strangely familiar. He
realized that he was dreaming and that some appari-
tion was about to appear.

As he watched, a wisplike cloud appeared at the
far side of the clearing in front of a stand of white
birch trees. The cloud, transparent at first, became
thicker and gradually began to assume a human shape.

Renno recognized the familiar figure of Ghonkaba,
his father. Instead of appearing to be years younger
than he had in life, as other shades had looked to
Renno in his dreams, Ghonkaba closely resembled
what he had been before his murder. His face was
pale and wan, however, and Renno was shocked
when he realized his father was still in the clothes he
had been wearing when the assassin struck. The
front of his shirt was still soaked with blood that
continued to ooze.

Ghonkaba extended his left arm. "Greetings,
my son," he said in a hollow voice. Renno tried to

respond to the greeting but found that he could make no sound.

Ghonkaba did not appear to be surprised, however, by his son's inability to speak. He acted as though the choking, gasping sounds that Renno made were normal and expected. "I have been reluctant to appear before you," he said, "but at last I find it necessary. You will tell no one of this visit. I particularly want no mention of it to your mother. She would be disturbed and would grieve, and I have no wish to cause her pain, now or ever."

"I hear you, my father, and I will do as you command me," Renno replied somberly, recovering his voice at last. "No word of this visitation shall escape my lips."

"That is good," Ghonkaba said, smiling. To his son, his expression looked more like a ghostly grimace. Renno fought a strong desire to shudder.

"I have stood on the near bank of the Great River," Ghonkaba said, a note of longing in his voice, "and have looked across at the inviting, green wilderness of the land of our ancestors. There, standing on the far shore, waiting for me and waving to me, were my father, my grandmother, and my grandfather. With them were those I have heard about mostly in story and song, Ghonka and Ena, my most illustrious ancestors. They instructed me to await transportation to the far shore. I did as I was bidden and I waited."

Renno nodded, totally absorbed in his father's description of life after death.

"I learned patience when I was a small boy in the land of the Seneca," Ghonkaba said, "and therefore I exercised patience. I waited for hour after hour after hour. But no boat came for me. Finally I determined it was the will of the manitous that I swim the short distance across the Great River. I plunged in, but I did not reach the other side. The current was so strong it picked me up and deposited me on the near shore. Three times I tried with all my might to swim across that narrow stream to the shore of the land of my ancestors. Three times I was frustrated. The current was so swift and so strong that it hurled me with great force back onto the near bank.

"Then, as I lay upon the mossy ground, I heard from the other side of the river the voice of our ancestor, the great Ghonka, who was passing judgment upon me and giving me advice. The manitous had decided, he said, that I was not to be admitted to the land of our ancestors until my death had been avenged. *By you!*"

Renno quickly sucked in his breath.

"It is decreed by the manitous," Ghonkaba went on slowly, "that I am to wander the face of the earth in torment until such time as Renno, my son, kills with his own hands the man who murdered me."

Renno repeatedly clenched and unclenched his fists.

"Tell me," Ghonkaba begged, "that you will be obedient to me, as you were in life. Tell me you will do as the manitous have bidden you."

Renno replied without a moment's hesitation. Bowing his head, he said, "I will do as the manitous have ordered, and as you have bidden me to do, my father. I will seek Ben Whipple, who cruelly murdered you, and obtain vengeance for you in order that you will be freely admitted to the land of our ancestors."

"Then go to the funeral pyre, where my earthly remains were consumed by fire," Ghonkaba said, "and there you will find an item of substance that will be useful to you in obtaining revenge."

Renno, confused, started to ask what he meant, but broke off to listen as his father's image began to fade.

"You will have ample reason, other than my murder," Ghonkaba was saying, "to kill Whipple."

His body was becoming transparent again, and it was possible for Renno to see the birch trees at the edge of the clearing behind him.

"Wait, my father!" Renno cried in consternation. "Do not leave me yet! First, tell me where I may find Whipple, so that I may obtain the vengeance that is needed to repay your death."

He received no reply. Ghonkaba's ghost was fading rapidly. Within a few moments, it was reduced to a cloud of vapor, which then blew away.

Renno awakened, bathed in a cold sweat. Because further sleep was impossible, he dressed and crept out of the house. He went to the palisade gate, where he saluted the officer in charge as he departed. Upon reaching the sanctuary of the forest, he made his way to his father's funeral pyre. There, by the half light cast by a partial moon, he made out the mound of ashes that constituted the last earthly remains of Ghonkaba. For a long time, he stood in silence, contemplating the results of the devastating fire.

When the toe of his moccasin touched a hard object, he bent down to pick it up.

Examining the object in his hand, he identified it as a piece of wood that had been in the fire but had only partly burned. About two feet long, it was an inch in diameter at one end, then tapered like a spike to a narrow end with burned edges that, when he tapped it on the ground, fell away. The solid wood that remained was chestnut. Tempered in the fire, it seemed as strong as steel. Renno had no idea what use he could make of it. Remembering the instructions he had received from his father's spirit, he slid the strange implement into his belt and then turned and started back toward the fort.

He knew now that his plans for the future must be changed radically. During the coming month, while Emily was being taught Indian customs by Toshabe and Ah-wen-ga, he would be absent. Alone in the wilderness, he would be searching for Ben Whipple, in order to avenge his father.

Gripping the strange wooden object so firmly that his knuckles turned white, he started walking with a deliberate, purposeful stride, his head high.

Coming in January 1986 . . .

BOOK XII IN THE WHITE INDIAN SERIES:

SEMINOLE

by Donald Clayton Porter

Awaiting their wedding day, Renno and his bride-to-be Emily are catapulted into stirring new adventure—and perilous danger—by the evil scheming of a renegade Tennessee militiaman.

Kidnapped by the murderer of the Seneca's revered sachem, Emily is taken far into the remote Seminole Territory of southern Florida. There, she must fight to survive the tribe's cruel bondage, while Renno follows a strange order from the Manitous as he goes in search of her, combatting the Spanish who occupy the area, pirates, Seminole war parties, and the perils of the Everglades.

And Rusog is the victim of a bizarre plot—and the charges against him bring Indian and white settlers to the brink of a war no one wants . . .

Read SEMINOLE, on sale December 15, 1985
wherever Bantam Books are sold.